R2003899552

W9-BYR-995

# THE COLOR OF DARKNESS

# THE COLOR
## OF
# DARKNESS

Volume Two in the
Book of Storms Trilogy

## Ruth Hatfield

Henry Holt and Company
New York

Henry Holt and Company, LLC
*Publishers since 1866*
175 Fifth Avenue,
New York, New York 10010
mackids.com

Library of Congress Cataloging-in-Publication Data
Hatfield, Ruth, author.
    The color of darkness / Ruth Hatfield. — First American edition.
        pages        cm. — (The Book of storms trilogy)
    Summary: "Danny thinks he's left magic and mystery behind, but Sammael, a creature of
terrible imagination, refuses to let him go. A strange new girl, Cath, enters Danny's world,
bringing with her a message: Danny's cousin Tom has sold his soul to Sammael. It's up to
Danny and Cath to find Tom and stop Sammael, who seeks to destroy humankind once and
for all"—Provided by publisher.
    ISBN 978-1-62779-001-7 (hardback) — ISBN 978-1-62779-002-4 (e-book)
[1. Adventure and adventurers—Fiction.    2. Soul—Fiction.    3. Supernatural—
Fiction.    4. Human-animal communication—Fiction.]    I. Title.
PZ7.1.H38Co 2016        [Fic]—dc23        2015018270

Our books may be purchased in bulk for promotional, educational, or business use. Please contact
your local bookseller or the Macmillan Corporate and Premium Sales Department at (800)
221-7945 ext. 5442 or by e-mail at MacmillanSpecialMarkets@macmillan.com.

Originally published in the United Kingdom in 2015 by Hot Key Books
First American edition—2016

Printed in the United States of America
by R. R. Donnelley & Sons Company, Harrisonburg, Virginia

10  9  8  7  6  5  4  3  2  1

*In memory of C, an inspiration*

# ~ CONTENTS ~

I haven't brought a spade.

*He stands in the moonlit woods, a thousand miles from any-where. How can you make a hole in the earth when you've nothing to dig it with?*

Perhaps I should go home.

Perhaps I should call my dad and ask him to come and fetch me.

Perhaps I should go back to bed, where the rest of the world thinks I am.

Perhaps I should—

Keep it?

*It is burning a hole in his pocket, trying to break through the material and cling to him like a limpet.*

*I am yours, it says.*

*Danny shudders, and a breeze picks up through the thinning leaves of the autumn treetops. There's rain on the air, soft and damp. Rain that might fall lightly or lash down from the growling clouds of a storm.*

*Storms, he thinks. If a storm comes—*

*And he is on his knees, tearing at the earth with his fingers, gouging shallow scoops from the soft patch at the base of a tree. The leaf mold is sticky and grainy, and smells of bitter coffee. The soil underneath is more compact, but his fingernails cut through the layers, scrape by scrape, until his hands are sunk up to the wrists in loose soil.*

Not deep enough. Not nearly deep enough.

*He drags the loose soil away and keeps digging. His nails pack with grit. Tiny thorns drive themselves into his fingertips. Twice he catches his thumb on something so sharp it makes him gasp with pain, but the hole needs to be deeper and he knows that the next time he stops he'll feel it there in his pocket, talking to him, and it will say, Please don't bury me. Keep me. I'm yours. You're mine. We belong together.*

*He closes his eyes and shuts it all out. The wind whispers away to stillness, the hooting owl closes its beak. Even the scraping of fingers through soil is without sound, as though the soil has begun to move itself silently out of the hole it knows must be dug.*

✦ ✦ ✦

*At last it's done.*

*It is so deep he can put his arm in it up to the elbow. It must be deep enough.*

*He stands back, puts his muddy hand into his pocket, and pulls the thing out. And without looking at it, he pushes it down into the earth at the bottom of the hole.*

*He fills the hole quickly, his head turned away, looking into the shadows lurking around the silver trees. When the hole is full, he kicks dry leaves over it and smooths them down with his shoe.*

*The thing has gone. It's out of his pocket. It's out of his world. It's at the bottom of a deep hole and it'll never see daylight again.*

*He widens his eyes to look for the path home, and it's a clear path, bright with moonlight, welcoming him toward it.*

*Out of the woods. One step, and another, and another, and each step takes him farther away from this place.*

*He goes as quickly as he can, and the forest watches him leave.*

✦ ✦ ✦

*Under the earth, a call begins. The days and weeks pass. Autumn falls prey to winter's claws; spring's green teeth gnaw away at the frozen armor of winter, and then summer sweeps yellow over the land.*

*And still it calls. Only one person hears it, but to him, it roars as loud as thunder.*

*Danny, it says.*

*Danny.*

*Danny.*

*Danny.*

## CHAPTER 1

# TOM

"Get down! They're coming!"

Johnny White barely whispered the warning, but Tom Fletcher instantly ducked his head behind a tree root and pressed himself flat to the forest floor. A flapping of wings beat up into the treetops, and a few leaves rustled as a creature crashed against a branch, then the dark woodland inhaled all sound with one giant breath and held it, leaving only the light air of a summer night, the gentle gray of a thin moon, and silence.

Next to Tom, hidden away in the moon shadows, Johnny pressed his pale face down into the leaf mold. No one would see his black hair against the night and the shadows of the birch trees. They had better not see it. If Tom and Johnny were seen . . . if Johnny was recognized . . .

Tom pulled his woolly hat farther down over his ears and waited. Stupid blond hair. He should have put camouflage paint on his face, but there hadn't been time to get any.

His keen ears scanned the woodland again. An owl let out the faintest whisper of a hoot, telling its chicks to be quiet. From the bank across the clearing, a few short grunts let Tom know that the badgers were shuffling around just inside the entrance of their sett, thinking about venturing out. Two of them tonight: the old boar and the heavily pregnant sow. His favorites.

And then the tiny *crack* of a dry holly leaf snapped halfway down the hill. Footsteps kicked leaves, and the damp scent of decay floated up on the breeze.

"Is the shotgun loaded?" Johnny barely breathed out the words.

Tom nodded. "Yeah. But there's loads of them. One warning shot won't—"

"Sssh!"

Tom was silent for long enough to hear the pounding of his own heart. Why had the forest gone so quiet? Once the men got up here, they'd hear his heartbeat and they'd find him. Why couldn't something squawk or cry out or flap around? Why had everything become so *unnatural*?

Three sets of footsteps tramped up the slope toward the clearing. The tiny pattering dots of a terrier's paws jogged beside them. And then the sliding, scraping rakes of bigger paws, straining at collars, scrabbling toward their prey.

They came into the clearing. Seven shadowy shapes.

Three men armed with spades and shovels, a terrier small enough to scramble down a badger sett, two squat fighting dogs ready to set upon whatever poor badgers the terrier flushed out, and a much bigger dog—a Rottweiler, or something like it—with a chain for a collar.

Johnny tugged at Tom's jacket. They had to get out of here. Those dogs would smell them, and they wouldn't care what kind of animal they were sinking their teeth into, as long as it had flesh.

But Tom shook his head. He couldn't go now, not when he knew what was about to happen. He had to at least try and stop it—that was the point of bringing the shotgun.

If he fired a shot . . .

He reached around to get hold of the shotgun. Small twigs snapped off a bush, crackling out into the still air.

The dogs' heads shot up.

"What's that?" one of the men hissed.

They listened for a couple of seconds.

"Nothing. An animal. Let's get Julie down to work."

The tallest man leaned down to unclip the terrier.

Tom cursed himself for not having got the gun to his

shoulder before the men had arrived. Now he'd have to wait until the dogs were distracted, which meant he'd have to wait until they'd flushed out a badger and started fighting it.

Johnny trembled beside him. When he'd found Tom at school and told him that some of the men from the Sawtry buildings were baiting badgers, he'd been boasting like crazy about how he was going to hunt them down and "give 'em as good as they gave." "It's sick!" he'd said. "Sending them dogs in, tearing animals apart just for fun. It's sick. Someone's gotta stop 'em."

But out here, he seemed hardly able to move.

For a second, the moon flashed out from a thinning gap in the clouds. The terrier shot forward as the leash came away. It scrambled down into the earthy entrance of the badger sett and disappeared.

Tom heard the growls of the badgers. If it has to be one, he prayed, please let it be the old boar. He was a fearsome creature, and he'd at least have a chance of fighting for long enough that Tom could get a shot fired in time to save him.

But it was the snarling of the pregnant sow that he heard loudest, as the terrier's hindquarters came powering backward up the tunnel and out into the clearing. The dog was dragging the badger by the scruff of her neck, and the badger was roaring in anger. As soon as they broke out into the open air the badger began to swing her head around, snapping her jaws around the terrier's legs, biting at its sides. But she was heavy, her pregnant belly holding her down.

"Get some light on 'em!"

One of the men switched on a bright light, directing the beam toward the fight. A laugh rang out as the terrier began shaking its head, trying to force the breath out of the badger.

"Go on, let Tyson go!"

Another leash unclipped. A bigger dog hurled itself into the fight.

Tom could stand no more. He grabbed the shotgun and yanked it up to his shoulder, not caring how much noise he made.

Johnny leapt up and pelted away into the darkness, crashing through the bushes.

Tom let loose both barrels of the gun.

His aim was wild against the glare of the light and the shots thumped into trees, but the deafening *crack* of the gun made the men yell startled curses. One of them ran forward to grab the terrier, kicking away, pounding his foot into the snarling fight until the animals broke apart and the barks of the terrier rose shrieking over the echoes of the gunshots.

"Run!" The man with the terrier rushed out of the clearing, but the others ignored him and stayed, standing over the panting body of the badger, gazing around into the night.

Tom kept his head low, watching them. The shorter of the two had a tough face with a double chin. The taller, with a fat paunch and dark hair, had eyes as silver-cold as knife blades.

"It ain't gamekeepers," said Cold Eyes. "There ain't keepers here."

"Let Elvis go," said Double Chin. "He'll flush 'em out."

"Go on, then."

Tom was on his feet and running before he heard the rush of the dog's paws, but he knew it was the Rottweiler, unchained. It didn't waste breath barking, simply bounded toward the sound of him sprinting away through the undergrowth.

He felt no fear. Tom knew this landscape better even than the sounds of the midnight woods: this was his farm, his work, and his life. He broke from the edge of the woods out into the fields and made for the stream at the bottom of the hill, slinging the gun over his shoulder as he ran. His legs were strong and fast: he had a head start, just enough of one, if nothing hampered him.

Behind, he heard the thudding of the dog's paws against the black grasses. Not far now. Not far. And then he was at the shallow stream, splashing through the widest point, running a few steps along the bank and back into the stream again, back out, back in, back out. He heard the dog splashing, stopping, listening, and he leapt out of the stream, hared across a narrow strip of grass, and vaulted over the fence into the lane.

His bike was where he'd left it; he pedaled away into the night, gripping the handlebars with a fury that kept him pedaling at top speed long after there was any further danger of being caught by the dog. He would go back there in the morning, just to check if the badger had survived, but in his heart he knew that she hadn't stood a chance.

And the baiters would be back. Tom knew how men like that operated—how violent and brutal they were, intent on finding ways to carry out their disgusting sport. He could call the police, but it would only be Tom's word against theirs— Johnny would never get involved.

The baiters would be back, and they'd kill more badgers unless he could take away the cover of darkness and shine bright lights onto their horrible cruelty.

I'll find some way of stopping them, he thought as he wrenched the bike up the drive to the farmhouse, his wheels spinning against the gravel. I'll catch them and I'll let them see that I caught them, and that it's *my* badgers on *my* farm that I'm protecting.

And then I'll make them pay.

## CHAPTER 2

# DAD

The dogs had dumped on the carpet again.

Cath Carrera woke up and didn't even have to sniff to know that they'd done it, right in the middle of the living room, close to the couch where she slept. The smell was rising, hot and eggy, into her nostrils. As she breathed, it shot into her empty stomach like a poison-tipped stick.

She sat up and gagged. "Yuck!"

Then she froze. She shouldn't have made a sound. If Dad or Macy woke, they'd make her clean up the mess before she went to school. Even if one of the other kids came into the living room and started screaming about the rotten smell, Cath would still be the one who had to clean it up.

She didn't want to do it. It wasn't fair that Macy's kids got a bedroom while Cath didn't, and it wasn't fair that Dad had kicked the dogs into the living room late last night when Cath had already shut the door, so it was even less fair to make her clean up after them. But if she tried to say no, Macy would probably have a fit and shove her onto the pile of crap, and then she'd have to go to school stinking, like last Thursday, when that English teacher with a neck like a string bag had taken her aside and suggested that she go into the washroom to see if she'd trodden in anything, and was everything quite all right at home?

Cath listened to the sounds of the apartment. One of the dogs was snoring in the corner. Macy was snoring in her and Dad's room, grunts muffled by the closed door. The kids didn't snore, but they always woke up early. There wouldn't be much time before someone else appeared.

She swung her legs off the side of the settee, looking carefully at the floor to avoid the mess. The snoring dog had a clump of pale gray hair stuck to its soggy jaw. Badger hair again, for sure.

Reaching for her school clothes, Cath tried not to breathe as she put them on. If she managed to get out of the apartment and didn't come back till late, someone else would have to clean the carpet. They wouldn't be able to sit in the living room all day with that horrible smell.

✦ ✦ ✦

She got as far as the hallway, and then the door to the kids' room opened and Sadie stuck her head out. Her blond hair was across her face, but her hard little eyes shone through the white strands. She looked at Cath.

For a second, neither of them spoke. Cath clenched her fist.

"Why are you going out now?" said Sadie, very loudly. "It isn't time for school yet."

"Shut it!" Cath hissed, grabbing for her schoolbag.

"WHERE ARE YOU GOING?" yelled Sadie, looking at the door of her parents' room. She pushed away the hair from her mouth and smiled at Cath.

Cath yanked the bag up from under the other schoolbags and turned the key in the front door. She pulled it open just as the bedroom door at the end of the hall opened.

"What the—?"

It was Macy, nightie strap hanging off her shoulder.

"Mum, Cath's going out!" said Sadie.

Cath went out. Running as fast as the walls and stairs would let her, she crashed into the angles of the stairwell and leapt down the floors.

"CATH! YOU LITTLE COW! GET BACK HERE!"

The yell bounced off the walls and zoomed past her ears. She ran, jumped, careered down the seven flights of stairs, slapping her hand on the metal handrail, swinging her bag around the corners of the landing. Macy wouldn't catch her. Macy wouldn't even bother to run—what did she care?

Cath's own mum had disappeared ages ago, long before Cath could remember, and the only thing Cath knew about her was that she was "wild."

"Enough sense to leave you, anyway," Macy liked to say when Dad wasn't around.

Cath shot outside into the early-morning drizzle. The Sawtry estate was quiet and cold, exhausted apartment buildings sagging toward the earth. Behind the thin rain, a stillness in the air spoke of a world that hadn't yet learned to move.

She slowed to a walk and looked up. She liked the Sawtry in the early morning. If only the day never got old. If only the sun never slunk its way up into the sky, shining light on all the dirty cracks of the earth below. If only nothing ever had to carry on—just to begin, and begin again, and go on beginning, and all the things that began badly wouldn't matter because you'd know they weren't going to carry on any more than just the beginning.

If that was the world—but that wasn't the world. Not this world, anyway.

She shrugged and grinned, baring her teeth to the silent clouds. For a second, she could almost feel the fangs of a wolf growing long from her gums, flashing white against the day. If her fingers were wolves' claws, if she could prowl and spring and sink her teeth into Macy's neck . . .

Shaking the wolf from her shoulders, she dropped the imaginary fur onto the pavement and was just about to turn the corner of the alley that went toward school, when a voice made her stop dead.

"You little . . ."

She knew the voice at once. It had said those words to her often enough.

Dad. Outside in the early morning, prowling around the Sawtry. It wasn't unusual, but it wasn't good.

Cath shrank back against the wall. Her chest contracted, trying to hold in the swelling beat of her heart. Her lungs bulged.

And then—somebody else.

"No! Please! Please! Don't!"

The second voice was whining and thin, and it came from down the alley. Johnny White, who lived four floors below. He did stuff for Dad sometimes, though he didn't seem very good at it: only last week he'd turned up at the door, soaked and shivering, with a panicked story about losing money.

At least Dad wasn't talking to her. She breathed out and in again, tasting the sweetness of the damp air. Her feet edged backward, trying to take her away from the alley. But Dad didn't know she was there. There wasn't any need to run.

She put her hands on the wall and peered around the

corner, trying to keep everything but her eyeballs out of sight.

"I told you to meet us," said Dad. "You owed me, big-time. Five grand you lost us last week. Five. Grand. And I said, be fair, give the boy another chance. Let him keep lookout for us while we have a little bit of sport. Nice and easy. Did you have trouble understanding me?"

Heavy and hairy, he was pinning Johnny White up against the alley wall with his massive forearms and solid round belly. Johnny White looked like a little piece of shivering straw.

"No!" Johnny whined, not even putting his hands up to try and push Dad away. "I was going to, I swear . . . I was coming . . . I got lost . . . I swear, on my mum's life . . ."

"You little maggot," said Dad. His face was so close to Johnny's that they might have been about to kiss. "Nobody could've known we was in them woods, unless you'd told 'em. Ain't that right, son?"

"No! I didn't . . . I swear! I'll prove it—I'll go on another job for you! Anything! Anything you want!"

"Too late now." Dad was fishing around in his pocket, bunching up a gloved fist. "You know, I don't reckon you lost that money at all. I reckon you stole it. You stole it from *me*. Didn't you?"

"No . . ." Johnny gasped, the skin around his mouth going gray.

Dad carried on. "You *steal*, you double-cross me—you ain't no good for nothing. No more guts than a *dead badger.*"

Then Dad pulled back his fist and punched Johnny in the stomach, and his other hand slapped itself tight across Johnny's mouth.

I'd bite him if he did that to me, thought Cath. Johnny's just standing there, and he's twice as big as me.

Dad's fist jerked away, and Johnny gave a strange grunt. His hands fluttered and went to hold his stomach. Dad stepped backward. A spark of wet silver caught the light.

Johnny dropped to his knees. Dad looked down at him, smiling like a rattlesnake, and threw a knife onto the ground.

And then Cath saw that a dark shadow was seeping along the sleeve of Johnny's white sweatshirt, a crimson flower unfurling its petals over the pale cloth. And she understood why Dad had taken his hand off Johnny's mouth. Johnny wasn't going to be shouting now. He didn't have the breath to spare.

Nobody got away with double-crossing Dad.

A piece of invisible fluff caught in her throat. She struggled for air and a sound rasped out, as raw as the croak of a crow.

Dad looked up.

His ice-gray eyes met hers. Cath couldn't look away, because he was Dad, because she saw him every morning, because he was the only thing in the world that she'd always known, because Johnny White . . . because Johnny White was bleeding . . .

Dad was on his toes in a second. And Cath ran.

Back over the estate. Over the roads, across the yards, past the benches and concrete planters. Over the cracks and past the railings, around the cars and through the doors. Out of the far doors. Out of the Sawtry.

"Cath!"

He tried calling her, once, in a gentle voice that she'd never heard him use. But she knew him. She knew what he'd do if he ever got hold of her again.

"CATH!"

Now he was calling her in his real voice, that hard, furious roar of anger. His feet smacked against the concrete behind her.

Cath ran. She looked ahead and kept her legs running. There was only one place to go to now, where she might get away from him, where she could bury herself deep in the undergrowth and cover herself with plants and bushes that would keep very still and refuse to give her away.

The park, down by the old railway. She'd crawled into the bushes one summer and found a hidden world of wildness: dark thorns and twisted branches and tiny pockets of space linked by foxes' tunnels. And after that, she couldn't keep away from it.

Normally, she only went when she was alone; she didn't want to risk anyone finding out where she hid. Normally, she could outrun Dad easily, what with his huge hairy shoulders and his fat arms and his heavy belly.

But nothing was normal now.

CHAPTER 3

# THE HARE

Breaking past the edge of the park, Cath ran straight across the middle, dived into a hollow at the base of a stand of cow parsley, crashed down onto her hands and knees, and began to crawl, crushing the long wet grass around her into a gaping trail that any human could follow, even Dad, if he could still get down on all fours.

He wouldn't be hurrying right now. He'd think he had her cornered.

She clawed her way under a tangle of brambles, wrenching her hair and sweatshirt free of a thousand thorns, her blood too full of panic to care about the pain. And then the ground dropped away into the old railway cutting and the thin stems around her became a thicket, knotted and dense.

She made for the bottom of the slope, following an animal's narrow track. The damp undergrowth smelled of lemons and cut grass and gasoline.

Down in the cutting she crouched, listening for the sounds of the morning and the sounds of Dad, putting her hands on the soil to feel for the vibrations of his heavy footsteps.

The earth was cool beneath her palms. A crow screamed out above her. She wasn't a wolf now, only a trembling mouse. The far bank of the cutting rose steeply up to a high fence crowned with rolls of barbed wire: there was no way out, except the way she'd come in. But she was invisible in here. If she sat tight, Dad would have to burn the whole thicket down to find her.

"You wretched thing . . . Get off me! Get off!"

Cath stopped breathing.

"I said, get off me! Let me go! Ow!"

"Sssh!" Cath hissed, hoping to scare whoever it was into silence.

There was a rattling noise, which turned into a clinking *bang*. It was coming from only a few yards away along the bank.

"Who's there?" The voice came loudly through the thicket.

"No one," she said. "Shut up!"

She inched backward and knelt on a thorn. It drove itself deep into the flesh of her knee, and she swore.

"Help me," said the voice. "Please. I'm stuck."

Cath wriggled her leg until she could pull the thorn out. A bead of blood pushed its way through the grime and began to trickle down her shin. This was it, then. Dad was bound to have heard that voice. He'd plow straight through the bushes, and she'd be found, even here. Was there never going to be anywhere she could escape to?

"All right," she said. "Whatever."

She crawled toward the voice, expecting the bushes to open up again, but the undergrowth was relentless.

"Oh!" A high-pitched squeal came from close to her right arm.

There was a lean brown hare stretched tautly away from her, ears flat against its head, black eyes hot with distrust.

Cath stared.

The hare stayed still for seconds. Too many seconds. And then Cath saw—its legs were caught in a tangle of leaves and wire, and it had pulled with all its strength to try and get free, so that the wire had tightened and was cutting into its flesh.

Moving as slowly as she dared, she reached out to touch the wire. What would Dad have done if he'd found this hare? Stamped on its head, probably, and said something with a laugh about putting it out of its misery. She could easily kill it. All she'd have to do would be to put her hands around its neck and squeeze.

Its bleeding legs were warm. They struggled as she touched them, and the hare scrabbled with its forepaws.

"Sssh," she said. "I ain't gonna hurt you."

The hare stopped struggling and stared at her.

"*You* can talk?" it said.

The hare's mouth didn't move, but Cath heard the voice, low and clear. Her heart threw itself against her rib cage. Everything disappeared: the dogs, Dad, Johnny White.

It was a hare, and she could hear it talk. And she'd thought for a second about killing it . . .

She pulled her hand away.

" 'Course I can talk," she said, keeping her voice to a low whisper. "Can you?"

"Well, of course *I* can," said the hare weakly. "But . . . you're a human! Why would *you* be able to talk?"

This was crazy. She was inventing things. Cath peered around the forest of stems, expecting to see some person lurking there, snorting with muffled laughter. But nothing was moving; not a leaf rustled out of time.

She looked at the hare's bleeding legs again.

"Want me to get that off?"

The hare twitched, and a tremor ran up its body.

"Yes, please," it said.

Cath found the end of the wire and began to unloop it

as carefully as she could, but her hand was shaking so badly that when she pulled the wire away from the skin, the hare trembled and moaned.

"There you go," she said, pulling the last loop off its hind paw. "Free."

The hare struggled with the urge to bolt away from her. It kicked at a few leaves and got perilously close to the wire again.

"Idiot," she said. "You'll get caught again. Don't do that."

She pushed the wire away. It was too tangled with the undergrowth for her to pull it out, so she did her best to twist it up into a tighter bundle.

"You have my gratitude," the hare managed. "How . . . how fortunate . . ."

"Go on," said Cath. "You're free. Run away."

But the hare crouched awkwardly on its sore legs and stayed where it was. It was silent for so long that Cath realized she must have been inventing the sound of its voice in her head, just like she'd invented the feeling of being a wolf. That wasn't surprising, really. Sometimes when the dogs barked at home, she thought she heard them shouting real words at her.

And then the hare spoke again, so quietly that she wasn't sure if she'd actually heard it.

"Are you . . . are you one of them? Do they really *exist*?"

Cath's ears buzzed, and the words repeated themselves to

her, again and again, until she knew beyond doubt that it was true. The hare was talking to her. Coldness ran over her skin, and she had to put her hands against the ground to steady herself. At least that was normal: the ground, wet and covered in trampled plants. Solid.

She frowned, trying to concentrate. "They? What d'you mean?"

"*Them.* The telas."

"What, like fortune-tellers? I ain't one of them." She scowled. The kids at school were always shouting crap about her real mum having run away to join a circus with all the other Gypsies, and living in a caravan rubbing a crystal ball and spouting a load of witchy rubbish.

"Not teller. Tel-a. The creatures who inhabit the places . . . *in between.*"

"What are you on about? What places? I live up the Sawtry."

The hare gazed at her, its black eyes steady. "Have you not heard the old legends? The telas begin life as ordinary creatures, but after a particular event they are thrown into one of the spaces *in between*—that is to say, between the usual divisions that separate creatures: human from hare, ant from skylark, grass from tree. After a tela has fallen into an in-between space, it can talk to whatever type of creature is lying on the other side of it. Perhaps that's what has happened to you."

Cath forgot to breathe. Visions of hares raced through her mind, gathering around her scratched knees, telling her stories of the world beyond town. They would know places she could hide, and ways she could live under hedges and around fields, never having to see another human. They would teach her how to fight with cunning and agility, to make up for the strength she didn't yet possess.

"So I can talk to hares? All hares?"

"Well, it would certainly seem so. Has something happened to you recently? Something shocking?"

Cath felt her back tense. Was this hare going to say something about Johnny White? It wasn't possible. A hare couldn't know about that. "Don't be daft," she said. "Nothing's happened to me. I'm normal."

It wasn't true, though. Johnny White's pale face came into her mind, and she knew suddenly that she wasn't normal. She was older than the earth itself.

"But . . . you are different," said the hare. "Why did you come here, for instance? Humans don't come crawling around here."

"No, they don't," said Cath, glad to push the thoughts of Johnny White away. "That's why I do. I hide."

"From what?"

Cath shrugged. "Everything. Everyone. Out there. And sometimes, in here, I think I can hear it—sort of—breathing."

For a second she heard it—the murmur of wind through

leaves, of water swelling inside tough stems. Maybe it wasn't only hares she could talk to. Perhaps she had crept into one of the places in between *everything*, and in a second, she would hear the whole thicket burst into a forest of chatter.

She listened for it, waiting, stopping her own breath. But really it was only the rumble of cars and the drizzle. And footsteps.

Dad's footsteps. And Dad's voice, speaking into a cell phone.

"Get your backside over 'ere, now. We gotta find 'er. If she gets away . . . ruddy little cow. You get 'ere. Bring Elvis."

Elvis was the neighbors' dog. Elvis was enormous and ferocious; he had a deadly nose. The only thing he ever looked like he might sing about was how many small animals he could murder in a morning.

Cath began to shake. It was stupid, being so scared. Of course she could still get away. She just had to make sure she was hidden so deeply in the bushes that not even Elvis would be able to get to her.

She tried to turn and inch her way backward.

"What's the matter?" said the hare. "Where are you going?"

"I've gotta go," Cath muttered. "He'll find me."

"Who will?"

"My dad. He's getting Elvis. I've gotta go." A bramble caught on her sleeve and she tugged at it. Her arm was shaking.

"Who's Elvis?"

Cath tore at her sweater in desperation, ripping a long gash in the sleeve. It was grabbed immediately by another bramble, thicker than the first. "A dog!" she said, yanking her arm out of the sweater. "A bloody horrible dog!"

"A dog?" The hare stood upright, snapping onto its injured legs. "Ah, I see. In that case, I had better make myself scarce. Can I suggest an alternative to your—er—rather unstructured method of departure?"

"What?" Cath tried to wriggle her other arm out of the sweater, but the brambles caught on her hair, anchoring fast to her head.

"Stay still," said the hare. "My name is Barshin. Remember it if you need to call out to me. And most important—touch nothing. Nothing! Your blood runs with many things, but they are all earthly. Touch nothing!"

With a jerk of its wounded legs, the hare leapt into Cath's arms. She caught it and clutched its warm body.

A strange sound came from Barshin's throat, low and rumbling like the growl of a cat. The dangling legs twitched and kicked out. For a brief second, blunt claws dug deeply into Cath's stomach, and the growl turned into a single, wild shriek.

The ground began to rumble and shake, and the air seemed to tighten, until Cath's skin felt stretched, as though she'd been burned by the sun. She wanted to scramble away, but Barshin squirmed and a flash of twisted colors stamped itself on the air, the same shape as the bundle of wire she'd rescued him from, only larger, much larger—bigger than the bushes, bigger than the trees—bigger than the whole park, a mass of bright, streaming color burning at the sky, so hot that Cath had to close her eyes and bury her face in the hare's soft fur to shield it.

"Open your eyes!" screamed Barshin. "Open your eyes and look!"

Cath threw back her head. The brambles were shrinking away, opening up a clear patch of moss that gleamed with the vivid green of springtime. Four dark pits appeared in the moss, quickly filling with brownish lumps that traveled upward, and upward, spreading and reaching out and painting the air into a solid block of color.

A giant, browny-gray horse had appeared inside the thicket, a lean-framed animal with knees as knobbled as tree roots and jutting hip bones under a hide as dusty as an old dirt track. His head hung low; his mane stuck out in tufts. Only his eyes were bright—eyes that held all the colors of the flash that Cath had hidden her face from.

"I am Zadoc!" boomed the creature, throwing up his head and trailing the colors of his ever-changing eyes across the sky. "Come to Chromos, if you dare!"

## CHAPTER 4

# CHROMOS

"Get on!" said Barshin. "Quick!"

He leapt out of Cath's arms and landed, safe as a cat, on the horse's back. Cath reached for a tuft of wiry mane way above her head. That wasn't going to work—there was no way she could pull herself up there.

But what was she even thinking? This couldn't be real. It must be her mind, sending her crazy. In a minute, Johnny White would walk up and get on the horse and sit there laughing down at her. She must have fallen over, hit her head, it must be a dream . . .

The horse rolled his eye, and then rounded his huge slab of a shoulder and lowered his chest, sinking to the ground.

"Get on!" shouted Barshin. "He can't stay long!"

Cath touched the horse's shoulder. It felt smooth and warm, as soft as old velvet with a pulse strong beneath the skin. Could it be real?

"Stop thinking!" said Barshin. "Just do it!"

She closed her fist around the gray mane, then scrambled up the mountain of rib cage and onto the ridge of spine. The horse stuck his legs out, heaved himself back to his feet, and shook like a dog. She grabbed at mane, neck—anything she could hold on to—and her legs rattled against the horse's sides, as rubbery as if they'd lost all their bones.

Around her, the sky flared into a mass of color. Red—orange—scarlet—turquoise—black—emerald green. For the first few moments she couldn't see anything except streaks and swirls hurtling about the air. But the horse started to move slowly, and the colors became paler.

They were crossing the park. The same park that she'd crossed only minutes before, except now the colors were all mixed up: the bright green of grass was splashed across the normally dark bushes; the yellow of buttercups was growing up the once-white goalposts, and the gritty gray of pavement was clinging to trees that only moments ago had been green and brown.

Where were they? What had just happened?

As if in answer, the horse began to move faster, lurching from side to side. Cath unloosed a hand long enough to reach behind and pull Barshin around to her front, where she could cling to him. He sank into the crook of her elbow gratefully enough.

"Hold on," he whispered, his head tucked against her chest. "Don't fall. You mustn't fall."

Like I'd want to, Cath was going to say, but the horse was off, bounding through town. Her butt bounced hard against his back, rattling her teeth. She concentrated on not biting her tongue.

As the last of the buildings slipped away and they broke into open country, the trees were purple and the roads red, and the yellow sky flashed with bursts of silver that stung Cath's eyes. The air seemed thin, but when she gasped, breath drew down into her lungs and tingled, as warm as sunlight.

"Where are we?" she asked.

"We're in Chromos," said Barshin. "On Zadoc's back. Zadoc is the guide for travelers through here. Just open your eyes and look around, if you want to know where you are."

It was no kind of answer and Cath's eyes were already open, but as she gazed around, the roads seemed to fade away and vanish, until they were walking across a wide plain, the sky spreading vast and cloudless overhead. The sun was warm and the ground was covered in bright grass. Through the grass, a wild herb was growing that kicked up a strong, dusty scent as they brushed past it—a bit like curry, but with the green smell of bashed-up leaves. Small herds of sheep, cows, and horses grazed in the distance, along with a few hairier animals whose name Cath didn't know.

Nothing was moving fast. But there was so much space—she felt she could take off in any direction, wandering slowly or urging Zadoc forward at top speed, and she would see any threats coming from miles away. Not that this place seemed to hold any threats. She was warm and her belly felt full. The land shone before her, grinning, calling her into it.

This is your realm, it said. Here, you can do anything.

In between the grasses there were patches of delicate blue petals, clusters of purple pompons, and great banks of thorny bushes with tiny yellow flowers. As they walked past the bushes, Cath longed to take one of the small flowers, just so she could tuck it away and bring it out when she wanted to remember the sky and the plain, and the feeling of being so powerful yet entirely at peace under a warm sun.

She reached out and touched a flower. A strong smell of coconuts burst into the air, and a flash of bright yellow shot up her finger. Zadoc jerked away. Barshin in her arms gave a convulsive start and scrabbled against her chest with blind paws.

"Ah," said Zadoc when he had moved so she was an arm's length away from anything. "Now, you see, I wouldn't normally be an advocate of doing what one is told. But in certain circumstances . . ."

Cath looked at her right hand. The first and second fingers bore a faint patterning of dark green leaves, spines, and yellow flowers.

"Well, you'll have something to remember us by," said Zadoc, a touch glumly. "Trouble is, remembering isn't always a force for peace."

Cath spat on her fingers and tried to rub the pattern off. It didn't budge.

Away to their left a castle stood on the horizon, mute and dark. To the right, hills and mountains. No tracks or roads ran through the land: Zadoc walked on the grass and flowers, and he walked in whichever direction she wanted him to go.

"Where's the town gone?" asked Cath.

"Who knows?" said Zadoc. "In Chromos, *you* make what you see. This is your country."

"But I live in town. I've lived there all my life. That's my country, ain't it?"

"Perhaps not," said the horse.

Cath let her hands relax around the clump of his mane. She felt sure she'd manage to stay on his back.

"But there ain't nothin' here. It's just empty."

As soon as she said this, she caught herself thinking, Does that mean I'm empty too?

"Empty? This?" said Zadoc. "This is . . . this is fuller than anything has a right to be. Look what you've made. You've made space in this plain and in this sky. You've made freedom, without any roads to lead you. You've made adventure, in the castle and the mountains—who knows what could be inside and over them? You've made an infinity of color and taste and smell in these plants. You've made *life* in the animals. And you say it's empty?"

Cath gazed at the sky and the plain, and heat burned through her chest. Could Zadoc be right? Had she really made all this? She'd never been anywhere at all like it in the real world. Everything stretched wide and bright before her, and the air was quiet. Even when a breeze picked up and she turned around, thinking that it must be the breathing of creatures lurking in shadows behind her back, there were only more plains and mountains and a flock of geese winging their way across the sky.

She couldn't have made this. She'd never imagined such a place could exist. She'd never seen enough to think that it was possible.

But all the things she dreamed of were there: a world to explore, entirely hers, with nobody to answer to and nobody to hate.

"Can we go anywhere?" she asked. Her shoulders were warm with sunlight, so warm that for a second she thought they might crack open and hatch a great pair of spreading wings. But she didn't want wings. She wanted to feel the power of Zadoc beneath her, beating his hooves against the earth. Real life had vanished: there was no need to look over her shoulder anymore. She could run for the joy of it.

"Anywhere—everywhere—or nowhere!" said Zadoc, throwing up his head.

Cath looked down at Barshin, who untucked his head from her chest and stared back up in silence. She thought hard. Anywhere? And the words poured themselves out in a jumbled, excited stream.

"When I'm at home—"

"Don't talk about home," said Zadoc. "Not here."

"Well, I just think about this place—a house, not big, just maybe two or three rooms, that's only mine. And then there's some fields around it, and then a massive dark forest with deer and pigs and horses in it, and the forest goes up the sides of these mountains, where bears and tigers live, and the mountains go so high that no one ever bothers to come over them. Then on the other side there's the sea, which is full of whales and sharks and giant squid and stuff, but the sharks know me so they don't kill me if I go in there, but they'd kill anyone else who tried. Sometimes I go and find all the animals and fish and stuff, and sometimes I build things in the forest, and sometimes I just go around the fields and lie in the grass and look at the clouds. And nobody else ever comes there, unless I want them to. And when I want them to go, they have to go."

She'd never said that to anyone at home. It was the stupid sort of dream that little kids had, until they grew out of it. But neither Barshin nor Zadoc commented on her words. Zadoc just began to move, gathering his great legs into a smooth leap, and then they were bucketing over the plain, so fast that the horizon ahead was shaken up into the waves of a choppy green sea.

Cath closed her eyes and missed, for a long while, what they were galloping over, because it was so good just to listen to the strength of her own powerful blood, beating warmth and courage through her veins. She'd never felt so strong. She knew that if anything came leaping across the plain toward them—armies, monsters, wolves, even Dad—she'd grow claws from her fingers and fangs from her teeth and a sword from each hand, and defeat them all, without fear.

When Zadoc slowed, she opened her eyes again. The plain had gone. They were on a beach, wide and white, with the sea to their left and some sand dunes crouching to their right. Beyond the dunes, at a little distance, the forest-covered slopes of mountains rose steeply into the pale sky, and seabirds screamed overhead.

Zadoc pointed his nose inland, and Cath saw a roof and chimney peering over the top of the dunes, with a narrow path leading toward them.

"Is it there?" she dared to ask.

"Of course," said Zadoc. "Or here. It's always either there or here. Shall we go up?"

Cath heard the distant call of a wolf. Her nose picked up traces of pine in the air.

"Yeah. Let's go."

They turned up the sandy path. Beyond the dunes crouched a low house with whitewashed walls and a thick thatched roof, and in front of it a garden bright with thousands of small flowers. The house was as much a part of the land as the trees and garden that surrounded it: the walls seemed to have grown out of fallen rocks, the roof from the tough sea grasses that fringed the dunes, and the window frames from sapling trees, planted in the corners of each window. It was almost breathing.

It was her house.

Zadoc was right! She'd made it up! She'd made everything—the land, the sky, this house, the animals, the freedom—these were her wildest dreams. And she'd thought they were *unthinkable*.

Cath's heart soared for a moment, out into the blue sky, swooping alongside the seabirds in their clean, free flight. Their feathers brushed against it, and it stretched toward them, purring with pleasure.

"Put me down," she said, trying to swing her leg over Zadoc's back. "I'm stopping here."

"No!" said Barshin. "You can't! This is Chromos, the land of colors! It's full of everything that could ever happen—all the things that never will, and all that might, and all the things that no one has even thought about yet. If you fall into Chromos, it'll swallow you down into a hole full of all the people you might have been and might one day be, and the person you are now will get lost among them. You must stay on Zadoc's back!"

"Says who?" said Cath, letting herself start to slide down toward the white path.

But Zadoc swung his huge head around and knocked at her roughly with his nose, barring her way.

"The hare is right," he said. "You can't walk the ground in Chromos. No earthly creature can. Your mind would eat itself up. Content yourself with your eyes, for now."

Beside the house there was a brick well with a metal bucket hanging on a chain. As they drew closer, Cath saw a dark patch of shadow spread over the ground next to the well, a thin layer of powdery gray fog clinging like mist to its surface.

The longer she looked at the patch, the heavier her stomach grew, until she felt as if she'd eaten a bagful of cold fries. Wisps of smeary smoke drifted up and collected in small whirlwinds above it.

"What's that?"

"It's a path," said Zadoc. "It links Chromos to the current owners of this house, wherever they are on earth."

"What? But you said this is just my dream, didn't you? I made it up."

"Oh no," Zadoc assured her. "What you see in Chromos is no mere dream. Many things here do indeed exist on earth. There is even a creature that makes a trade of mixing Chromos and earth, and it is he who is responsible for that path. Sammael, they call him, the Master of the Air. His business is none of ours, but thanks to his work, if you jumped down into that patch, you'd land on earth right next to this house. Or your mangled corpse would, anyway. Probably your brains would have exploded out of your ears on the way down, but most of you would get there."

"What if you take me?" asked Cath, letting herself feel hopeful for a second.

"Oh no," said Zadoc. "My colors would get all jumbled up and I'd die. Not immediately, but soon enough."

Cath didn't see how the house could possibly be real if she couldn't go to it. Zadoc was lying to her—this was something she was imagining, and very soon she would have to stop it and go back to the Sawtry, which did exist, and was where she really belonged.

At once the plain lost its greenness and darkened into khaki, and then dusty violet. The sky became streaked with yellow, and black clouds swam up from the horizon.

"Don't," said Zadoc. "Don't compare it to what you're used to seeing. Don't call that reality. *This* is reality, right now . . ."

But suddenly Zadoc's hooves were clattering against pavement. He stumbled on a sharp stone and began to run away in pain, tripping and falling over his own feet, galloping faster and faster.

"No . . ." Cath tried to say. "Barshin, don't let him . . . Make him stop . . . I want to stay . . ."

Barshin had his eyes closed and his head pushed into Cath's armpit, and she had to cling to Zadoc again to keep on his back, his wide, lumpy ribs rolling from side to side, bouncing her painfully on his spine. Her head snapped up and down so hard she thought her neck would break, and then they were falling through endless space.

✦ ✦ ✦

Zadoc came to a sudden halt, and Cath pitched over his shoulders, and then she was standing on the old railway line in a clearer part of the thicket, holding a hot, struggling Barshin in her arms. The hare's legs kicked against her until she dropped him, then he leapt high into the air and jack-knifed twice before settling back onto the ground. His entire body was shaking.

"Oh—oh dear," he stammered. "Oh dear, I'd forgotten— I'd forgotten—quite how blinding that place can be."

"Where's Dad?" said Cath. "Is he still here?"

Now that her feet were on the ground, her legs felt as if they'd been drained of their blood. She scanned the edge of the bank, but Dad wasn't standing there, and neither was Elvis the dog. How much time had passed in that place? Was it really long enough for Dad to have given up and gone home?

"I've got to go there again," said Cath. "I've got to go back. What *was* that place?"

"Chromos," said Barshin. "It's the land of colors. A world made of our minds—of our imaginations, if you like. But not an imaginary world. It is another land that sits on top of our world, in exactly the same place. Everyone sees a world unique to themselves in there, though. And apart from you, only Zadoc knows what you see. Because what *you* see in Chromos is the color at the core of your very being: what you imagine most deeply—your desires, and your fear."

"How does it know?" Cath shrank for a second at the thought that something had seen inside her, looked deep into the thoughts she always kept well hidden away.

Barshin shook his head. "It just knows. That's what Chromos is made of—the longings and the dreams of every creature that has ever lived, and much more besides. It just knows."

Dreams. Did that mean she could do things there? Make things? Become things?

"I want to go back," she said.

Barshin nodded. "Of course. You can escape into Chromos whenever you like, if you know how. You can't always control it, mind—you might spend seconds in there, or hours, or days. You might travel only a few yards, or hundreds of miles. You might see just as you see on earth, or you might see another world entirely. Anything is possible in Chromos.

You just have to know how to call Zadoc, and then you can come and go as you please."

"Can't I go by myself?"

Barshin twitched his whiskers and said, "Oh no! As I warned you—you must always be on Zadoc's back, or touching him, at least. He ensures that you only see the strongest possibility in your mind. Imagine if you were to see all of them! You'd go crazy on the spot. But I could call Zadoc again for you, if you wanted. I can always call him."

"Yeah," said Cath. "Call him now. Maybe Dad's coming back. I should go now."

The colors still danced before her eyes. That wide plain, the animals, the house—was that really out there, somewhere? Could she really find it again?

"Well, you see, the thing is, I need a favor. Perhaps you could do something for me? And then I'll call Zadoc for you, whenever you want."

"Do what?" Cath didn't take her eyes off the hare, even though she knew she should be looking out for Dad.

"I need to get a message to someone. I was told he might be a tela, too, but I've tried talking to him and I don't think he can hear me. Do you think you could give him the message?"

There was bound to be a hidden bit. There always was, if anyone ever asked you to pass on a message. That was the sort of thing that happened all the time on the Sawtry.

"I can't," said Cath. "The minute I get out of here, Dad'll find me."

"He won't," the hare assured her. "I promise you. Didn't I say that time passes strangely in Chromos? Look—the sun's higher, and the morning dews have gone—we must have been away for a while this time. They'll have searched and not been able to find you, nor to follow your scent out of here—how could they, when you didn't leave? I'm certain they won't still be waiting. If they are, I promise to take you straight back into Chromos. And I'm not asking you to go alone, I'll come too. I just need you to speak for me, so that this message is heard and understood."

Cath considered Barshin for a moment. He might be lying. But what reason could he possibly have to lie?

"Okay," she said grudgingly. "Who is he, this guy you want?"

She half expected the hare to say Dad, or one of the guys on the estate, although there wasn't any reason to think a hare would want to say anything to them. He didn't look like a gangster hare.

Barshin said, in a curious, tight voice, "A boy. He's called Danny O'Neill."

The name rang a bell. It wasn't a bell of alarm, though: Danny O'Neill was just a boy in her year at school, a small, pale boy who never had much to say to anyone. Cath hadn't looked at him more than twice in the two years she'd been there. Not that she'd looked at any of the boys much. They weren't as vicious as the girls, but they were still stupid idiots who hated her just because she was Cath Carrera and dared to exist.

"I know him," she said. "What's the message?"

"His cousin is in danger," said Barshin. "His cousin Tom is in great danger—there are hideous rumors flying around the world. And Danny O'Neill is the only one with the knowledge and power to intervene. Something has gone horribly wrong, and it is his duty to set it right."

"Jeez," said Cath. "Don't ask much, do you?"

"It isn't a question of asking much." Barshin twitched. "It's a question of what's wrong, and what must be done in order to fix it. So, will you tell him my message?"

"Sure," said Cath. "Don't mean he'll listen, though."

"He'll have to listen," said Barshin. "He has no choice."

"Come to school, then," said Cath. "That's where he'll be."

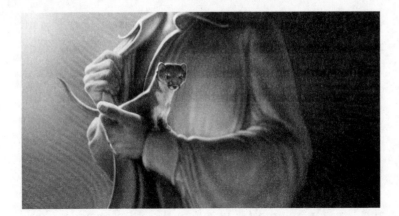

## CHAPTER 5

# SAND

"Sand. What harm can you do with sand? Throw it in someone's eye? Scratch their eyeball? Sand's harmless! And it isn't even very much sand!"

"Be quiet, stoat."

The tall, humanlike figure closed his fingers and opened them again to look at what he held. A few grains of brownish sand.

The stoat peeped out from where she sat, tucked inside his shirt collar, and chattered angrily. "Rubbish! You're telling me you can destroy the world with a few grains of sand? It's rubbish! You're useless! Powerless! I need someone who's strong and vicious and mean and savage! They told me Sammael was the one to come to. And all you've got is sand!"

Sammael's fingers twitched. His arms were as thin as broomsticks inside his white shirtsleeves, and a low shine lit up his close-curled black hair, but no sun or moon hung in the sky. Here in Chromos, no lights followed him, only shifting clouds of darkness.

"You misjudged me, stoat, if what you wanted was blood and fire. I'm the master of a better kind of revenge. Could you do this with a sword?"

He opened his fingers and let the grains of sand trickle down onto the floor. They bounced for a second, and then a gray patch began to spread around the place where they lay.

"It's just another path," muttered the stoat. "You've shown me them before. They don't do *anything* bad."

Sammael stepped back to the edge of the patch, and then leaned forward to peer down it.

"This one's different," he said.

The stoat craned her neck. For a second all she saw was the real earth below, the world she'd come from and been normal in, until terrible things had happened.

The wide, green earth, a field, a couple of humans walking through it.

Humans. Hated humans.

The stoat bared her teeth.

And then a great puff of colors—scarlet, green, purple,

yellow—rose up from the floor at Sammael's feet, and rolled over, tumbling into the hole and streaming down through the sky toward the earth.

The colors pounded down in a waterfall into the earth, and others swarmed to join them—blue, gray, orange, and pink—and the humans shrieked. They turned to each other, but neither seemed to notice the colors falling onto their heads. Instead, they stared madly into each other's eyes, then began to dance, legs stamping and beating the heavy soil. Closer and closer they got, until their legs and arms became tangled together and they fell, shrieking and yelling.

And then they began to fight. One tried to strangle the other. The second put up fists and feet, kicking and punching at his friend. They choked each other with mud. They hit each other with stones. They shouted and screamed and roared. They did not stop until one of them was dead and the other was lying beside him, bruised and exhausted.

Still, neither noticed the colors that continued to fall from the sky and soak away into the earth.

"The human mind turned inside out," said Sammael. "Madness. Violence. Chaos. Was that the kind of revenge you were imagining?"

"Hah!" screamed the stoat, her blood hot with excitement. "That's better! But it's only two of them. More must die! Do more! Do it to all of them, right now!"

"Patience," said Sammael, turning away from the hole. If

only the earth didn't absorb the colors of Chromos as fast as they fell. If only they would spread about its surface like a flood, then no more holes would be needed. But that wasn't the way things worked. He needed more holes. A hole as big as the world itself.

"More!" shrieked the stoat. "I want to see more!"

Sammael's fingers reached up to his collar. He closed them around the stoat and held her little brown body in front of his face, looking into the glinting black eyes.

"I said, patience. I need exactly the right sand to make these kinds of holes. It doesn't grow on beaches."

"Well, find more! Come on!"

The long fingers clenched, and the stoat squirmed in a spasm of pain.

"Softly, softly," murmured Sammael. "I'll be getting a whole lot of it, quite soon." He contemplated the angry animal, and then his impassive face softened. "But maybe you've got a point. No harm in trying to hurry things along a bit, is there?"

He put the stoat back inside his collar and began to walk through the floor of Chromos, down and down, as smoothly as if he were striding down the long slope of a hill toward the solid earth below.

## CHAPTER 6

# NATURE AT YOUR FINGERTIPS

Tom was mending the fences around Hangman's Wood. Sweat ran between his shoulder blades as he slammed the mallet down onto post after post. The rain had stopped for a moment, but a stifling thickness in the air spoke of a coming storm. Still, the sky was now pleasantly blue with white clouds scudding across it, and even if the fence line did stretch on ahead of him and there were a hundred more fence posts to beat into the ground, it was good to be working. And to have something to hit.

Johnny—*thud!*—what a coward—*thud!*—running away and leaving him to it—*thud!*—those dogs leaping on the badger—*thud! thud!*—those men laughing—*thud!*—and he, Tom, had run away—*thud!* Running away—*thud!*—what kind of a thing was *that* to do?—*thud! thud! thud!*

Sometimes, in the pauses between thuds of the mallet, he heard the rapid rattle of a woodpecker in the wood, and earlier there'd been a few soft hoots from an owl, unwilling to close its eyes against the morning. The skylark had grown used to the sharp bangs too, and was hovering high above him bellowing a crazy jumble of tumbling song. Crows and magpies were cawing irritably at one another as they prowled the corners of the empty field.

He stopped hammering for a moment to let his arms and back recover a bit. As he leaned against one of the new fence posts, a woodpecker fluttered down from a tree at the edge of the wood. It began poking its beak into the ground to look for grubs, so silent and focused that he thought it must be alone until he heard a squeak behind it and saw another, younger woodpecker tumbling down the tree.

"Mum!" the squeak clearly said. "Mum! Mum! Feed me!" The young woodpecker bounced up to its mother with its beak open. "Mum! Feed me! I'm hungry!"

The mother woodpecker sighed and stuffed a few ants into its beak.

"Mummy! I only like fat ants, and these are thin! Get me fat ants!"

"Stick your beak in the ground, you useless bunch of

fluff," said the mother woodpecker tartly. "It's not the science of flight, for tweeting out loud. Just stick your beak in and get the fat ants yourself."

Tom grinned to himself. Not every sound was a cry of pain, then. And his grin broadened as he thought about it: he, Tom Fletcher, could understand the woodpeckers, the owls, the badgers, the starlings, and the sparrows—every single thing they said. He had spent the past year learning the calls of hundreds of birds and animals. Last week, after days of struggle, he had come to understand the endless poetry of the skylarks, who sang for hours as they soared over the wide fields. Yesterday, he had pretty much got to grips with the crows.

One day soon, he would understand every creature that shared his land, or flew in the skies above him.

He was thinking about this so strongly that he didn't notice how the woodpeckers froze and shrank into the shade of the tree trunks when the man stepped out of Hangman's Wood. All Tom noticed was that Sammael was back—Sammael, whom he'd met a year ago, and who'd given him the book of bird and animal calls that had led him to this happiness.

His heart leapt with joy as he saw the tall figure in the white shirt.

"Hello!" he called out. "You've found me again! Welcome to my farm!"

Sammael came forward with an open, smiling face. He shook Tom's hand in a vigorous way.

"Hello! How's it going? You still having fun with that book?"

Tom grinned. "Never put it down. I'm almost at the end, would you believe it? A handful of pages left. How lucky you came up here today! What brings you?"

"Ah." Sammael cocked his head back toward the woods. "Please excuse my trespass. I'm looking for badger setts. I think there's some baiters around—I found a new sett earthed up, down in that little copse on the other side of the valley. Thought I'd check up here."

Tom realized that his hand had clenched around Sammael's and he pulled it away quickly.

"They've been here," he said, and the sunshine seemed to fade.

"Already?"

"Last night. I saw them. They killed a pregnant sow by the sett at the top of the wood. Evil men."

Sammael's face, too, lost its cheerful air and became pinched.

"Evil is one word for it. I could think of a few others."

"So could I," said Tom. "But what's the use? People like that—"

"Oh, come now." Sammael raised an eyebrow. "You can't be thinking of letting them get away with it?"

Tom reached out to the fence post, more just to touch something solid than because he really needed to lean on it.

"No!" he said. "Of course not! I just . . . I don't know what to do. I knew they were coming last night. My mate told me. I tried calling the police, but they wouldn't do anything. So we went up there and waited. I even took my shotgun, but I couldn't shoot at the fight in case I hit the badger, so I went for the guys but I missed, and then they turned one of the dogs on me. I had to run away. Stupid!"

Tom bit back a pointless curse and made himself loosen his grip on the fence post, trying to remember the feeling of listening to the woodpeckers. But it was right to be angry about cruelty. Maybe if he did shoot one of the men next time, he'd get away with arguing it was in self-defense.

As if he'd seen into Tom's thoughts, Sammael gave a bitter laugh. "A shotgun? That's a bit dramatic, isn't it? There's not much point in trying to fight angry men with dangerous dogs. You're bound to end up getting hurt yourself. I think you need to be a bit more creative."

Tom eyed him, not liking the half smile on the older man's face. Was he being patronized?

"Oh yeah?" he said eventually. "How's that?"

"Well, isn't there someone who could help you? If you could get a few people together, the baiters might not want to take you all on."

"There were two of us last night," said Tom gloomily,

thinking of Johnny White's panicked flight. "The other guy was the one who told me about them. But he got scared and ran away as soon as they let the dogs go."

"What about your family? They own this farm, don't they? That brother you were looking for when I met you last summer—surely he'd be brave enough to help you?"

Tom snorted. "Danny? He's not my brother, he's my cousin, and he's scared of the sound of a leaf falling! And he doesn't care a fig about badgers. Maybe Mum might help, I don't know . . . I think she'd just keep calling the police, though. And my sister, Sophie, is at university now. She used to like animals, but she's not been near the woods since she discovered wedge heels."

Sammael's lip curled in scorn. "And that's it? No giant brass-knuckled dad or tattooed uncles?"

Tom shook his head.

"Well then, we'll have to do it ourselves. What about your book?" Sammael indicated the thin paperback sticking out of Tom's tool bag. "Knowledge is a powerful tool, you know. Couldn't you start making use of your new knowledge?"

Tom frowned. "Understanding bird and animal calls? How's that going to help me stop dogs killing badgers? I can already understand the badgers, and it didn't help last night."

"There's got to be a way," said Sammael, looking toward the edge of the woods and falling into a thoughtful silence. Tom waited, and then a streak of sunlight caught the pale green hazel leaves and they blazed up for a second, shining with hope.

Sammael turned back to him. "I've got a sort of half-formed idea. But it would require some preparation. Maybe leave it with me, for now. Have you seen the kingfisher down at the Tybourne brook? I've just come up from there this morning—she was sitting on a willow branch over the stream when I left."

Tom took his hand off the fence post to reach over for the book. He smoothed his fingers over the cover and read the title for the thousandth time: Nature at Your Fingertips.

"Kingfishers!" he said, flicking through the pages. "I haven't seen one since early spring. The stream at the bottom here is too shallow once the weather improves, so they don't come here later in the year. Where exactly was it?"

He found the page of the book, stroked it, and listened to the kingfisher's quiet calls. A vision of electric-blue plumage and a bright orange chest came strongly into his mind.

"I'll have to show you—it's difficult to describe," said Sammael, shrugging. "I'll take you there one day, when you're not so busy."

"Oh, this doesn't need to be finished now—it's more of a deterrent than anything else, and I know it won't really work. I can leave it for a bit, easy. Why don't we walk over to Tybourne now? It's only a couple of miles."

Sammael looked doubtful. "If you're sure . . ."

"Yeah, of course. I learned the kingfishers' calls when they were here before, but I'm not sure I really got all of them. I've been wanting to check for ages. Come on, let's go!"

Tom picked up his T-shirt, laid the mallet down, and shoved the book into his pocket. He didn't bother getting his phone out to send a text to his mum. She wouldn't worry—it wasn't unusual for him to go wandering off. Sometimes you had to break free.

✦ ✦ ✦

The kingfisher was still there. They watched as it swooped down over the brook and rose up to perch on the willow, waiting and then swooping again. The sun vanished, but even under the dull clouds the bird's feathers shone sapphire-bright.

"Easy does it," it chirruped, settling back down onto its branch and staring into the water. And then, louder, in a single cry, "This branch is mine! Don't even *think* about it!"

Whatever bird it was calling to stayed hidden in the tangled copse behind the far bank of the stream, and Tom heard no answering challenge.

"Did you understand it?" asked Sammael, leaning back against the smooth trunk of a wild cherry tree.

"Every word," said Tom. "They're quite easy, those calls. Very clear. I don't know why I thought I might not have got it right."

"Ah, it's a good book, if I say so myself." Sammael held out a hand, and Tom passed the small paperback over to him. Its brown cover was still clean, despite the thousands of times he'd thumbed through it.

Sammael opened the book, stroked a few odd pages and listened to them, then passed it back to Tom.

"The magic doesn't fade, does it? How far have you got?"

Tom smiled the forced little grin that he kept for occasions when he tried to ask himself how the book actually worked. The word *magic* was stupid. He couldn't think of another explanation for it, though. Stroking a book, feeling the pages turn into a bird or animal, and hearing the sounds of that creature—it shouldn't be possible. But that was what the book did, and he was happy with that unless he started to think about it too much.

He went for the more sensible question. "I've almost got to the end. There are so many groups of birds that share the same calls—it's sort of like dialects of the same language, isn't it? So it didn't take nearly as long as I thought it would. There are a few things left, though. Some animals, and golden eagles. They'll be hard—I need to find a real one to listen to, if I can. Recordings don't really work."

"Ah, yes, I remember finding that when I was writing it. No, there's no real alternative to finding something out for yourself, is there? Well, that'll be an adventure for you, at least. Look!"

Sammael's finger flicked out toward the far bank of the brook, and there was the kingfisher, returning to its perch with a silver fish crushed in its sharp beak. The bird threw back its head and snapped the fish down into its orange throat, then rustled out its wings in satisfaction as the sun broke through the clouds.

"Brilliant!" whispered Tom. "She's so beautiful!"

Sammael dipped his head in acknowledgment, his eyes warm with delight. For a moment, both Tom and Sammael gazed across at the kingfisher, a glistening jewel against the dusty green willow leaves.

"But there are still so many ugly things in this world," said Sammael. "Badger baiters, for a start."

"Yeah." Tom looked into the running brook. "Yeah, I haven't forgotten."

The water bubbled darkly over the mud of the streambed. Tom noticed clumps of rotting grasses by his feet, teeming with squat black beetles, and the sun disappeared again. He shrugged and looked down the path toward home.

"Well, I'd better get on with that fence while I can. I want to be up in the woods again tonight, in case they come back." He put the book in his pocket.

"I meant what I said," said Sammael. "I think there's another way we can go about it. Leave it with me. I'll come and find you—tomorrow, say—and hopefully by then I'll have a fully formed plan B we can try."

"We? You'll help me?"

"Of course." Sammael nodded his dark head briefly. "I want them stopped as much as you do. Till tomorrow, then. Good luck tonight. Stay safe."

He walked away from the bank, his feet making so little noise on the rushes and grasses that the kingfisher sat undisturbed on its willow branch until Sammael's white shirt and scuffed boots were well out of sight.

And then Tom moved, and at the first rustle of his shoe against a twig, the little blue bird leapt from its branch and flew off into the safety of the trees.

## CHAPTER 7

# DANNY O'NEILL

"That's him over there," said Cath. "On the bike."

The boy coming out of the alleyway was scrawny with close-cut brown hair. His bike was shiny and new and too big for him. As he swung the bike around and pedaled out across the road, Cath saw that his helmet was clipped through the straps of his schoolbag. Trying not to look like a geek. Failing.

She opened her mouth to call out to him.

"Danny!"

But another voice got there first, a boy's, and the tone was slow and mocking.

"Oi! Dan-nee! Danny Oh-Neeill! Oi!"

The boy was walking with a small group of others. It was Paul Barnes, who Cath would have said was Danny's friend. But Danny wasn't turning his head. His face was set steely pink, and his eyes looked straight ahead. He stood up on his pedals to push them faster.

"Oi!" yelled Paul. "I'm talking to you, weirdo!"

The group with Paul laughed. He picked up a stone from the pavement and chucked it at Danny. With deadly accuracy, or perhaps just luck, it hit Danny on the butt. Everyone screamed with laughter.

"Want to talk to the trees?" shouted one of the girls. "Here!"

She grabbed a stick from the base of one of the plane trees and lobbed it at Danny. He was too far away now for them to hit him, but the others began flinging more bits of broken stick at his diminishing backside, so that for a couple of seconds there was a volley of flying tree parts. Then Danny turned in to the school, tried to cycle off across the playground, and was shouted at by Mr. Berry, the vice principal. The gang dropped their sticks before they were seen.

Cowards, thought Cath. Frightened by a teacher.

It began to rain. A few dark spots peppered the pavement and Cath lingered under the last plane tree.

"Take me in there," said Barshin. "Take me to him. Together we can explain everything."

Cath breathed in the swarms of children and concrete and damp iron railings. Nobody noticed her there, standing with a small brown hare, but they would once she was inside the school gates. She swung the bag off her back and crouched down, pulling out the thin schoolbooks and holding the bag open.

"Get in," she said.

Barshin took a deep breath and hopped into the bag.

Inside the gates, Danny O'Neill had vanished. Gone straight off to class, probably. Cath tried to slink past the door of her classroom and go after him, but the teacher was waiting outside, rounding up reluctant children.

"We'll go after this class," Cath whispered to Barshin, although she wasn't sure if he'd heard above the chattering and scraping of chairs. Trying to put the bag on the floor gently so as not to injure the hare, she moved so slowly that the teacher asked if she'd hurt herself.

"Nope," said Cath. The teacher wrote something in her notebook.

The bag at Cath's feet began to wriggle. She prodded it with a toe. There was a frantic scrabbling sound from underneath the table and a smell floated up, briny and hot.

"What's that?" said the teacher.

"Nothing." Cath prodded the bag. The scrabbling was replaced by a thin ripping *screech* as Barshin found one of the many small tears and used his powerful paws and teeth to gouge a hole. His head shoved itself into the open, nostrils wide, eyes wet with fear.

For a moment, Cath had no idea what to do. Then the bag began to move across the floor and a foreleg came punching through another hole, and she grabbed at it. Barshin's struggles were surprisingly strong.

She swore. "Don't do that!"

"Let—me—out!" gasped Barshin.

Cath twisted the bag, trying to find the clip.

"Catherine CARRERA!" shouted the teacher. "Get that OUT OF HERE!"

"I am!" said Cath, yanking open the bag. Barshin's head was stuck through the hole he'd made. Cath tried to push him back through, but in his panic he scratched at her hand with claws that were sharp and stubby and made her bleed. She pulled her hand away.

Somehow the hare freed himself and dashed from corner to corner of the classroom, bashing against table legs and walls in his panic. Cath dropped the remains of her bag and ran to the door, wrenching it open.

"Come on!"

And for a moment, only the two of them existed in the world—she and the hare, hearts leaping. They would escape—they'd escape together! We're exactly the same kind of creature, thought Cath. All we need is to get away!

Barshin saw the gap and shot through it, and Cath ran

after him with the howls of the teacher smarting in her ears. Down the hallway, down the stairs, out into the sweet air of the concrete yard, and then they both stopped. The air was heavy with the forced quietness of hundreds of children in classrooms, hunched over desks.

The hare was gasping a little. "That bag . . ." He shuddered. "Never again."

"You were safe, you know. But I guess—you were in a bag," said Cath, understanding what it was to know and to fear.

"Where's Danny O'Neill?" said Barshin, looking around. "Was he back there, in that room?"

"No, he's in another class. Up there." Cath waved a hand toward the upper corner of the opposite building, and then the door behind them swung open and her teacher came screeching through.

"Shoo!" the teacher yelled, waving her arms in a windmill and clattering toward Barshin. "Shoo! Get away!"

Barshin leapt into the air with a compulsive kick, crashing against Cath's elbow. Together they bounded through the double doors of the building opposite.

"At the end, on the right!" she panted to Barshin, who accelerated so quickly that she barely saw him reach the end of the hall. He launched a flying kick at the classroom door with his long hind legs, and Cath sprinted after him, knowing that she was running into a room with only one exit but that Barshin would scorch his way out if he had to. And where he went, she could follow.

When she got there, the door had been opened and Barshin was somewhere under the sea of tables and chairs and legs of all kinds. Children were leaping up, pushing back the furniture, struggling to trace the path of the crazed hare.

"It's here!"

"There! There! Get it!"

A high shriek as the animal came too close to someone who'd only ever watched hamsters through the shiny mesh of a cage. A girl scrambled up onto a table.

"It touched me! It touched me!"

Only one person in the classroom sat unmoving. He was at a table by himself because his desk mate, Paul, had moved away to sit with another boy, and he had turned his eyes away from the chaos, as though he had decided that if he did not look at it, it could not come near him.

But all too soon the hare was underneath his chair and every eye in the room turned toward him. The children backed away, one step, then two, and the shouts died down with a hiss.

For a long second, Cath stared at Danny O'Neill. His face was white. He was gazing at a fixed point on the wall ahead. His fingers were curled around the edge of a piece of paper, which looked more like a drawing than a sheet of history notes.

Cath had no time to try and see what it was. The teacher's hand grabbed her collar, twisting it around into a choke hold.

"Is that animal yours?" he hissed. "Get it out of here!"

Danny O'Neill's gaze flicked away from the wall and he caught Cath's eye. Why was he still just sitting there?

"Run!" Cath shouted at him as shrieks began to rise again around the room.

Danny pushed back his chair, crushing the paper in his fist. He stumbled blankly toward Cath.

"Oh no you don't!" yelled the history teacher over the hubbub. He tried to take a step toward Danny and tripped over a chair leg.

Danny shot forward like a cannonball.

The teacher let go of Cath's collar more in surprise than pain, but before he could compute Danny O'Neill's peculiar charge, Danny and Cath and Barshin the hare were running for their lives toward the same target: the school gates.

## CHAPTER 8

# THE MESSAGE

They dodged out into the road and ran along the pavement, the plane trees passing by in a blur. At the end of the street, Cath turned to the right, away from the Sawtry, and Danny to the left, away from the center of town, so they collided and stopped running, breathing hard. Cath's right sock was soaked from splashing into a puddle, and now that she'd stopped running she saw that it was still raining, a little steadier. Danny's face was glistening wet.

"We can't stop," he gasped. "He'll find us."

"Your teacher? Nah, he'll only have run as far as the phone. Fat fool," said Cath. People like that didn't run.

Barshin hopped up and down the curb a couple of times, shaking his paws as the raindrops landed on his fur. Danny wasn't looking at him, although Cath could see by the tilt of his head that a part of him wanted to.

"I can hear him!" said Barshin. "He talks too! He must be a tela! Why doesn't he—"

But Danny evidently couldn't hear Barshin, because he broke in halfway through.

"I don't mean my teacher . . . I mean, we'll get into trouble," he said.

"So?"

"So I don't want to. I'm going back."

Cath stared at him. "Are you scared 'cause we ran out of school?"

"Yeah," said Danny. "I'm scared. I'm a coward. Go away and leave me alone."

"What about him?" said Cath. She pointed toward the hare, who was trying to brush raindrops off his whiskers. "Can you hear him? He says he can hear you."

Danny stared at her. *What?*

"He says he can hear you. Says you must be a tela, like me."

"It's a hare. People can't talk to hares."

But he didn't say "hares can't talk," thought Cath. That's what anyone else would have said.

"We can," she said. "Can't we? Me. And you."

Danny looked away. "You're being stupid. I'm going

back," he said, and turned in a direction that wasn't away from school, but wasn't toward it either.

What was wrong with him? Cath was used to feeling like she was some kind of alien, but this boy didn't make sense at all.

She reached forward and snatched the paper from his hand. He lunged to get it back, but she dashed around the corner into a bus shelter. And Danny just gave up. He stood outside the shelter in the rain, his shoulders sagging and his thin face set, as if he were trying not to cry.

Cath smoothed out the picture. It was a tree, twisted and black and dead, and there was a streak of lightning coming down from the top of the page, driving itself into the crook of two branches.

"What is it?" she asked.

"It's . . ." Danny put a hand up to brush away the rain from his face. He seemed tired. "It's the tree in my back garden," he said. "It got hit by lightning in a storm, a year ago."

"Is it for art?"

He shook his head, holding out his hand for the picture. Cath didn't give it to him.

"Have you seen this?" she asked Barshin. The hare hopped out from under the seat, and she held the paper down for him to sniff.

"I've seen others like it," Barshin said. "It's that tree again, isn't it?"

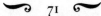

Danny lunged forward and tried to snatch the paper. "Give it back!"

Barshin leapt in surprise, but Cath jerked the picture quickly away. She was used to being quick.

"Give it!" said Danny weakly, not bothering to reach out again.

Cath shook her head. "Nah. Anyway, I've got a message for you."

"Yeah? Let me guess . . . is it from Paul?"

Cath remembered the morning, the sticks and stones. She didn't ask why Paul hated Danny. It was clear now why anyone would hate Danny—he was a spindly, mealy-mouthed small kid who couldn't stick up for himself and didn't seem to want to try.

"Nah, not him. Him." Cath pointed at the hare.

Danny looked at the hare, and the last traces of color in his cheeks faded to gray. The rain had flattened his hair to his skull and his short bangs were spiked along the top of his forehead, each point holding its own raindrop.

He mumbled something that Cath couldn't hear.

"What?"

"I can't talk to it," Danny repeated. "I know hares can talk. And I could hear them, once. But it's finished with, all that. I can't do it anymore."

"He can," said Barshin. "He's lying. I can hear him. He must be able to hear me."

"He says you're lying," said Cath.

"No!" said Danny, putting his hands over his ears. "No! I can't talk to that thing! Leave me alone!"

"Calm down," said Cath. "He ain't some evil monster."

Barshin sat wisely still, twitching his whiskers.

"You don't know anything about it," said Danny. "Nothing at all."

"About what?"

Danny looked at her with his scared-kid eyes and took his hands away from his ears. He opened his mouth, seemed as though he might say something interesting, and then abandoned it in favor of a quick gulp of breath.

"Nothing," he said. "Go away."

"Okay," said Cath. "*He*'s called Barshin, and he says to tell you a guy called Tom's in danger. Big trouble, all that. There. Done. Bye!" She took a couple of steps, out into the rain again. "Oh yeah, and he says you've got to sort it out. As if."

She was about to walk away when Danny O'Neill punched the side of the bus shelter so hard that it gave a great cracking sound. It didn't break, but his hand must have hurt like hell.

Cath swung back. Barshin had gone skittering into a hedge and was peering out from under drenched leaves. Danny was staring at his knuckles, which were flashing a rapid shade of red.

Funny, thought Cath. I'd have put him down as the crying sort.

"People are stupid," Danny said. "Everyone's stupid. Adults are stupid. Even people who don't look like they're stupid are still stupid."

Cath wasn't sure what he was talking about, but she didn't disagree. Except maybe *stupid* wasn't quite the right word.

"It's Sammael, isn't it?" said Danny, looking over at Cath. "I knew something would happen. I knew he wouldn't just give up. That animal's come from him, hasn't it?"

Cath shook her head. "I don't know nothing more. That's all he said to tell you."

"How come *you* can talk to it?" Danny asked. "Did you find something?"

"I told you." Cath shrugged. "He said some people can, that's all. He calls them 'telas.' He says something happens to them, and then they can talk to some other kind of animal. You're one too, ain't you?"

Danny shook his head. "No, I'm not. And how do you know he's telling the truth, anyway?"

How did she know? She didn't. But she knew when people weren't telling the truth: she'd seen plenty of that. And Barshin had an honest feeling about him, something strong and clear.

Cath turned to the hare. "He don't believe you. We might as well go."

"No!" said Barshin. "This is important! Tell him I came to learn of this from a hare in a place humans call Great Butford woods. That hare saw Tom there, meeting with Sammael in the dead of night, in the middle of a storm. Since then there have been many stories, here and there—Danny O'Neill must know how these stories reach around, like the tendrils on a creeping plant—and I have spoken to many hares to try and find the truth of them. I have my own reasons for fearing Sammael. He made a bargain with a hare I knew, a long time ago, and I saw what came of that. But the danger for Tom is greater still. Danny O'Neill is the only one who can reach out to Tom and stop him. It is vital that he take on this responsibility. Please tell him that."

Cath shrugged. "If you want."

She told Danny as much of what Barshin had said as she could remember. Danny didn't answer. Instead, he left the bus shelter and went over to the hare. He didn't seem to notice the rain either. Cath liked him a little bit for that. She didn't like that he clenched his fists when he looked at Barshin, though. She'd kill Danny O'Neill if he tried to hurt Barshin.

A car splashed along the road. The driver turned her head sideways to stare at the two children out of school, both standing in the rain. Hopefully she was going too fast to see they were talking to a hare in the hedge.

Cath shivered. The rain had soaked her to the skin. She

was cold, and there wasn't enough of her to make herself warm again. And she was hungry, too, and her ribs were hurting. People were stupid, Danny had been right. They were stupid, and they stood in the rain and got cold and didn't give each other enough to eat, and these were some of the things that made life rubbish.

It hadn't been raining in Chromos. She hadn't felt cold or hungry—her body hadn't seemed to matter much at all. Why couldn't Danny O'Neill say what he had to say and do what he had to do, so Cath and Barshin could go back to Chromos?

"This rain's horrible," said Danny. "Let's go somewhere dry."

✦ ✦ ✦

They went to the wasteland next to the supermarket and crawled into a huge drainpipe that had been dumped in the corner by the road. Danny went and bought hot fries from the burger van, and Cath ate most of them before anyone had time to speak. Barshin wrinkled his nose at the warm, fatty smell, but didn't ask to try one.

Danny cheered up as soon as he was in the pipe, eating fries.

"I can't do anything about it," he said. "I know what's happened. Tom's been e-mailing me since last summer, loads of junk about birds and badgers and trying to get me to visit his farm, because he's got all this stuff he wants to show me. He never did that before—I knew something was up. But if that hare's right, and it's to do with Sammael, then there's only one thing Tom could have done, and there's nothing I can do about it. Really, nothing."

"Geek," Cath said, not really caring and wishing that there were more fries. "You're scared of everything, ain't you?"

"Yeah," said Danny. "I am scared. You've got no idea what Sammael did before. Tom never wanted to believe it either— he just told me I was being a stupid little kid. Now he can find out for himself."

"What are you going on about?"

Danny looked at her and then at the circle of wasteland and gray sky at the end of the pipe.

"Sammael took my parents," he said. "He was going to gather a massive storm and destroy everybody, but I found out and stopped him. And I thought that was it, trouble over. But of course it wasn't. I know he's still alive somewhere, and this is just the next thing he's trying to do. I'm not going to fight him again. Somebody else can stop him now. You can, if you're so worried about it."

He flicked a fry at Barshin. The hare declined to touch it, and it lay in the dirt at the bottom of the pipe. Waste of a fry, thought Cath.

"But Sammael's in Chromos, ain't he?" she said. "He ain't here."

Danny's face stopped in baffled surprise. "Where?"

"Chromos," repeated Cath. "That place with all the imaginary stuff."

But Danny ignored the strange name. "*Have you seen him?*" he hissed, dropping the rest of his fries and pushing himself away, ready to spring into escape. "*Did he send you?*"

"Nah," said Cath. "Don't be an idiot. I don't know nothin' about him. What are you so scared of, anyway? If you stopped him before, he can't be that bad."

Danny gave her another sharp look and then turned to the drizzly sky again.

"I killed his dog," he said. "I didn't mean to, but I did. And he is bad, in every way you can think of. He's making my life hell. He's put all this stuff in my head and now I have nightmares every night, and I can't be normal because I know too much about everything, and I know what horrible things can happen, and sometimes I make mistakes and say something weird so no one at school likes me now. And I got my parents back, but then all I could think about was that tree, so my dad got rid of all the dead wood and covered the patch in grass, but I still can't get it out of my head. My parents keep having to come into my bedroom to wake me up because the nightmares make me scream my head off, like some stupid baby. It's *ridiculous*. I hate it. But it's in my head and I can't get it out."

He turned back to Cath, his dark eyes lost. Were those tiny pinpricks of color in his black pupils?

"Okay, okay," said Cath, thinking that he sounded like a little kid whose mummy told him to go out and play with the big boys at the end of the street. "Ain't it this guy Tom you ought to be telling that to, though?"

Danny shook his head again. "There's no point. He'll just say I'm being stupid."

Cath gave up and turned back to Barshin. "He's right," she said. "There ain't no point. He ain't going to do anything. So I gave him your message, didn't I? Can we go back to Chromos now?"

"No," said Barshin. "This is important. We must persuade him to intervene with Tom. I won't take you back to Chromos until we've made him understand."

Cath thought desperately, trying to find some small clue in what Danny had said. "What about— You said this Sammael's mad at you because you killed his dog, right? So why don't we go into Chromos, and you can imagine up his dog and give it to him in there. Seriously, it's dead easy. In Chromos, you see what you really, really want, so if that's this dog, then it'll be there. And then if he gets his dog back, maybe he'll let this Tom guy go in return. That okay?"

But Danny's face was set in the stubborn expression she'd seen when he'd punched the bus shelter.

"No way. No way am I going anywhere weird. Never. My

mum and dad and me all promised each other that none of us would ever go missing again. And anyway, if it was that easy, he'd just have imagined up the dog himself, wouldn't he?"

"He can't!" said Barshin. "Tell Danny he can't! Sammael isn't mortal—he doesn't have dreams, like we do. He can't use Chromos for his own benefit—he can only put its colors into earthly creatures and watch their dreams fly free. He does know his dog is dead—but Danny's imagination could certainly bring a vision of her to life in Chromos. It's a great idea. Tell Danny he should definitely try it."

Cath did.

"No," said Danny. "I said, no weird places. No and no and no."

Cath shrugged to Barshin. "Told you."

Barshin, having given in and nibbled a bit of a fry only to find it not to his taste at all, gave five tiny sneezes and hopped a step closer to Danny.

"All right," the hare said. "If he won't try that, then how about this: Sammael gave Tom a book. If Tom doesn't finish reading this book, Sammael will have no power over him. But if he does read the entire book and learn all its contents, then the moment he comes to the end of the last page, he is lost, and there will be no going back. Tom will be free for only as long as the book is unfinished. Danny *must* persuade him to stop reading this book."

Cath repeated this. Danny sighed and ran his greasy hand through the spikes of his wet hair.

"A book," he said. "It's not called the Book of Storms, is it? No, it wouldn't be that. There's no Book of Storms anymore. But there're other books. Of course there are."

He was silent for a long time, staring out of the end of the pipe at the wet parking lot with all the shiny cars trundling around puddles, their engines spitting out raindrops. At last he nodded to himself, and seemed to square his shoulders a little.

"Okay," he said. "If it'll get you off my back, I'll try."

"And if it don't work," said Cath, "then we can go to Chromos and get the dog."

If Danny went into Chromos to help Tom, Barshin would have to let her come too. And once she was there, she would imagine herself up another Zadoc, and get on his back and never leave.

Danny didn't answer her. He just shrugged and said, "We'll have to go to the farm. Tom's hardly ever at school. The farm's miles away. And I don't have any more money for the bus or anything."

"You ever get anywhere on your own?" said Cath, curling her lip.

"No. I don't need to. *My* parents look after me."

Barshin hopped quickly between them, knocking against Cath's hand.

"Okay, okay." Cath scrambled to her feet to stop herself from punching Danny O'Neill's skinny runt of a face. "We'll get a lift."

✦ ✦ ✦

Cath walked up to the road. She didn't try to stop any of the clean, new cars that zoomed past, spraying up blades of brown water. Instead, she waited till a greenish-gray car came along that looked to be made more out of rust than actual metal, and stuck her thumb out.

"He'll never stop," said Danny.

The car stopped.

"Now what?" Danny hissed.

The driver rolled down the passenger window, all thick neck and shaved scalp. "Cath Carrera," he said. "Someone's looking for you."

"Hi, Stan," said Cath. "Yeah, I know. I don't want him to find me. Can you take us someplace?"

"Maybe. Where?"

Cath looked back at Danny. "Where is it?"

Danny swallowed, his voice barely audible above the engine, and croaked out a few words.

Cath repeated them to Stan. "Sopper's Edge. Out on—"

"I know where it is," said Stan. "Who's yer friend?"

"Kid from school. Go on. My dad'll kill me if he gets me."

Stan considered it for a minute and said eventually, "Your dad's a piece of work."

He nodded his head toward the backseat, but Cath opened the passenger door. Danny stood frozen behind her.

"What?" Cath got in and looked out at him. "Got a problem?"

"I'm not getting in there," said Danny. "I don't know who he is."

Cath snorted. "What you gonna do? Run behind?"

"He looks like a . . . like a *drug dealer,*" hissed Danny. Stan bared his teeth like an Alsatian at a cat.

"What you scared of, kid? You'll be safe with Cath. She's tougher than ten of us."

Cath grinned for a fraction of a second. The shock of seeing her smile seemed to stun Danny into silence. He opened the back door of the car and Barshin hopped in gamely, leaving Danny with no choice but to follow. He slid down onto the seat.

"Where's the seat belt?" he said nervously.

"Dunno," said Stan, pulling off the hand brake and stamping on the wheezing accelerator pedal. "Been wondering that since I got the car. Let me know if you find it."

In the rearview mirror Cath saw Danny's arms: rigid, going straight downward. He was gripping the edge of the seat as though it were his last hold on life.

She took her eyes off him and watched the town dwindle away around them. It felt good to be driving away from Dad. Away from Johnny White.

If only she never had to go back.

CHAPTER 9

# THE FARM

Stan swung the car up a driveway beside a sign that said SOPPER'S EDGE FARM. He bombed over the potholes as if his old clunker were a jeep. The floor scraped on the earth as it shuddered over the ruts, but Stan didn't care. He slammed to a halt as soon as the driveway widened out into a gravelly yard and cocked his head.

"Scram," he said.

Cath got out silently. What could she say, anyway? Don't tell my dad? But if Stan was going to tell, he'd tell, and if he wasn't, she didn't need to ask him not to. Everybody understood how it was.

Maybe Dad wouldn't find her here. They were miles away from town. There was a redbrick farmhouse that looked like it had been kicked about by the winds and rain and snow for longer than anyone had ever been alive, and there were some black barns behind it, and loads of fences and puddles and bits of metal machinery around the place. The rest was fields, with a strong smell of cows. From somewhere on the damp breeze, Cath heard a long, mournful moo.

Danny got out of the car, and Barshin slowly hopped down after him, his long ears drooping. As soon as Danny closed the door, Stan turned around and shot off down the driveway. They stood for a second and watched him go.

"That guy . . . ," said Danny. "Is he, sort of, a friend of your parents or something?"

He thinks Stan is lowlife scum, thought Cath. And he thinks I'm the same.

"You ain't got a clue, have you?" she said, without anger. "Go on, then, where's your cousin?"

Danny shrugged. "I dunno. He's normally doing something with the cows. Oh crap, there's Aunt Kathleen."

A tall, rawboned woman with a horsey face and wild toffee-colored hair walked around the side of the house. Her hair was struggling out of an elastic band, her clothes damp with smears of greenish slime. Her cheeks were as red as a smacked butt.

"Danny!" she said, looking confused. "I thought you were

the postman. What are you doing here? Why aren't you at school?"

"I need to see Tom," said Danny. His voice sounded weak, as though he didn't really mean it.

"Why?" said Aunt Kathleen, going from confused to suspicious in a nanosecond. Sharper than she looks, thought Cath.

"Um," said Danny. "Nothing, sort of. I just need to see him."

"Do your mum and dad know you're here?" snapped Aunt Kathleen, moving on equally swiftly to irritable. "And yours, whoever you are?" She swung around to Cath, and then noticed Barshin lurking by Cath's feet. Her face froze.

What were they all so scared of?

"Danny," Aunt Kathleen said in a low, warning voice. "You haven't been up here for months. What's going on?"

Danny squirmed under her glare. He'll crack, Cath thought. He's the sort who runs sniveling to his parents the moment anything goes wrong. But to her amazement, he pulled himself together enough to shrug.

"I was just . . . busy," he said. "This is Cath, the hare's her pet. She's from school."

Aunt Kathleen narrowed her eyes and looked at her nephew, the girl, and the hare. She gave Cath the longest look of all.

"Tom's up by the wood, seeing to the fences," she said.

"He'll be down in a minute. You can come in and have some lunch, and I'm going to give your mum a call. I know you're nearly a teenager, Danny, but you're still a child as far as the law and your school are concerned."

Cath scowled and balled her fists, ready for the questions about where she lived and who her parents were. But the ugly horse-faced woman merely raised an eyebrow at her, went over to the side door of the farmhouse, and opened it.

"In," she said. "Where I can keep an eye on you. *All* of you."

✦ ✦ ✦

Inside, it was soft and cluttered and comfortable, with sofas and chairs covered in magazines and papers. There was a gentle animal smell, as though the furniture might be alive and warm, heating the house with the fumes of its breath. The kitchen had a big wooden table in the middle, half-covered in letters and bills, but Danny sat down at the clear end as if he did it every day of his life. Barshin crept into the darkness underneath the table and lay with his belly along the floor tiles, nostrils quivering, ears flat along his skull.

Aunt Kathleen put the kettle on, plonked a fruitcake down on the table, and gouged off a few thick wedges with a bread knife. Cath reached out and wrapped a hand around the biggest slice.

"Where did you get that hare?" said Aunt Kathleen to Cath.

Cath was stuffing cake into her mouth. She didn't stop to answer.

Aunt Kathleen gave Barshin a hard glance but the hare was still lying motionless on the cool floor, resting his chin on his forepaws and trying to recover control over his shaken stomach, so she gave up and made the tea. She put some mugs on the table and sat down, cradling the warm pot in her hands. There was a long silence while she stirred the tea bags and poured the tea into three mugs. Danny didn't touch his mug. Cath took a gulp of hers to wash down the cake. The tea was brick red and tasted of iron pipes. She covered the taste with another slice of cake.

"What do you want Tom for?" repeated Aunt Kathleen.

"Just . . . stuff," Danny said.

"About the hare?"

"Sort of. You know . . . he likes animals."

"He does," agreed Aunt Kathleen. "Very much. So much so, in fact, that since last summer he hasn't stopped looking for them. I hardly see him. Oh, he never misses a milking and he cleans every cut and scrape the cows get, but outside of that—he's out all day, sometimes all night, for weeks on end. He doesn't even call Sophie anymore, and they used to be thick as thieves. What's going on, Danny?"

Danny stared down at his mug. "I dunno," he mumbled. "Why don't you ask him?"

"I have. He says he's watching wildlife. But I know

something else is going on—I *know* it. Can't you give me any clues?"

Cath glared at Danny for a sharp second. Just tell the old bat, she wanted to say. Tell her so she'll sort it out and I can get back to Chromos and be free. But Danny O'Neill was silently struggling with himself again, staring down at the table.

Cath's fists clenched. Why did this weak little kid who was scared of everything get to sit at this table like he owned it? Why did he get to have an aunt who put plates of cake in front of him and gave him tea he was too fussy to drink?

Well, she wouldn't like to be the kind of person who was scared to get in Stan's car, or scared to run around on her own. She reached for another bit of cake and stuffed it into her mouth, partly just to stop herself from speaking. With any luck, she could eat her fill and escape out of here before anybody found out where she was. She'd go up into those woods at the top of the hill and hide for a bit, until Barshin agreed to call Zadoc again.

"Right," said Aunt Kathleen. "I'm going to call your mum. Don't leave this room, either of you. There's bread in the cupboard, if you want sandwiches."

She got up and went out.

"What cupboard?" said Cath.

Danny fetched the bread and some ham from the fridge. He chucked it across the table at Cath and she tore open the packets, making squashed wedges of bread and ham.

She tried offering a bit of ham to Barshin, but the hare flared his nostrils in disgust, so she sat back up and concentrated on feeding herself.

"What's that?" Danny's quiet voice broke through her furious eating. He was looking at the hand that was mechanically cramming bread into her mouth.

He'd seen the flowers on her skin. For a second she thought about spinning him some lie—he'd believe it, of course. She could just say it was a stick-on tattoo. Then she remembered that fist against the side of the bus shelter. He wasn't as stupid as he looked.

"I touched something in Chromos," she said.

"Chromos?" He frowned. "What *is* Chromos?"

"It's where I went. Barshin took me there—we was running away. It's this place where you can dream up things, and they . . . I dunno . . . they're just *there*. Like, all the stuff you really want but don't think you can have."

"Like what?"

Cath didn't want to tell him that. He wasn't Barshin or Zadoc, he was a person, and she didn't trust him. Instead she just said, "Anything. Whatever's in your head. But you can't touch any of it. There was this bush, really spiky, with all these yellow flowers that I really liked, but when I tried to touch it, it sort of burned its way into my hand. It don't hurt, though."

She grabbed the last bit of cake before Danny could get

it, but Danny seemed to have forgotten the food entirely. He shook his head as though trying to dislodge a fly in his ear, and then Aunt Kathleen came back in from making her phone call.

"Seems like you've got the whole town out looking for you," she said to Danny.

Cath stopped chewing. But maybe it was okay. The people looking for Danny O'Neill weren't going to be the ones looking for her.

"Sorry," mumbled Danny into his plate. He wasn't so bad when he was by himself, but he turned into such a sniveling little snot bag whenever grown-ups were around that it made Cath want to puke up a whole bucketful of scorn.

"Have you had enough to eat?" Aunt Kathleen asked.

"Yes, thanks," said Danny.

"No," said Cath.

A tiny smile flicked across Aunt Kathleen's mouth. "I think your friend is hungry," she said to Danny. "Though decidedly lacking in manners."

And instead of starting to screech like Macy would have done, Aunt Kathleen went across to the other side of the kitchen and opened a cupboard door.

"Here, Hollow Legs," she said, plonking half an enormous meat pie in front of Cath and giving her a knife to cut it with. "Fill your feet. I can hear the ATV coming down now—that'll be Tom."

✦ ✦ ✦

Tom was almost as tall as Cath's dad, but much thinner and blond, and his face shone with cheerful distraction. He opened the side door and slammed it behind him, stamping into the kitchen and heading straight for the fridge.

"Worse than I thought," he said, as though this was brilliant news. "Whole back edge of the fence on High Top is rotting. Going to take days to get the new posts in. Where's that pie, Mum?"

Swinging to survey the kitchen, he caught sight of the extra people at the table and his face froze for a fraction of a second. "Danny! Long time no see! What brings you here?"

Then his face quickly moved again and he recovered his easiness, advancing on the meat pie and giving Cath a broad grin. Cath scowled. Tom cut himself a wedge of pie and took a bite out of it, leaning back against the kitchen counter.

"Danny and his friend Cath are here to see you," said Aunt Kathleen.

"Oh yeah?" said Tom, chewing rapidly. "What about?"

Aunt Kathleen raised an eyebrow at Danny, but Danny stayed silent, his cheeks reddening. His aunt held up her hands.

"Right, okay, okay, no more interfering aunt," she said, heading for the door. "I'll go and finish cleaning out the henhouse. But don't you dare set foot out of this kitchen, any of you. Your mum's on her way, Danny. No running off, okay? Losing you once was enough."

With that, she left the kitchen. Danny, Cath, and Tom were silent until they heard the door close.

"You met Sammael," Danny whispered.

The pie paused halfway to Tom's mouth and then swiftly carried on. Tom bit again and swallowed before shrugging. His face had lost the easygoing smile.

"Yep," he said in a low voice. "I met him. He's nothing like what you said. He gave me a book. I would have shared it, but you're not really into finding stuff out, are you?"

"Not that sort of stuff," hissed Danny. "It's an evil book. You can't read it."

Tom snorted.

"It's a book of bird and animal calls, not some kind of brainwashing cult manual. It just means I can learn to understand them all and learn what everything's up to. What terrible evil is that going to do to me?"

"It'll make you his," whispered Danny. "You'll belong to him. He'll do whatever he wants with you."

"Oh, don't be thick, Dan," said Tom, letting his voice rise to a normal level and going over to fill the kettle. "Sammael isn't some deadly creature of the night. He's just a bloke who likes nature. You're only scared of him because he doesn't live in a suburb and drive a car and watch TV like everyone else. Just because he isn't conventional, it doesn't make him wrong, you know."

Cath cut herself more pie, but she did it quite slowly, so she could have something to do while she thought. Sammael did sound interesting. Maybe when she got back to Chromos, she could find him and see what everyone was talking about.

"You don't get it!" Danny frantically crumbled a bit of piecrust between his fingers. "You never listened to anything I said about him! He isn't even a *person*—that's just what he wants you to think! He asked you for your sand in return, didn't he? Do you even know what that is? It's your soul, Tom, your entire soul. He'll find some way to kill you, then take it and use it to put dreams in people's heads. To give them *nightmares*. Horrible nightmares . . . Oh, I knew this was a stupid idea."

"Why come, then?" said Tom, getting out a mug and a tea bag. "Sammael's not going to kill me—he's given me a book to make me *live*. Mum's already on my back half the time—I think she reckons I'm going to go as crazy as you have. Well, I'm not. I'm just having fun and learning about the fantastic world out there. If you're still too scared to come and see what it's got to offer, just go back to your video games and leave me alone."

"Yeah," said Danny in a sharp, sarcastic tone that Cath hadn't heard him use before. "I would've. But then *that* came along."

He pointed at Barshin, who had nervously struggled into a sitting position under the table. Tom, pouring water into a mug, looked around and kept pouring for a second too long. Hot water splashed onto the counter, flying drops scalding his arms. He put the kettle down.

"Wow," he said softly. "Where did he come from?"

"*He* came to warn us that you were in danger," said Danny, throwing pie crumbs down against the wooden table. "Don't you get it?"

"Yeah, right," said Tom, raising an eyebrow. "Pull the other one, it's got bells on. It's just another of your crazy tricks. That's no wild animal, it's just something you got from a pet shop."

He turned away to get a cloth for the spilled water.

Cath looked down at Barshin. "It ain't working," she whispered. "He don't believe it."

"Try the other idea," said Barshin. "Maybe Danny'll agree now."

Cath shrugged. "Come on," she said to Danny. "Tom ain't gonna listen to us, is he? Let's go to Chromos and get that dog and deal with Sammael ourselves."

Danny was silent for a few seconds. Tom finished mopping up, threw the cloth into the sink, picked up his mug, and turned back to them, lifting the tea bag in and out of the darkening tea.

Cath almost thought Danny had ignored her, but then he said, "Okay, I'll do it. We'll go off to some weird, dangerous place where Sammael lives and I'll risk my life *again*. Because it wasn't enough for me just to save my parents, was it? Apparently I've got to go around saving all my family, even though they're adults and I'm twelve. Fine. Brilliant. That's what I'll do, then. Let's go."

Tom laughed. "Please," he said. "Don't trouble yourself on my account. This week alone, I've dealt with badger baiters, stampeding cows, and an angry mouse in a feed bin. I'm pretty sure I can save myself from the perils of reading a book."

"What's so good about this book?" asked Danny, his voice rising. "What's so good about this book that it makes you so completely *dumb*?"

Tom gave a tight smile, and his pleasant face became sharp and clever. "Oh, you know, just the possibility of learning more about the natural world than anyone's ever known before. A small thing, really. You're not the only one in the world who gets to have adventures, Dan."

"I don't want adventures," said Danny. "I just want to be left alone."

"Well, toddle off, then," said Tom, chucking his tea bag in the garbage. "In fact, I think I can hear a car coming up the driveway. That'll be Mummy, won't it? Come to take Dannykins and his Bunnykins home, and make everything safe again."

He got some milk from the fridge. Nobody spoke as the

sound of wheels crunched up on the gravel outside. A car door slammed, and footsteps came toward the house.

Tom smiled mockingly at Danny and went out into the hallway to open the front door.

"Where's that girl?"

A voice, uglier than a jagged knife wound, burst through to the kitchen. Cath leapt out of her chair and sprinted for the side door, but her legs were suddenly tangled with something warm and furry that squealed, and she was sprawling forward onto the floor, banging the side of her face against the table. A crash of pain battered into her temple and she tried to ignore it, scrambling to her feet, but her head spun with whining nausea and the room filled with tiny spots of color.

For a moment Cath's heart leapt—Chromos! This was Chromos! She'd stumbled back into it again and in a split second Zadoc would pound his way into the kitchen and lift her up, away from this whole place—all she had to do was focus on the spots of color, not let them fade away and die, to reach out for Barshin—

Something yanked her up from the floor. Its presence was much darker than she'd remembered Zadoc being, and it was roaring like a sea lion, clods of sound wailing around her ears. Instead of setting her on her feet, it swung her against the wall, so that the other side of her head cracked against the plaster and a picture frame came crashing down, its corner stabbing into the skin above her eye. The frame tumbled to the floor and the glass inside it smashed, but Cath was already being dragged to the hallway, out into the open air, and there was a voice of protest, the gentle, deep voice of Danny's cousin Tom, but he was just a boy against this hulk of fury— what could he do? What could any of them do?

No one could beat Dad in a fight, not without a weapon deadlier than any animal on earth. Dad was a grizzly bear, his claws sharper than iron spikes.

He slammed Cath against the side of his car and the last breath was smashed out of her lungs, as he'd meant it to be. He opened the car door and threw Cath inside, closing it with a furious bang. She wouldn't be running now. She wouldn't be trying to find the door handle of the car to jump out and escape. She'd be lying on the backseat, thinking only about how to pull breath into her body and how to stop her head from spinning in a galaxy of tiny white stars.

"Don't even think about calling the fuzz," Dad said to Tom, who had followed him outside. "I know where you live. I'll torch this place to the ground."

✦ ✦ ✦

Danny clung to the edge of the door frame, unable to move.

"Stop!" yelled Aunt Kathleen, running out into the yard. "Stop that!"

She ran down toward the driveway, toward the car,

toward the man. She ran without any hesitation in her step, and her arms were waving in the air as though she were reaching out to Cath, trying to pull her away and save her.

The man looked up and for a terrible second Danny thought he was about to get out and attack Aunt Kathleen. Instead, the car shot down the drive in reverse, leaping and bouncing as it hit potholes. The man leaned out to shout something at Aunt Kathleen, then he swung the car into a gateway, turned it around, and screeched off toward the main road. A smell of burning engine oil sat waxily in the air behind him.

Danny stood in the doorway, biting down hard on his knuckles to stop the tears of panic spilling down his face. Something pulled at his chest, tugging and tugging, and when he looked down at himself he realized that it was his own lungs, begging him to breathe.

Tom swore, his stunned hands raised to clutch at his blond hair. He kicked a bit of metal clean across the graveled yard and then kicked the ground.

"Who was that? Who was that man? I'm calling the police now. He can't do that to a kid. Jesus!"

He swung around on Danny. Danny, knuckles still in his mouth, couldn't think of a single word to say. He didn't know anything about Cath Carrera other than that she was from the Sawtry estate. That man must have been her dad. Stan had gone straight off the farm and told Cath's dad where she was, even though he'd been friendly and kind and Cath had seemed to trust him.

Danny didn't understand any of it. That hare— He looked around for Barshin, but the hare had disappeared. Maybe he'd gone after Cath. Yes, Barshin would go after her, Barshin would help her. Maybe Danny could just go back home . . .

Down at the bottom of the hill, Danny watched a familiar blue car turn up the driveway. His parents' car, with his mum at the wheel. Soon he would be inside that car, sitting in the seat next to his mum, watching the world scoot past from behind the windshield as they drove home.

Of course the hare would help Cath. They'd both go to this Chromos place and live happily ever after. And Tom would read his book and belong to Sammael. And Danny would go home and never have to see any of them ever again.

Danny's mum got out of the car. Something in Danny's brain sent a vision of himself running over to her and hugging her, burying his face in her coat and feeling the rough fibers against his cheek, and everything—the feel, the smell, the sound of it rustling—being the essence of home.

But his actual, real body stood in the yard and watched her close the car door neatly, and he realized with a huge, sickening lurch that she was just a person, and he was another person, and that even if she wanted to, she couldn't solve this for him.

"Darling," said his mum. "You should be in school. Why did you come here? What's wrong?"

She put her arms around him in a warm hug and pulled him gently toward her. Not angry, not threatening, just loving and kind. He'd run out of school and gone off without telling her, exactly as he'd promised never to do again, and she didn't have a cross word to say to him. A year ago, she would have at least yelled a bit. Was this still his mum?

I have never really known any of these people in my life, thought Danny. They are complete strangers. There is only one creature whose face I can picture. And I'd give anything to get that face out of my head.

But that wasn't quite right. The face of Sammael had been joined by another picture now. No matter how many times Danny shut his eyes, he knew he would never forget it. It was Cath Carrera's skull thudding against a wall.

Danny turned away from his mum and was quietly sick.

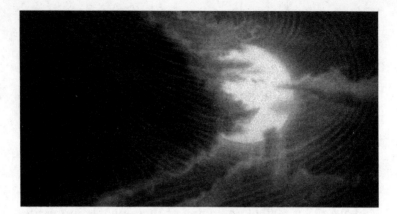

## CHAPTER 10

# THE STAG

"Had enough yet?"

The face above Danny's was almost indistinguishable from the night around it. He knew what it looked like, though. He knew every angle of the sharp, lean cheeks, the slanting black eyes, and the close-curled hair.

Was he awake or asleep? Did it matter?

*If I'm awake, he's in my room. And if I'm asleep, he's in my head.*

On the whole, it was better not to know.

"Leave me alone," he managed to say. "I'm sorry about your dog. I've said I'm sorry. I don't know what else I can do."

"How about . . . ," said the face, coming closer to Danny's own, "how about giving me something in exchange?"

Danny's skin began to feel cold. Was it the night breeze coming in through his bedroom window? Or was it the puff of ice clouding Sammael's figure, stretching out toward him in soft wisps? He shivered.

"I won't give you anything," he said. "It wasn't my fault. I won't give—"

Sammael put a hand on his chest and pushed down gently.

"I know an old lady who swallowed a fly," he said, his thin lips close to Danny's ear. "I don't know why . . ."

Danny's arms stayed by his sides. Why couldn't he lift them? Maybe if he concentrated on only one . . . He pushed all his thought into his right hand—just bend one muscle, one finger . . .

". . . she swallowed the fly . . . ," said Sammael.

Danny's hand refused to move. His finger refused to move.

"Perhaps . . . ," whispered Sammael, touching his cheek to Danny's cheek.

A scalding burst of heat shot through Danny's brain and scorched its way down his neck, out to his limbs. His arms and legs went rigid, held in place by rods of pain. A cough swelled up inside his chest and tried to break free, but it couldn't force itself up his taut airway. He began to choke.

"I haven't got the taro . . . I'm no threat to you

anymore . . . ," he tried to say, but it came out as nothing more than a stream of dribble.

". . . she'll die!" said Sammael, right into Danny's ear, in a whisper as shrill as the grating of ancient machinery. "You've always got the taro, Danny. Don't you even know that by now? And weapons in the hands of fools—they're the most dangerous of all."

Sammael's hand pressed down harder on Danny's chest. Danny tried to gasp. A thick bubble of spit rolled from his mouth, and he tasted the hot metal of blood.

"Please . . ." He gulped. "Please . . ."

And Sammael's cheek next to his own cheek pressed closer and closer so that Danny couldn't feel anymore where he ended and Sammael began, and he thought, he's melting into me, I'm melting into him, and soon we'll be one and the same, and I will have black hair and black eyes instead of my own brown ones, and I will have a face that looks like it's been carved out of rock, and I will wander around the world and never come home again, and spend the rest of my life searching for my dead dog . . .

✦ ✦ ✦

The bedroom window slammed into its frame. Danny was alone, as usual, in his bedroom, and outside a breeze had picked up. He hadn't put the catch down and the window was banging as the wind grabbed at it.

What was inside his head? Sammael, of course. And Cath. And Tom—but Tom was a lost cause, wasn't he? No, there was something else, something he'd been trying hard to forget—something his brain, even now, didn't want him to think about.

Sammael's hand pressing down on his chest. *I know an old lady who swallowed a fly.* Sammael's cheek melting into his own. Sammael's dog . . .

And the taro. You've always got the taro . . .

Except he didn't have it. The taro was the thing that had caused all the trouble in the first place. The taro was a small, innocent-looking piece of stick that had been lying in the ashes of the burned sycamore tree. When Danny had picked it up, he'd found out about Sammael. And Sammael had seemed just as evil then, just as threatening, so Danny had chosen to bring him down.

But Sammael was still here.

Danny swung his legs out of bed and went over to the window. He couldn't do anything now. It would have to wait until the morning, of course. Except that in the morning he'd leave for school, and suddenly he knew that in the morning school would seem like a much better idea because he would be rational and sensible and afraid in the open light of day.

He stared out at the moonlit garden, the trees waving wildly in the silver night. There'd been a moon like this when he'd left the farmhouse with Tom, last summer on the first night of June.

The moonlight. The trees. The wind. So many things he'd never looked at before last year. He'd kept his head down and looked at his house, his small family, his school, and his friends' houses. These other things—the mysterious dark and the howling anger of the wet wind—they made him want to turn his eyes back to his bed and crawl inside it. But he couldn't stop looking.

Before him in the moonlight he saw them all—Shimny the horse, Paras and Siravina the swallows, the river in Great Butford, Sentry Hill, the great, gathering storms; all the companions of that summer's journey came back to him in a black, tingling flood, and he shivered as sharply as a cat.

If only Tom were here, tall and cheerful, they could pretend they were just going on a midnight badger watch, or up to the top meadow to watch bats at dusk. Danny had never really enjoyed those kinds of trips, but at least Tom's merry whistling had pierced the darkness and covered the sounds of dog barks echoing across the night.

None of that mattered, he reminded himself. He and Tom weren't even really friends anymore. Tom was having his own adventures, and Danny was alone.

But Cath was alone, too, somewhere. And she'd risked a lot to deliver the hare's message and go to the farm with him. Both she and Barshin clearly thought that the message was important.

He had to save Tom.

Go into another world, dream up a gray lurcher called Kalia, and offer her to Sammael in exchange for Tom's soul.

It was a crazy idea.

Danny thought about standing in front of Sammael, trying to find words to say, Here is this imaginary dog, I'll give it to you in return for the life of my cousin, I know I'm cheating you, and you'll probably find out sooner or later, but hey . . .

His stomach churned with fear. Forget it, he told himself. Forget anything beyond the next task. One step at a time. That's the way to get things done.

Because, before crazy worlds and gray lurchers, before even Tom, there was somebody else he had to save.

He set his face against the moonlight and began to get dressed.

✦ ✦ ✦

He took his bike from the shed and waited until he was out in the road in front of the house before switching the lights on. He could see quite well by the streetlamps and the moon, but the sky seemed like a wide black cloak waiting to throw itself down on top of him at any moment. Somehow the bike lights convinced him that he could fight it off. Or at least have a chance.

The bike was too big for him: even with the seat at its lowest, his feet only just touched the pedals. Danny paused before throwing his leg over the crossbar. Should he leave a note for his parents, in case anything happened? Maybe. But they hadn't left him a note when they'd disappeared in the middle of the night last summer. Let them find out what it was like to wake up and have your family missing.

He got onto the bike, turned his face to the wind, and pulled the zippers of his coat right up, so his chin was sitting inside the collar. Without looking back, he kicked the pedal and cycled off into the raw night.

✦ ✦ ✦

It was easy to remember where he'd buried the stick. He almost wished it had been harder. But as soon as he stopped his bike and saw the little wooden gate that led to the nature reserve, he felt its presence in the midnight air, calling to him with an anguished pull as rough as his own racing heartbeat. He left the bike by the gate and took the front light to use as a flashlight.

What was he walking toward? It was a sound, but not so much one that his ears could pick up. More like a humming taste in the air—the thin, hard, woody taste of bark mixed with burning sap. His palms itched.

At the base of the tree, the dry leaves and moss were disturbed, as though a dog had been having a root around. The earth was rough and mounded and didn't want to be where it was, piled uneasily over the alien growth he'd tried to make it hide.

Danny dug with his hands. It was deeper down than he'd remembered—he'd obviously been trying to put the stick so deep in the earth that it couldn't call to him, or make him want it back. Fat lot of good that had done.

And then it was under his fingertips and leaping into his hands, shedding the soil under which it had lain.

The world came to life around him. For a second he was surrounded by so much sound that he couldn't think how to listen to any of it. And then he remembered—turn his thinking toward one thing, and the rest would recede a little. The whispers of the breeze through leaves became whispered words. The groans of the trees were real groans—conversations about other trees, about the lack of sky and the salty edge to the stormy air.

". . . Such a long spring this year. So many leaves to hold on to. And that wind last week—would you believe that wind? I had to hold on to my leaves like a whelk to a rock . . ."

There it was: he'd forgotten how they talked about things they couldn't possibly have seen for themselves. It was because they spent their lives talking to one another—stories flew from tree to tree, or grass to grass, crossing vast distances. Often they squabbled, too: the plants around his feet were doggedly arguing. A small tendril of ivy above them was clinging to a tree and giggling.

"Hee-hee! Squee-eeze! Hold on tight, boys, and squee-ee-ee-eeze! Hee-hee! Round and round and round we go, climbing high and creeping low . . ."

The babbling. The chanting. He'd forgotten about that, too.

An owl hooted out a wicked greeting, boasting about the fat mouse it had caught in a territory outside its own. The earth bristled and sighed with a thousand tiny voices chattering away underneath it. Danny became aware of a soft music drifting up from the forest floor. Of course. It was the worms.

They ate the soil and sang tales of the lives that the soil had once been. It wasn't a very nice thought, really, but it had been useful to him before. The songs that came out often seemed quite random: the first time he'd heard a worm, she'd been singing "Cockles and Mussels." And now, from just in front of his knees, perhaps because it had his name in it, he heard:

> "Oh Danny boy, the pipes, the pipes are calling,
> From glen to glen, and down the mountainside,
> The summer's gone, and all the roses falling,
> 'Tis you must go . . ."

And then another worm began to chant like an ancient monk, and voices piled on top of one another, dozens and dozens of songs and shouts and whispers, from worms and grubs and beetles so small they could hide under leaves in their thousands, until Danny's ears began to buzz so loudly that he could no longer think what anything was, or hear any particular voice. He had to let the stick fall from his fingers just to find some quiet. He knew he wouldn't lose it in the darkness.

Why do I have to do these things? he asked himself. Why can't it be someone else? But he was asking the question of himself, turning his thoughts toward himself, and there was no plant or tree to give him an answer.

✦ ✦ ✦

He knelt beside the hole he'd dug, waiting for his head to calm down a bit. And then, from behind a tree across the small clearing, a stag stepped out into a shaft of moonlight.

It was a fine, slender animal with thin antlers, and it wasn't quite as big as he'd have expected a stag to be. But it seemed impossibly powerful, standing with its head high, thrown-back antlers piercing the silvery moonlight.

For a long moment it listened to the woodland creaks and rattles, and then it put its muzzle down to something on the ground and curled its lips around whatever it had found there. Danny heard the soft tearing as its teeth crunched its food, and the rustle of its hooves through the undergrowth. Could he speak to it? Should he speak to it?

And then he remembered the words of the old sycamore tree so many months ago. *Be careful who you ask.* Which had been a dying tree's way of saying: Sammael is every-where. Some creatures are on his side, and you never know which ones.

Regretting his own cautiousness, Danny watched the stag for as long as it stayed in the clearing. In his place, Tom would have spoken to it, he knew. But then Tom would do a lot of things Danny would be too scared to do. And per-haps that wasn't always a good thing.

✦ ✦ ✦

His front bike light ran out just as he got back to his bike. But away to his left there was a bluish tinge to the sky that suggested it might, in an hour or so, start turning into dawn. The road was deserted. Even the wind had dropped slightly.

Danny's eyes wanted to close. His skin felt heavy. He fought it off—there was no time for resting. He had to save Cath. Then at least *she* would be safe.

He got on his bike and thought, once more, of the moment he'd seen the stag stepping out into the moonlight. Once this was all over, he'd go back and find the stag again. He was sketching deer in his head as he stood on his pedals and kicked the bike forward into the slackening darkness. Stags with antlers and does with soft eyes—a passing herd of them, traipsing by and chewing at the vegetation. Hesitating only slightly, he mentally sketched himself sitting astride the biggest stag with the tallest antlers. He smiled to himself.

In the night so many more things seemed possible.

## CHAPTER 11

# IACO

In a shaft of early-morning sunlight, the calf struggled, fell, scrambled in its panic to get back onto its feet, then lifted its tail and let out a stream of liquid dung: the only answer it had left to give.

"Sssh. Silly girl. I'm only trying to take a look at you. Sssh now, you've cut your shoulder."

Tom tried to calm the little calf with the sound of his voice. She wasn't struggling anymore, but whether that was due to his efforts at calming her or the fact that she was now lying on the barn floor with three of her legs pinned down, he couldn't tell. No matter. At least he could clean her up now.

It was a quick job, which was more than could be said for the washing of his overalls after the calf's shocked flood of green slime.

"Is this a good time? You look a bit . . . occupied."

Sammael stood in the doorway of the barn, framed by the light. Tom clenched his hand around the calf's foot in case she should be alarmed by the stranger, but the animal had gone limp in his arms, her eyes soft and trusting. Of course, Sammael was one of those people whom animals instantly felt easy with. He knew how to move around them, and the tone of his voice was gentle.

"Just a sec," said Tom. "This lady's got a cut on her shoulder, and she's nervous as a field mouse. I'll finish up while I've got her quiet."

"Here." Sammael came forward and stepped neatly between the rows of pens, bringing the fresh morning air in with him. "I'll give you a hand if you like?"

The calf was almost in a trance. Her eyes quivered and half closed as Sammael ducked through the rails and came up to her. When he put his hands on her, she gave a sigh, shuddered, and lay back on the straw, as if sleeping beside her mother.

"Nice," said Tom, cleaning the last of the cut.

"Lovely calf," said Sammael. "Looks well bred."

"She is," agreed Tom, finishing up and putting the lid back on the antiseptic spray. "My granddad started this herd fifty years ago. They're as good cows as you'll find anywhere."

Even when both Tom and Sammael took their hands off the calf and got to their feet, she still didn't move. She lay in the dung-splattered straw, her chocolate eyes gazing up at Sammael.

Tom wanted suddenly to gather her up in his arms and offer her to the thin man. He wanted to offer up the whole farm, to say, Won't you take it, and live here, and work your magic on the whole place? The cows would grow fat, happy, and calm. The wild animals that lived in the hedges and ditches and copses would come out to flock closely around. Sammael would teach Tom about the plants, too: what to use to heal the cows, to make their bones sturdy and strong, their udders full of milk. Sammael's magic would bring a clean, bright life to the farm, a step higher than the endless rounds of milking and mending.

Tom saw a tiny face peep out from the neck of Sammael's white shirt. It had round ears and dark brown fur with a tinge of white showing underneath its chin.

"Is that a stoat?" he said. Stoats were one of the shyest creatures he knew; he'd seen them around the farm from a distance, but they disappeared in a flash when they caught wind of him.

"Meet Iaco," said Sammael, putting his hand up to his neck and pulling the little creature out of his collar. He sat it on his forearm where it glared at Tom with hot anger in its eyes.

"A tame stoat? Where on earth did you find it?"

"She was wounded. I took her home and healed her. Her family were killed by men with terriers out ratting."

Tom reached out a finger to the stoat, which arched its sleek back and bared its tiny teeth at him.

"Not keen on people, then?" He tried to smile but a thudding in his chest was choking him. If only the stoat would jump onto his outstretched arm, tuck herself into his collar, and feel safe with him. For a second his blood ran green with envy. But if he stayed friends with Sammael, he could have this too. He was sure of it.

"Not keen on people. But I think she might help you."

"How?" Tom pulled back his hand and the stoat chattered, then relaxed along Sammael's shirtsleeve.

"I think if you could learn to understand the way stoats talk, she might go with you and round up other stoats. If you had an army of them you might be able to divert the dogs, once they'd set on the badger. If you still want to stop the baiters, that is."

"Of course I do! But . . . I mean, I know I'll easily learn to understand stoats—I just haven't quite got to them in the book yet. But could I really learn to *talk* to them? I've never tried that with anything else. I didn't think it would work. My voice must sound so different from theirs, whatever noise I try to make."

Sammael smiled and put up a finger to stroke Iaco's back. The stoat bent herself to his touch.

"I'm sure I could help with that. It might take a little time, though. Could you take a day or so off from your farm?"

Tom never took time off from the farm. The milking was his job, and he did it come rain or shine. He'd done it since he was twelve. Five whole years without a single day's vacation.

"Sure," he said, not liking the way the word stuck in his tight shoulders. "Of course I could. Mum'll understand. She hates the baiters too. I'm sure she'll understand. I do need to finish up a few things here first, though."

"As you like," said Sammael. "I've got plenty of time. Maybe I can start trying to explain things to Iaco, and you can come and find me in the woods later, when you're ready."

He turned to leave the barn and Tom followed him, wanting desperately to say, I've changed my mind, let's go now. But as they walked out into the damp yard and Tom saw every familiar thing, old troughs and fences and the puddle by the drain that never quite dried up, he couldn't help feeling that the plan was a bit crazy.

"Do you really reckon it'll work?" he said. "I mean, stoats are so territorial. They'll just end up fighting one another, won't they? Wouldn't we be better off trying to chuck water on the dogs or something?"

"Depends on how well you think you could learn to command wild animals, doesn't it?" said Sammael. The stoat ran back up his neck. "Depends on how creative you want to be in your approach."

"But . . . *stoats*?"

Sammael turned and smiled his thin, easy smile, and Tom's doubts vanished.

"Imagine," said Sammael. "If you could."

And with a brief salute, he walked out of the yard leaving Tom staring after him, hope soaring in his heart.

✦ ✦ ✦

Up in the ether, Sammael stepped out of the air into the doorway and stamped into the cold room, hardly noticing as Iaco leapt from the neck of his shirt and raced behind a high stack of boxes. He was muttering to himself, a long stream of words the stoat couldn't follow.

The walls of the room had changed color again. Today they were a moldy green, the sort of color that gobbled up light.

Iaco's paws were still shaking from the horrors of the journey. They'd traveled through that awful, blinding world, wild with evil men and evil dogs. She'd had to hide inside Sammael's shirt and stay close to his chest again, just to stop herself chewing her own paws off in terror.

She found something that looked like an old lump of bread and gave it a tentative gnaw.

"Humans!" spat Sammael. "Humans!"

The stoat's fur prickled along the ridge of her spine. She burped, and a stream of tiny shovels flew from her mouth, in all the various colors of the rainbow.

"Iaco!" snapped Sammael. "I warned you—don't touch things you find here. You're still a creature of the earth—if you're going to be witless and dumb, not even I can help you."

The tiny shovels dwindled away, although they were followed by a single curving scythe, and then Iaco could breathe properly again.

"I'm not dumb!" she yelled, leaping up and down in fear and fury. "You haven't explained a thing about this place! I can't eat, I can hardly breathe, and every time I move a claw something even more disgusting happens to me! Last week—those giant pink slugs falling from the roof—ugh! This isn't what I asked for! The deal's off! I'm going home!"

"Go on, then," said Sammael. "Off you trot."

Iaco crouched against the ground, sniffing with hatred.

"I can't," she growled. "You've trapped me here. You've tricked me."

"Oh, get over yourself," said Sammael. "You and I want the same things, and we'll get them very soon. Just don't be a dimwit in the meantime."

Iaco arched her back and flexed her claws, growling at the insult. But Sammael reached out a hand and picked her up, and she felt again the powerful warmth of his skin. He set her to rest on his forearm, and gradually her back lost its tightness as she lay along the strong bones.

"Those humans will get what's coming to them, don't you worry," he said, raising his arm to his face so she could look into his hard black eyes. "When I get his sand, I'll rip a hole in Chromos so big you'll be able to push the moon herself through it. And those pure colors will pour down on every inch of earth, bringing every nightmare and terror scream-ing out from the darkest corners of people's minds. All the stupid, ungrateful people, all the dull, unimaginative cow-ards, and the brainless, backward fools who won't look at the world in case they see something that they don't understand—*none* of them will survive."

A vision of her babies came into Iaco's mind: the first one opening his eyes, beginning to struggle onto weak, shaking legs. His brothers and sisters following his lead, clawing out into the world beyond their fur-lined nest. How small they had been. How fragile.

Iaco's tiny heart sat as heavy as stone, and for a moment she couldn't breathe.

"I know something about death, too," said Sammael in a tight voice. "The last human who stumbled on some minor unearthly powers was so afraid of the whole thing—so afraid to even *look* at me—that he murdered my innocent dog. I know what it's like when the world takes and takes and takes from you, and gives nothing back."

Iaco closed her eyes. "Will it kill other creatures, too?"

And Sammael nodded. "I should think so. But they've all had enough chances. And the brave ones might make it through, the creatures who aren't afraid of the wilderness. Hardly any of them are humans, though. Humans are the most cowardly creatures of all."

"But . . . but what if the men and dogs who killed my babies survive? What if *they're* brave, in some way, somehow . . . ?" Iaco screwed her eyes tighter shut, trying to push away the thoughts of the heavy-booted feet, the pattering of the terriers' paws, the sounds of danger stamping through the undergrowth.

"Bah!" Sammael shook his arm, sending the stoat flying through the air and tumbling onto the ground. "People like *that? Brave?* Don't be absurd! And don't question me! There's too much that a sniveling shrew like you could never understand."

"I'm not a shrew!" spat Iaco, recovering her feet and baring her teeth. "I'm a stoat!"

"Hunger making you snippy, is it?" said Sammael, picking up a box and opening it. He set it down in front of the stoat. "Here. Dinner."

The box was full of a yellowish-gray fine sand. Iaco trembled at the smell. It had the cold scent of age and a mummified dryness that clung to her nostrils.

"What's the matter? Lost your appetite?" asked Sammael. "The souls of long-dead humans not tempting you today?"

The stoat shuddered and gulped, trying to gouge pinholes in the floor with her claws. Sammael was a creature to be scared of—she knew that. The old legends were full of stories about him turning day into night and squashing mountains into the sea. He'd performed countless acts of strength and wild impossibility, and he'd behaved exactly as he liked since the dawn of time. She didn't expect him to be nice to her. But his changes of mood were terrifying.

It didn't matter. As long as she stayed with him she'd be safe. He'd help her take her revenge. Nothing else was important anymore.

Iaco watched as Sammael turned away and began to run his fingers along the stacks of boxes, pausing for a second on each one as if listening to its contents.

"Nope . . . nope . . . nope . . . ," he muttered to himself. "None of you will do. But as soon as he's finished the book, I'll get his sand. And when I've got that—then you'll see."

## CHAPTER 12

# ESCAPE

Cath sat in the corner next to the settee, hugging her knees to her chest. Her neck ached from where the sweater had dug into it, and her stomach was bruised. She concentrated on those two lines of pain, shutting out any memories of yesterday. Yesterday was worse than any pain: the single day in which she'd let herself think she might get away from Dad.

Sadie stuck her head around the door frame and put her tongue out.

"Yeah?" said Cath. "Come here and do that."

Sadie smirked. "You're in *so* much trouble!" she said,

retreating safely to the doorway of her bedroom. The words floated up the hallway and mooched around the living room, but Cath hardly heard them. She didn't need Sadie to tell her anything.

Macy came in wearing a leopard-print dressing gown. She sat down on the settee, rubbed makeup-crusted sleep from her eyes, lit a cigarette, and turned the TV up.

"Yer Dad's getting up," she said over an audience-fake-booing noise. "And then he'll sort you out. And you let the dogs crap in here again. I ought to rub your dirty little face in it, teach you some manners."

Cath swore at her.

Macy took another puff of her cigarette and said, "I'll tell that to yer dad, will I?"

"Yeah," Cath said. "Go on."

"You're a waste of space," said Macy. "No wonder yer own mum didn't want you."

Cath tried to get up but Macy was on her feet, quick as a terrier.

"Don't you get any ideas, missy. You just sit there and keep yer mouth shut."

Cath sank back down to the floor. Where was Zadoc, who could lift her up and carry her high above the world? And where was Barshin, who'd put all those strange talking thoughts in her head, so that she'd seemed to be having a conversation with him? It couldn't really have been true.

She'd just been going crazy. People did go crazy and started seeing things, and talking to things that weren't there. That must have been what had happened to her. But it was all over now.

The bedroom door clicked and squeaked, and Dad's footsteps thumped over the junk in the hallway. A tang of stale air floated into the living room.

"Sadie!" yelled Macy, getting up. Sadie came slyly in, smirking at Cath. "Watch her. Yell if she moves."

There was something said in the kitchen. Macy's sharp voice and Dad's low, hard one, and then more footsteps.

Sadie stepped backward, and Dad filled the doorway. He looked at Cath. There was nothing on his face, just the same blank look he'd give to a dog in the road.

"I've got school," said Cath, trying to make her shaking voice sound defiant. "I've gotta go."

"Oh yeah? So you can run away and get the pigs on me, is that right?" Dad said quietly. "We'll see about that."

Cath looked down at her feet pressed against the floor. There was a hole in one of the toes of her socks. If she looked very hard at it, so hard that she could convince herself the sock hole was another way to Chromos, with Barshin and Zadoc waiting just on the other side of it—if she could imagine that, maybe she could forget about Dad.

That spiky yellow plant with the coconut smell. She saw the bush as clearly as if it were growing from the living room carpet, yellow flowers holding tightly to the air. She breathed in and something pulled at the corner of her mouth.

Dad grabbed the top of her arm and yanked her to her feet. Cath's shoulder swung forward, arm twisted behind her. She bit her tongue.

The yellow flowers. The thorns. If her fingers were thorns, poking out into Dad's face . . .

Dad lifted her up against the wall. And then there was a knocking sound and he dropped her, stomping out of the room. For a second she lay frozen on the carpet.

In the hallway someone opened the front door and someone else spoke. A boy's voice, light and nervous.

Danny O'Neill? But he couldn't be here. He didn't know where she lived.

The door slammed shut. Cath's chest felt heavy. What else had she expected? Danny O'Neill, rescuing her?

Dad stomped off to the kitchen. Cath heard the mumbling of his voice but not the words. Maybe if he kept on talking for long enough, she could get out of the apartment.

She inched toward the door. The dogs began to bark from the kitchen and rushed out into the hallway. Cath froze. But it wasn't her they were heading for. They threw themselves against the front door, frantically slapping their great paws against the plastic.

"I told you, she don't live 'ere!" bellowed Dad, stomping through again. Cath tried to whip her head out of the way, but she wasn't quick enough. Dad gave an outraged yell and thundered toward her, fist raised.

A rattling sound came from the door. Dad stopped, turning his head.

The door was hissing like a basket of angry snakes. Behind the noise of the dogs' barks and scrabbles, the whole thing had begun to shake.

Cath thought she heard a squeak, but maybe it was just another dog claw. No—there was another squeak, and another.

A small black patch appeared at the bottom of the door, and a rat leapt through, hurling itself into the air above the dogs' heads. As they threw up their jaws to snap at it, another rat ran in, and another, and another. The black patch grew and grew, and the whole bottom half of the door turned into a writhing sea of brown and black rats pouring into the apartment. They engulfed the dogs, the piles of junk, and the entire hallway in a dark, shimmering flood.

"Cath!" Danny yelled into the apartment. "Cath! It's me! Come on!"

Cath ran out, grabbing at a coat from the hook by the doorway.

"Oh no you don't!" yelled Dad, straining to reach out and get hold of her.

"Get the man!" shouted Danny to the rats.

The rats swarmed in a bunch up Dad's body and raced

along his flailing arms. One perched on his head, two more hung on to the tops of his ears. One ran daringly down the bridge of his nose and leapt off. Soon they were all following, running along Dad's nose and dive-bombing into the swarm of rats below.

"Bye!" shouted Cath. She was already laughing as she shoved past Dad, dodged the howling dogs, yanked open what was left of the door, and threw herself out. Her feet, as precise as a pianist's fingers, pounded down the stairs with such joy that Danny, scrambling and sliding, couldn't keep up with her at all.

She burst into the open air and slowed for a second or two so that Danny could catch up.

"How did you find me?" she yelled, dancing backward.

"Asked . . . at . . . school." Danny panted, his thin legs flapping over the concrete.

Cath grinned at him. Wobbly legs and all, he'd found her, and he'd gotten her free.

"Rats!" she said, her eyes shining. "Ha-ha! Them dogs covered in rats. *Dad* covered in rats! Ha-ha-ha!"

And she was sprinting off again, her coat swinging against her legs. She dodged along the side of the playground and hurdled over the bicycle barriers at the entrance to the footpath.

"Wait!" Danny shouted. Cath swung back to see that he was having trouble running. His legs were swinging as if he'd drunk too much.

Behind them, the apartment building doors swung open and Dad roared out, shaking rats off his arms. The rats flew through the air, squealing with joy, and ran straight back at his trouser legs. He had to slow down to shake them off, but he wasn't stopping.

Cath swore. "Barshin!" she yelled.

And there he was, loping out from underneath a fence. He came a little slowly, but his eyes were chips of steel.

"Barshin! We need Zadoc!" Cath shouted.

The hare stopped at her feet. "Zadoc's coming," he said. "But we won't all get on, you know. He can't carry two humans."

"He'll take us," said Cath. "We're not heavy."

"It isn't the weight of your bodies," said the hare. "It's the weight of your minds."

And the air was dissolving around them, the world bending away. Zadoc's hooves appeared, then his legs, and the tired old carpet of his hide.

Danny O'Neill stared in horror.

"Get him up there!" hissed Barshin. "He's the one your father will catch first. I'll come back for you."

"No way," said Cath.

"You can run. Hide where you did before. No man would harm his own daughter," said Barshin.

Wanna bet? thought Cath. But she grabbed Danny, shaking him roughly out of his stare.

"Climb up!" She held out her hands, clasped together for Danny to step up on.

"It's made of dust . . . ," Danny mumbled, still half-frozen.

"Nah, it's just Zadoc. He'll get us away."

"Where?"

"To Chromos, of course!"

And Dad was roaring closer, Irish dancing with the rats in his trousers. He'd be there in moments.

Danny closed his eyes and reached out.

A jet of pale light shot up his arm, as bright as a firework. Wisps of smoke leapt from Zadoc's hide toward him, flaring into flames. Danny tried to reach out again, but instead leapt back and screamed, throwing up his arms to protect himself, and Zadoc reared up on protesting legs.

"No!" Danny gasped. "No! Go away!"

"Get on!" urged Cath, and Danny screamed again, fighting off something invisible to her eyes, something huge and leaping, that was going for his stomach, his legs, his face—

"No!" he yelled. "No, Kalia, no!"

"Don't be daft, it's only Chromos!" Cath pushed forward, scrambling up along the horse's leg and onto his dusty back. Barshin took an almighty leap, bounced off Zadoc's knee, and threw himself up in front of her. Cath held out a hand to Danny. "Come on, quick!"

But Danny's hands were up in front of his face, protecting his eyes, and then he lashed out at her, knocking her away. Did he think she was attacking him?

"Time to go!" boomed Zadoc, his legs beginning to disappear.

"Danny!" Cath tried one last time. "Come on, just get on!"

Danny pushed out with his hands again, waving them wildly at the empty air.

"Kalia!" he gasped. "The dog—"

He took a shaking step backward, then another, and then turned on his heel and ran.

Cath set her jaw and clutched Barshin to her chest. Fine, she said silently. I'll go on my own, then. Coward. You don't know what you're missing.

The world pitched into darkness, and they leapt into Chromos.

## CHAPTER 13

# A WARNING

At first Zadoc galloped wildly, careering in a zigzag through alleyways and narrow streets, hurdling fences and gates and traffic barriers. Then the strange colors of the town grew dingy and dark, and the horse's pounding hooves began to slow until he was moving hesitantly, stumbling a little. Cath looked down at his feet. A pale mist rose from the earth, growing thick so quickly that within seconds she could no longer see where he was treading.

Before she could look forward again, a hand smacked the horse's shoulder, nearly hitting Cath.

She yanked her knee away. That hand . . .

"Cath!"

And that voice . . .

"Catherine!"

She didn't dare turn her head. Her arm clenched Barshin's squirming body, and her heels drove themselves into the horse's flanks.

"Go!" she yelled, sure that the horse would gather up his legs and spring forward, shake off the hand, and gallop away from the voice that was calling her name.

But the horse slowed abruptly, threatening to stop.

"Go!" she shouted again. "Just go!"

"What is it?" Barshin squeaked, trying to struggle out of her arms.

"It's him!" Cath almost choked on the word. And still the horse didn't move. The harder she kicked, the more his body turned solid against her.

"Who?" gasped Barshin.

The hand reached toward Cath's knee. In a second he'd be touching her. In two seconds, he'd have her leg between those fat-tentacle fingers.

"Dad!"

The word hurt her throat. She tried to say it again.

"It's D—"

"He's not here!" squealed Barshin. "He can't be here! You're imagining him!"

The hand stopped just short and trembled.

Was she? Was that even possible? No—it was Dad's hand, rough and strong. It was definitely his.

The hand moved another fraction.

"No!" shrieked Barshin.

And the fingers were around her left leg, clinging as tightly as cornrows of hair on to a scalp. Cath tried one last time to pull herself away, but it seemed as though the horse was almost helping Dad—his shoulder dropped, he leaned sideways, and Cath slid down his ribs. Her right heel came up to the horse's knobbly spine and slipped over the top of his back so that both her legs were dangling on the same side. And Dad grabbed them both.

She tried to see what she was sliding into, whether it was hard ground, or mud, or water. But there was nothing down there except darkness, a thousand colors blending into a starless night.

Dad's hands tugged at her. She tried to wriggle away, and he pulled her toward him, off the horse's back, away from Barshin. Barshin—she couldn't let go of him—he was her friend, her protector . . .

Her guts exploded with a burst of slime that spattered wide across Zadoc's flank. Looking down, expecting a ragged hole in her belly, she saw a shadow climbing up the front of her sweater, hot as lava. It was burning her away, eating into her skin, and she saw suddenly and certainly that she was dissolving into the darkness. Dad had got her, and she was disappearing.

She had always wondered if he might actually kill her one day, and now he had.

Pain tore at her shoulder and she flew upward, as smoothly as water. Her butt hit something, and her hands came to rest on a wiry scalp. The horse's mane, right in front of her.

The horse had picked her up in his teeth and thrown her up onto his back again.

He had saved her life.

The world stopped. Cath didn't dare breathe. And then a furry body crawled into her arms and pushed itself against her chest, tiny heart fluttering as fast as the running paws of a mouse.

She opened her eyes.

"Close them!" said Barshin. "Close them now and listen to me."

Cath wanted to look around, to see how near the hands were. If only the horse would move on again.

"No!" said Barshin. "Keep your eyes closed. Listen! I told you not to get off Zadoc!"

"I didn't get off," said Cath. "The hands pulled me off."

"They aren't here," insisted Barshin. "No one else is here, only you and me and Zadoc. Every other creature you see is in your head."

"He pulled me. I felt his hands."

"No," said Barshin. "If you couldn't survive on the ground in here, how do you think anyone else could? You pushed yourself off. I saw it. I tell you, nothing can survive here."

"Then why did you let me come, if it's so bad?" said Cath.

"You needed to get away," said Barshin. "And you saw before—it isn't bad. It's just Chromos."

"All I saw this time was hands." Cath shuddered. "Horrible hands."

"That's because when we came before, you were hopeful," said Barshin. "You were scared, but you thought deep down that you *could* get away. This time, you let yourself fear that you couldn't. And of all the things in your mind, the things you're scared of are the most vivid, so they come to you first in here."

"I didn't look for anything," said Cath. "It just came."

"But you can stop that." Barshin squirmed upward, so his face was pressing against her cheek. "Always think forward. Don't look back for safety, just think of what you want! I told you before—just put your dreams in your mind's eye and that's what Chromos will always be for you."

"Dreams?" Cath felt something sting at her heart and it fizzed inside her chest. "That's easy. I want to go to my house, between the sea and the mountains."

"Then open your eyes," said Barshin. "But be careful."

Cath opened them, and Zadoc began to run.

✦ ✦ ✦

The great plain of Chromos passed by in a blur of emerald green; Zadoc didn't stop to let Cath gaze around at the world that sprung out from inside her. He headed fast in one single direction, but Cath didn't worry: it all made sense to her. He was taking her to her house again.

She tried to see where the sun was, so that she would at least know the vague direction to take once she was back on earth. Lemon yellow, it hung in the sky up to her left, staying constant beside her. Good: she could set out from the Sawtry and keep the sun in the same place, and then she'd get there eventually.

But suddenly, her heart slammed into the pit of her stomach and she felt a tearing inside her tangled guts. They had gone past the house, or turned away from it, she wasn't sure which, and they were heading somewhere else. Somewhere she didn't want to go. But how could that be?

If it wasn't something she wanted, then it must still be something she feared.

Zadoc slowed, changed direction, and began moving east. Now the sun was rising, trying to break through a sky the same smeared green as the mold that grew on the wall behind the couch at home. For a moment Cath thought she saw the shapes of the Sawtry apartment buildings looming up from the horizon. He wasn't taking her back there, was he?

She kicked her panicked heels into Zadoc's sides. "Oi," she said. "Don't you dare take me home! Dad's after me. Take me to my house!"

"But you don't know where it is," said a voice.

Not Zadoc's voice.

Cath's skin went cold. She swung around just as Zadoc stumbled over a bump in the ground and stopped. They were in a low meadow next to a river, and the grass was just about green and the river just about brown, though farther afield the land was lumpy and purplish.

A few meters away, a figure was leaning on a tree. It was a tall, thin man with close black curls and a face paler than Johnny White's as he'd lain on the ground losing his blood. This man was wearing a white shirt and black trousers tucked into battered boots that stopped just below his knees. He looked a bit like a highwayman, but his face was ugly—it held something of Dad in the way his lips twisted and his eyebrows pulled together in a scowl.

"I said," repeated the figure, "you don't know where it is, do you?"

"Who are you?" asked Cath, feeling Barshin like a lump of rock about her neck.

The figure smiled exactly like Dad did when someone came to the door of the apartment with a fistful of money.

And then she knew.

Zadoc snorted and took a step backward.

"Oh, don't be feeble," sneered Sammael.

"Get lost," said Cath.

Sammael eyed her with slight interest. "I was talking to your noble steed," he said. "He's always found my presence rather challenging. You don't know where you're going, do you?"

"Yeah," said Cath. "I'm going back to my house. The one I saw in here before. That's all."

Sammael took three steps toward Zadoc's side and then he was there, looking up at them. But he was taller now, and Zadoc had shrunk, and Sammael barely had to lift his eyes to be staring into Cath's.

Up close, he was even uglier. But she felt no fear.

"You're a long way from home, aren't you? What makes you think a mere human girl like you can get what she wants from Chromos?"

"I don't think nothing," said Cath. "Barshin brought me here, and I saw that house. Now I'm going to find it and live there."

Sammael smiled. His teeth were very white. "It's always interesting what people find up here. Some find their wildest dreams and fantasies. Some find things that are boringly real. I'd have thought *you* were made of wilder stuff. A house in the middle of nowhere—a real house, somewhere *safe*—that's the sort of thing I'd have expected from Danny O'Neill. Tell me, did he even try to come up here with you?"

"Yeah," said Cath, still not knowing whether she ought to be more afraid. "He tried. But then he started screaming and going on about—"

She broke off, biting the word *dog* away from her tongue. A swift lie came easily, covering her hesitation.

"About some fire burning him, and he wouldn't get on Zadoc. I dunno—I didn't see no fire or nothing, just a bit of light from Chromos."

Sammael sneered. "I thought that might happen. You can't come to Chromos if you don't want to. And you can't fool it by just pretending that you do, either. Chromos knows what's really inside you. Only those who are prepared to embrace the unknown can thrive here. Danny O'Neill wants to sit in a dark corner with his eyes shut. He would be eaten by his fears the moment he came near Chromos. What use is there in a person like him?"

"He saved me," said Cath, surprised to find herself defending Danny.

"Oh, through some great act of bravery, no doubt," said Sammael. "Did it all by himself, did he?"

"He got rats. They chewed down the door."

Sammael snorted. "Rats! How appropriate. Except I wouldn't do a rat the dishonor of comparing it to Danny O'Neill. I suppose he came running in at the head of them, then?"

Cath shook her head. She wondered why Sammael was bothering to ask questions when he knew all the answers already.

"Shall I tell you why Danny O'Neill doesn't want to come to Chromos?" asked Sammael. "Or have you worked it out for yourself?"

Cath shrugged. "He's just scared, ain't he? It's normal."

Sammael cocked his head and considered her. "Top marks. But you aren't scared. Do you think that's normal?"

Cath shrugged again.

"Okay," said Sammael, gesturing toward the hazy horizon with his long thin hand. "See that out there? You must know by now that what you and I see, what your little rabbit friend sees, and what Zadoc sees are all entirely different things in here. Because you know that Chromos holds up a mirror to the soul. If you've ever imagined yourself as more than you are, cleverer, more inventive, more full of life and ideas, then Chromos has everything you need to show you how to live. But to see anything good in here, you have to be brave."

"Danny's brave," Cath said. "He came back to find me. That was brave."

"Danny O'Neill is scared of everything!" Sammael spat. "What does it matter what he does? Inside, he is scared. He is scared of badness, scared of the cold, scared of the dark. Oh, he isn't so different from most other creatures. Darkness is always scary at first. But all living creatures on earth have darkness inside them, right inside their souls—you can't escape that fact. Most creatures leave it well alone, they don't look at it, and they don't face it or try to understand it, so it grows powerful inside them. Then in here, it rises up and blinds them. Because in their own hearts, the thing they are most afraid of is *themselves*."

Cath felt Zadoc tremble underneath her, but she didn't

mind the idea of darkness. There was plenty of it about in the Sawtry buildings. And Sammael was right, in a way—worse things seemed to happen when people tried to pretend it wasn't there. Like Dad, saying he was only angry at Johnny White, and not at the whole enormous world. Dad couldn't kill the world. But he could kill Johnny.

She looked at the yellow flowers on her hand. "How come I can deal with it, then?"

Sammael tilted his head. "It is the way you are. There is a wildness inside you, and you aren't afraid of it. I am an ancient creature: I saw what would happen to the world once humans came along. People do not like wildness; they are obsessed with controlling things. I've made Chromos trickle onto the earth, so those cramped minds can rise up and spread their wings. And I'll keep doing it—making new links between the two realms. Imagine it: with every new link, earth becomes more like Chromos. One day, you'll be able to think up anything and it'll exist! You'll fly, ride clouds, run faster than the speed of light, change trees into lions and lions into stars. You'll live in palaces, jungles, at the bottom of the sea—anything you want, you'll dream it up and make it, right there in front of you. I'm going to keep opening Chromos until earth is so soaked in color that nothing is impossible. And you—you're just the kind of person who'll thrive there. That's why those flowers only stained you instead of eating up your arm. You're wild and free and won't be satisfied with a small life. People like Danny O'Neill are so stupidly afraid. They don't know that if you want to see the stars you have to tear your eyes away from the wolf that's chewing up your feet. *They* think that happiness lies in safety. *Safety!* Paradise isn't a green field where the sun always shines. Paradise is fire!"

His eyes blazed, and the flames were dark.

"*You*'ll make a fire of your world, if you're worth anything at all. You'll fight the grayness and the drizzle and the nagging fear, and you'll set alight everything you touch. There aren't many like you."

Cath shook her head. "Burning things ain't right," she said. "It's what people like my dad do. That ain't good."

Sammael curled his lip and stepped back in disgust. "Bah! You don't know what you're talking about! But what do you matter? *I* am the creature who walks across Chromos, and *I* decide how much of it gets onto the earth. You humans always look for good or bad, for right or wrong. That's why you have your grubby little earth. But when Chromos comes pouring over you, you won't know good from bad. You won't even know up from down. Chromos doesn't care about right and wrong. It cares only for the burning fires of imagination! Remember that."

With this, Sammael hooked an arm around Zadoc's shrinking neck. Grabbing a handful of Zadoc's mane, he dragged the horse a short distance away, twisted his arms in a quick shrug, and kicked out a leg. Zadoc stumbled. Cath saw too late what the horse had stumbled into: a smoking gray patch just like the one she'd seen next to the well.

Zadoc plunged into the boiling gray soup, Cath clinging to his neck, and Barshin to Cath. They drew in their breaths, held them, and disappeared.

## CHAPTER 14

# ISBJIN AL-ORR

"**O**i! You little scumbag!"

Cath's dad pounded behind Danny, still shaking rats from his trousers, but every one of his giant strides was as big as two of Danny's and the ground shook as he thumped his feet onto the cracked concrete.

Cath had vanished completely into the fiery air, and with her had gone the vicious, snarling fury that had prevented Danny from following her: the fury of a creature he'd thought he'd never see alive again.

Danny had no time to think about Kalia, or to wonder how she had returned from the dead and leapt at him, teeth bared, trying to snap her jaws around his flesh. He saw his bike where he'd chucked it down at the entrance to the apartment building, sprinted to it, and threw his leg over the crossbar. His foot slipped on the pedal as he tried to start the bike—once, twice—and his hands were shaking so much that he couldn't keep the handlebars straight. But somehow he got the pedal hard against his shoe, and then an arm reached out, grabbing his shoulder—

Danny stood on the pedals, bounced down a curb, and felt the strong kick of his sturdy bike. Good bike. All it needed was to be kept straight and pedaled, and it wouldn't let him down. He pushed as hard as he could, kinking around parked cars, flying out of intersections without stopping to look. Luckily the roads were quiet and he didn't hear any cars slamming on squealing brakes or annoyed horns beeping, although a lady trundling a shopping cart did have to take a step backward to avoid him. But then he was wheeling along a street of terraced houses and out of town, into the countryside.

Unable to resist glancing back over his shoulder, he hit a pothole that grabbed the front wheel and sent him spinning into the grass shoulder. He landed in a heap, feet and ankles all twisted up in bike and wheels, and the bike had become such a part of him that for a moment his fuzzy head felt the whole tangled mess as though it were full of blood and nerves, attached to his body like a centaur's legs.

He kept his head down and waited for Cath's dad to come running up the street toward him, but there was no sound of approaching footsteps. He must have gone farther than Cath's dad could run. Facedown on a damp shoulder with grass up his nose and dandelions in his ears, he was finally safe. From Cath's dad at least.

What was that digging into his leg? He put his hand into his pocket. Of course: the stick. It hadn't broken in the fall, but then he didn't think it would ever break. It didn't seem to be made of breakable matter.

Pain shot up his ankle. He swore, then, too late, realized he was still holding the stick.

The grass rustled with a gasp of surprise that rose and echoed around the shoulder, and it all came back to Danny in a sickening flood: Kalia, Tom, Sammael, the dreams—there was no way of getting away from it. He had helped Cath escape, but that was only the beginning of what he had to do. If he was going to try and use Kalia to get Tom free, he had to find a way of getting into Chromos that would let him talk to the dog and tame her. He certainly wouldn't be able to get up onto the back of that strange creature of dust who had carried Cath away if Kalia was intent on killing him before he got close to it.

He remembered the bristling world around him and the things that had spoken to him on his last journey. Trees, rivers, grasses—everything seemed to know something new: he'd learned that quite often all you had to do was ask.

Well, the stick was in his hand and the grass had already heard him: he might as well turn his mistake to some good advantage.

"Hey," he said softly. "Can any of you grasses hear me?"

There was another small, rippling gasp, and then a silence. Danny still found it much stranger talking to plants than to animals.

"I said, can you hear me?"

"Of course we can," said a clipped voice from beside his right ear. "Do you know who you're talking to?"

"Yeah. You're the grass. I'm Danny O'Neill."

"Danny O'Neill? But of course."

Of course they knew it was him. Was there anything that the grass didn't know?

"I need to get somewhere," he said, struggling into a sitting position while trying not to squash the grass too heavily.

"You need directions? We grasses know the way to almost anywhere on earth. Where is it you need to go?"

"A place called . . ." He swallowed. Even the name was hard to say. "A place called Chromos. Do you know how to get there?"

There was some angry muttering among the grasses, and then the same voice spoke out again.

"Chromos isn't a place on earth—you must know that. And you are Danny O'Neill. Getting involved in your schemes, whatever they are . . . it sits badly with some of us.

Some say that you are trying to take control of the world of grasses."

"Of course I'm not!" said Danny, sitting back on his heels. "What good would that do? This talking thing was just an accident. But Sammael's after me. He wants to kill me. I need to go into Chromos and get something to try and make him stop."

"Sammael wants to kill you?" said the grass. "Why, for the love of oats?"

"It's a long story," said Danny. He felt a spot of rain on his neck and looked up at the clouds, but they were white rather than gray. "Just believe me, he does. So please could you help me?"

"Well . . ." The grass considered for such a length of time that Danny looked back down the road again, worried that Cath's dad might have had a chance to catch up. But there was no sign of him.

After much muttering and whispering among the grasses, too tangled for him to follow, the grass that seemed to have appointed itself spokesperson said, "You do not ask *where* Chromos is, but *how* to get there. So I am supposing you know that the answers to those questions are significantly different. And we grasses know *where* Chromos is—it is over us, around us, and inside us. It is a world made by the collective minds of all the living creatures on earth, joined together. But *how* to get there—I am afraid we have less information about that. It is known that creatures can travel through Chromos on the back of a guide made by the colors, although the secret of how to call up that guide has long been lost to us. And apart from that, only Sammael can travel into Chromos. Why, we don't know. It isn't his world—he must have discovered some device or other that allows him passage, otherwise it would swallow even him up. But we don't know what that is."

Danny tucked his chin into his sweatshirt. "And you don't have any ideas?"

"Ah, no, sorry. But there was a story, was there not, that you managed to take his coat off him? That, surely, was a thing that held much power. Where did that power come from? And how did you find out about it?"

The river in Great Butford. It had told Danny that there were many stories about the origins of Sammael's coat, some about an ox called Xur, some about the eight stags who pulled the moon across the sky—

Stags, he thought. That stag, silver in the moonlight.

"I heard some stories," he said. "But won't this be something completely different?"

"Who knows? It might be, or it might not."

Eight stags that pulled the moon across the sky. Maybe the stag from the woods would at least know something about that. It was the tiniest of hopes, but the only one he had.

"Okay," he said slowly, feeling the syllables grind up from the bottom of his lungs and break reluctantly into the air. "I guess you're right. I think I know who to ask."

There was another whispering among the grasses and the single voice floated up again.

"One last thing, Danny O'Neill."

"Yes?"

"These are strange times. Rumors abound. And you come here asking about Chromos, and some of us are not surprised."

A cold chill crept up Danny's spine. He knew that, whatever the grass was about to say, it wasn't going to be good.

"You humans know little of Chromos," the grass continued. "You are closed to such things. But some are talking of a time to come, when the barrier between Chromos and earth will be broken. Not with small holes, but with one vast rip that will see the colors of Chromos pouring, pure and free, onto the earth. Who would possibly do such a thing, no one wishes to say. But if it should happen, it's certain that the humans will come off worst of all, for of all creatures they are the most blind to the true chaos of the world, and they breathe the most life into their own fears. Chromos will not help those who fear: their fears will turn on them and drive them mad. We do not tell you this to frighten you. You talk to us of Chromos—we say only that if you are involved in some scheme, if you are meddling with Chromos, you should be aware of these stories. You should consider what kind of power you are meddling with."

The words brought Cath's eager, fearless face into Danny's mind, and for a second he watched her talking about Chromos, plunging heedlessly back into it, disappearing from the Sawtry's concrete yard. And then the vision of Kalia leapt in front of her, lips drawn back from sharp, biting teeth, and Danny knew that Cath was the odd one out, not him. He was the same as most other people, and Chromos was a dangerous place.

"I'm not meddling with it," he said. "Although I reckon it's not hard to guess who is."

"You are thinking about Sammael," said the grass.

Danny got to his feet, brushing the dirt off his hands and legs, trying to swallow the dryness in his throat. He thought about the stag's silver-shadowed neck, those branching antlers.

His heart leapt with something shocked and bright.

"Yeah. But what do I know? Maybe it isn't Sammael. Maybe I'll only find out once I get into Chromos. When I do, I'll let you know."

Wedging the front wheel of his bike between his knees, he bashed the handlebars back into position and swung his leg over the crossbar, noticing that his trousers had a huge rip down one calf. His mum wouldn't like that, but what did it matter? He wasn't going home just yet.

✦ ✦ ✦

The herd of deer were grazing at the edge of the woodland among a cloud of cow parsley. The stag stood a little way off, pausing between mouthfuls of grass to raise his head and glance around, but Danny, on his belly, managed to creep to within twenty feet of the animal before he sensed him, jerked his head up, and stood alert, flaring his nostrils.

Danny gripped the stick and whispered inside his mind. "Hello?"

The stag seemed to recognize the voice as that of a deer, because he didn't run away.

"Who's that?" he said. "Are you come to challenge me?"

"No," said Danny, wondering how far he'd get in a fight with those antlers.

"Are you known to the herd of Isbjin al-Orr?"

"No," whispered Danny, his heart beginning to fail him. Was the stag about to challenge him to a fight?

"Identify yourself, and your business in greeting me," said the stag, tossing his head so that his antlers appeared to shoot, for an instant, up into the white sky.

"I'm not a deer," said Danny. "I'll come out. But please don't try and fight me."

"What?" said the stag. "You're not a deer? Impossible. Show yourself."

Danny got to his feet, brushing the dirt off his knees. He

felt small and shabby in comparison with the stag. He could run him through with a single antler if he wanted to.

He stepped forward, treading as quietly as he could.

"I'm Danny," he said. "Hello."

The stag eyed him, sniffing at the air.

"I am Isbjin al-Orr, head of my herd," he said. "But I don't understand. You are a human—a young human male, if I observe correctly—and yet you can make words and speak in sentences. It was my understanding that humans could only make a series of indistinguishable sounds and communicate the finer points of their meanings through body language. But you—you have learned to talk?"

"I could always talk," said Danny. "People talk all the time to each other. But I can talk to you, too. Now I can, anyway."

"But how?" asked Isbjin al-Orr, one of his front hooves tapping twice on the green earth.

"It's . . . it's . . ." Danny floundered. He'd never actually told the truth about the stick to anyone except Tom, who hadn't believed it, and he didn't particularly want to start telling the truth now. ". . . It's to do with Sammael . . . ," he said, almost stumbling over the name. "Not anything bad, though. Just to do with him, so I can talk to things."

Sammael. What kind of an excuse was that? It left a dirty taste in Danny's mouth. He didn't want to link himself to Sammael in any way whatsoever.

A rustling in the trees made the stag turn his head and flick his rounded ears.

"What is it?"

"Just a sound," said Isbjin al-Orr. "I listen to them all. Sammael, you say? He is a creature of our young fawns' fairy tales. How on earth would that make you able to talk to me?"

"It wasn't him, exactly," said Danny. "I sort of . . . got . . . hit by lightning. Yes, that was it—I got hit by lightning, and then I could understand everything."

"It's lightning now, is it? Not Sammael?" The stag flared his nostrils.

"No—well, yes, it was. Lightning. It was when Sammael could control storms, and I got struck by lightning then. So it is sort of his fault. But I don't have anything to do with him now." Danny stopped hastily, not knowing where his lies were leading. In a moment he'd say something so preposterous that the stag might feel tempted to lower those branching antlers and thrust them toward him.

"Anyway . . . ," he said, trying to think of a subtle way to bring up the subject of Chromos and quickly deciding that more lies were a bad idea. "I heard about this place, Chromos, where Sammael lives. And I need to get there, so I wondered if you'd have any ideas about how he gets there."

"I do not believe you," said the stag. "Your tongue is certainly not silver. More an obvious shade of furry pink from what I can see. However, we deer do not hide things; it is not our way. Neither are we in the habit of inquiring into the affairs of strangers. In simple answer to you, therefore—in our stories, Sammael does not live in Chromos. He travels through Chromos to his home in the high ether. Our stories say that he has been playing with Chromos for thousands of years, ever since the death of the Great Ox, Xur."

"*What?*" said Danny.

"Oh, it is the seventh of our legends," said Isbjin al-Orr. "It's a tale about Phaeton, the son of Apollo, the Sun God."

"Tell me," said Danny. He leaned back against a tree and rested his head against the bark, breathing in the wriggling life of the woodland air.

"Very well," said the stag, and he began.

## CHAPTER 15

# PHAETON

"So we say that back in the beginning of the world, in the time when everything was new, the Sun God, Apollo, drew the sun across the sky each day, riding in a chariot pulled by eight magnificent stags. And Apollo had a son called Phaeton.

"Phaeton was a keen, curious boy. He craved to ride with his father in the chariot, and he begged Apollo to let him climb up beside him, but Apollo always refused.

" 'There is only space for one,' he would point out. 'Where would I put you? Would you ride on the back of a stag?' And he would laugh and turn away, and give Phateon a harness to clean.

"The truth of the matter was that Phaeton's mother was a mortal human, and Apollo knew that his son could never withstand the heat of the sun close at his back, but he didn't like to discourage the boy so early in his life so he kept him at bay with smiles and jokes.

"Phaeton grew sulky and began to desire, more than anything, to drive his father's chariot across the skies. And one morning, more silently than a mouse on a velvet carpet, he crept to the stables where the eight stags were dozing, harnessed them quietly to the chariot, then clambered up onto its narrow platform. The thick reins seemed impossibly large in his hands. He could barely close his fists around them.

"A sense of glory came upon him. As the stags stepped through the gateway, he felt as though he had found what he had been born for. I am the son of Apollo, he thought grandly. I am the son of—why, the son of the very sun itself!

"To begin with, the great sun only glowed warmly. But of course gradually it gained heat and strength, and as it grew hotter, Phaeton's back began to burn. Crying out in pain, he dropped the reins and clung to the front of the chariot, trying to cower away from the sun's great flames. The stags, free from any restraining hand, at once doubled their speed. With no charioteer to guide them, they galloped closer and closer to earth, the flames roaring out in their wake, and the mountaintops began to scorch and shrivel as they passed overhead.

"Closer still they came. Trees caught fire, the grass

crumbled, and the hillsides became barren. The seas began to steam. The creatures on earth screamed in fear at this terrible sight, but what could they do? They ran away, they tried to hide, but there was no escape. Soon the world was ablaze.

"One creature wasn't affected by the fire, though—a creature new to the world, who bore the name Sammael. He had an affinity with the skies and came to the world's aid by gathering together a great storm. This storm sent out a sleek thunderbolt that, with one sharp *crack*, knocked Phaeton from his perch and sent him tumbling down to the earth below. He fell onto the horns of the Great Ox, Xur, and was so deeply pierced that all his blood drained away into the earth and he died.

"The stags, their load lightened, let the skies draw them upward again and continued their way back to Apollo's stables. But when Phaeton did not return with the chariot, Apollo went searching for his son, hoping despite everything that he might find Phaeton alive. Alas, he found only his son's bloodless corpse, with Xur standing beside it.

"Now, nobody knew much about Xur, save that he was the Guardian of the Earth, and the gods had all sworn never to harm him. But Apollo was seized by grief and rage, so he killed Xur with one blow of his battle-ax, then carried Phaeton tenderly home to receive the last farewells of his mother.

"Sammael, who had been following these events, came in

search of Xur's corpse. He regarded the huge body with interest.

"'That's a fine ox,' he said to himself. 'And intriguing. It'd be a shame to let it go to waste.'

"So he skinned the ox and cured its hide. In time he made himself a pair of boots out of its skin. These boots had powers that no other creature could have foreseen. Various legends began to spread across the world: that the creature who wore them could control minds, that he could control the moon, the stars—even the course of the very sun itself. Some legends told how, when the race of humans came to cover the entire earth, the wearer of these boots could walk between all of them in a single stride.

"Who knows whether any of these stories are true. But one story above all was told and retold, countless times: that over and beyond the earth there exists a land called Chromos, where all the wonders and disasters of hope live in a thousand colors wrapped around the things of the earth itself. And those boots gave Sammael dominion over that endlessly colored world."

✦ ✦ ✦

Danny's blood had run as cold as his pinched skin. The rustling of deer in the cow parsley became louder, and faint chewing sounds scratched at the air.

Sammael's boots. Made from a legendary ox killed in the

first days of the world. There was no way he'd be able to steal them, use them to get into Chromos, take Kalia, and try to make a bargain with Sammael for Tom's sand. It was a crazy idea.

But if what the grass had said about Chromos was true, then simply getting Tom back wouldn't be enough. Danny would have to stop Sammael as well. Getting his boots would be the perfect way to do it.

Once Sammael couldn't travel through Chromos, he'd have to stay up in the high ether, where he belonged. All this would stop happening—Sammael controlling people's minds, making them sell their souls, making them try to kill each other. All that fear would be gone.

Danny saw it—the ending to his story. Sammael banished, Danny O'Neill free. No more trees struck by lightning. No more Toms with guilty, secretive faces.

"How could I get the boots?" he said abruptly, forgetting that he was speaking out loud.

The rustling sounds stopped immediately, as did every other sound in the forest except the hissing wind.

Isbjin al-Orr stayed still, as though the sound of Danny's actual voice was not much of a surprise to him.

"It's only a story," he said. "Sammael doesn't exist. If he did, he'd be hundreds of thousands of years old by now. Millions, even. Or billions."

Danny shook his head. "Something exists," he said. "And it calls itself Sammael, and it wears boots just like you said."

"I have always known that humans were strange," said Isbjin al-Orr. "But stranger still are you. I tell you, child, it is a story. It has been repeated so much over the entire length of the existence of deer that its origins must have been different entirely. I told you the story we have now, at this moment in time. It is not the same story as it was when it began, that is for certain. So it cannot be the whole story. It is only our version, for our time."

"Did you know that grass talks?" said Danny. "It's so sharp that anything one blade says can get repeated millions of times by others, and it stays the same. How do you know your story is wrong? It sounds right to me."

"Because I have seen time," said the stag, and as if to confirm this, the sunlight glinted on the gray hairs gathering around his nostrils and mouth. "I have watched the days rise and set, and the moons come and go, and the seasons turn by in their endless change. Nothing is ever the same as it was the previous year—I have seen the woodlands shrink and the crops grow tall. I have heard the voices of my sisters and brothers, and I have seen them appear, live, and die. I have seen the world, and I know that words are never true."

"Yeah?" said Danny. "But you've never seen Sammael, have you? And I have."

"You have?" The stag lowered his head, and Danny saw that, despite the gray hairs around his muzzle, his eyes were deep and strongly black. "Tell me, then. Tell me your story."

So Danny told him, in as few words as he could manage,

about the summer before. He left out the part about the sycamore tree but told all the rest—the hunt for his parents, the discovery of the Book of Storms, the great storm in which he'd battled Sammael—as though it were he, not the stick, that had the magical power of speech with all nature. He knew, as he told it, that he was recounting a legend with himself as the hero. It was easy to make yourself sound heroic if you left out the parts about feeling alone and scared, and never really being all that sure of what to do.

When he had finished, Isbjin al-Orr raised his head again and looked up to the sky.

"It is a good story," he said. "To hear of such things, I—who have been bound by the earth all my life, tied to its seasons, and its laws—I shiver with delight. To hear that some of our stories have a truth about them, when I have long supposed that they are all fictions for the entertainment of young fawns—it makes my heart sing with wonder."

Danny smiled, happy to have impressed the stag. It was something, to stand in the bright morning air, next to such a creature, and to hear it sing your praises.

Isbjin al-Orr sniffed, drawing the smells of the green-leaved trees into his nostrils, and continued.

"The world is magical, beyond doubt. I feel it, but I rarely see it. And you have shown another small part of that magic to me. I thank you deeply. If I can be of any further assistance to you, please find me again. I have a strong desire to break out into the unknown and to throw up my antlers against whatever I find there. And as I have not long left in this world, it would be a shame to miss such an opportunity."

Danny rested his palm flat against the tree behind him, feeling the roughness of its bark. Could he get the stag to help him somehow? The warnings of the grass rang in his ears. Chromos pouring onto earth, humans going mad . . .

"Can you think of any way I could get those boots?" he asked again. "Now that you know that it's possible."

"I cannot," said Isbjin al-Orr. "Nor can I think that such a move would be without severe consequences."

And Danny knew he couldn't embark on a quest against Sammael without knowing that Tom was safe. Not when Sammael had the promise of Tom's sand firmly in his hands.

Tom first, he decided. Get into Chromos, get Kalia, make the bargain with Sammael, and get Tom. Then stop Sammael, once and for all. Easy.

"I have to get into Chromos," he said. "I don't suppose you know of any other way? Are there any more stories about it?"

"There is only one other way of which I know," said Isbjin al-Orr. "And that is to summon up the guide of Chromos and get on his back."

"Yeah," said Danny. "I had a feeling you'd say that. Any idea how?"

"Oh no." The stag shook his antlers gently. "I don't think

any mortal creatures know that. I've certainly never heard of one."

"Oh, I have," said Danny. "And we tried it. Trouble is, there was something in the way of the guide, and I couldn't get near it."

"Something in the way?" Isbjin al-Orr looked at him, the black eyes keen and hard. "If you've managed to get that far, surely there can be only one thing getting in your way?"

"Yeah? What's that?"

"You're a human. You're too scared."

Danny raised his palm to the sky. "I can't help being scared!" he said. "How could I possibly help that?"

"Well," said Isbjin al-Orr. "You can't help feeling scared, I suppose. But there are three basic responses to being scared, aren't there? One is to flee and hide. The second is to stand the ground bravely, shaking but solid, refusing to be moved."

"And the third?"

"The third?" The stag tossed up his head and stamped his hoof hard on the ground. "The third is to bring gladness into your heart and run toward whatever you fear, bellowing at the top of your voice. Perhaps that's your way into Chromos, my friend. It seems as though you have no other options left."

"Run toward it?" said Danny. "But that's stupid."

"Perhaps," said Isbjin al-Orr, raising his nostrils to twitch at the breeze.

Danny waited for the stag to finish the sentence, to agree with him, to nod and say that it was right to be cautious.

But Isbjin al-Orr stood and sniffed at the wind, and took in all the scents of the faraway world that drifted through the air toward him.

And his eyes shone with silver.

## CHAPTER 16

# DOWN TO EARTH

As Cath fell out of Chromos, Zadoc's legs hit the ground and crumpled, and his nose banged against a pile of bricks so that his whole body jerked in a spasm of surprise. Cath was thrown into a mess of wire. It snaked into the holes in her sweater and pulled at her as she sat up, seeing the last fragments of Zadoc's hooves dissolve into the air as he leapt straight back into the place he belonged.

Where was Barshin?

The hare was close by, trying to find somewhere solid to put his feet in a mound of broken wood. Deftly avoiding rusty nails and splinters, he managed to balance on the end

of a plank and stood trembling, the wood shuddering underneath him.

Cath reached out a hand to steady the plank, sending
nervous Barshin leaping into the air. "What was *that*? How
did we get back?"

"He pushed us into a gray patch. We fell out of Chromos."

Cath remembered Zadoc's words, and panic leapt into her
throat. "Did Zadoc die? He said he'd die if he went down
one of those patches. He can't die!"

"Oh no." Barshin settled himself uneasily back on the
plank. "I think it was quite an old patch—the colors were
slow. He'll only have started to die. It will take him a while
to finish."

A swell of sickness rose up Cath's throat, and she tasted
sour bile. It was just hunger, she told herself, and closed her
eyes to make it go away. Barshin didn't sound that sure, really.
He was probably being dramatic. Zadoc would be fine.

When she opened her eyes, she saw that they were in some
kind of junkyard, piles of broken stuff all strangled with
grass and rubbish. Away to the right there was a fence with
barbed wire along the top. The fence was old and sagging,
but the barbs were shiny and stretched taut between the
posts.

Then Cath knew where she was—the allotments behind
the Sawtry, where the old coffin dodgers spent their lives
shaking their fists at kids who got through the fences and

waged war on their vegetables. Cath had stomped on a rotten old pumpkin here once—her foot had squelched into a pile of smelly mush that stank like ripe old fish guts.

She shook herself off and got up, trying to put away the thoughts of Zadoc. "Can't we—?"

"Oi!" came a shout from behind her. "Oi! You! Ruddy kids! Just you wait . . ."

Cath ran. There was a gap in the fence at the bottom corner where the plots were overgrown. She dodged around the edge of the rough scrub that passed for the gardens of the Sawtry and ran on, liking the way her legs lifted and her feet touched only lightly on the ground, as though she were flying, just touching the earth to remember that it was still there.

"We've got to get back to Danny!" Barshin loped easily beside her, bouncing smoothly over the wasteland. "We've got to save Tom's sand. You've seen for yourself now—Sammael's *evil*!"

Cath slowed as they reached the next fence and gave Barshin a shrewd look. "Ain't I done enough? I gave Danny your message, didn't I?"

She crouched, lifted the wire mesh fence, and put her head down to scramble underneath it. It was an easy enough slither, although all the rain-damped dust had turned into a layer of fine sticky mud that smeared itself over her face, sweater, and jeans. She wiped some of it off her cheeks and stood up, watching Barshin wriggle elegantly through the gap she'd made.

Barshin shook mud off his hind legs and gazed up at her.

"Come on, teach me how you call Zadoc," Cath said. "You said you would. I've gotta know how to get to that house."

Barshin sat back on his haunches. "I will," he said. "But only once I'm sure that Tom's sand is safe. And as for Zadoc dying—when he does, there will be another guardian to replace him, eventually. You will get to your house in another few years or so. I'll come back and find you when I've seen to my duty. Good-bye."

He turned away and hopped along the fence line in the direction of the estate.

Cath watched him for a frozen second. Another few *years*? When the Sawtry buildings came into her field of vision, she almost threw up at the sudden cold in her stomach, as though someone had filled her full of old rice pudding and then punched her.

"Barshin!" She choked on the name and had to dig her fingernails into her palms to stop the ice spreading through her veins.

The hare stopped, his back to her.

"Teach me now!" she yelled. "You have to! You know I can't go back home!"

The hare hopped on, farther and farther away.

"Stop!"

The farther he went, the smaller he became, shrinking against the dark outline of the buildings. If he went into the complex, she'd have to go there and find him, and she'd never get into the Sawtry without being seen . . .

"Stop!" Cath tried again, but she knew it was no use. Barshin had got his message to Danny; now he didn't need her anymore. She was the one who had nowhere else to go.

This time she didn't bother to shout. She thought Barshin might hear her anyway, somehow.

"Okay, I'll do it. You win."

The hare turned and came bounding solemnly back. He settled close to her feet and looked up at her, putting his head back and laying his long ears down his neck.

"This is it, okay?" Cath said. "I'll try and help him once more and then that's it. I like Chromos. This ain't my war."

"Maybe not," said Barshin. "But perhaps it is your battle, whether you want to fight it or not. Come, we will ask the hares that live on the edge of town if they know where Danny might be."

He's not right, thought Cath savagely as she followed him in the opposite direction. It's *not* my battle. There's only one battle for me—how can I make sure that one day soon I'll wake up and know I never have to see the Sawtry again?

And she felt the buildings behind her, bunched and ready to pounce, like a wolf watching a straying lamb.

✦ ✦ ✦

It didn't take too long to get up to the nature reserve, although Cath had never been that far out of town. Getting out of town seemed such a huge thing when you were in it; even getting off the Sawtry seemed impossible sometimes. But it turned out all you had to do was start walking and keep walking.

The woodland was strangely tame, in a way that the railway cutting in the park wasn't. The trees were tall and glossy, the forest floor covered in clumps of small shrubs around clearer patches of earth. Not many brambles, the only plant Cath knew by name. There were even signs up with maps and pictures of flowers and animals you might see there. Cath ignored them. Time enough to learn the names of things when she was living in her new house.

She stamped after Barshin and heard a great, sudden rustling, followed by the thudding of hooves. Nothing like Zadoc's hooves, though. Not even enough to make a single hope leap in her heart. These hooves were small and they raced away before she had time to see what they belonged to.

Danny was leaning back against a tree. He looked up sharply at Cath's arrival, and then swiftly at Barshin.

"You got away, then?" said Cath.

Danny nodded his head. "Your dad chased me for a bit. I lost him."

He seemed to be thinking very hard about something, turning it over in his brain. Cath wasn't going to ask what.

"I saw Sammael," she said.

Danny flinched, but he didn't set his face into that expression of not wanting to know that he'd worn yesterday outside school.

"You saw him?" he said. "Where is he?"

"Chromos. I dunno where, though—we were going too fast. He don't like you, does he?"

Danny leaned his head back against the rough bark of the tree, his short brown hair messy with wind and bits of leaf. Underneath his flushed cheeks, his face was gray with tiredness.

"What did he say, then?"

"He told me about Chromos—how he uses it to put ideas in the world. He wants to keep doing it, so that the world gets to be more and more like Chromos and nothing is impossible. Imagine it . . ."

Danny shook his head and shuddered. "That would be terrible," he said. "Imagine if all the worst things that could happen came true."

"But it might be the best things," said Cath. "Chromos is a weird place, yeah. But kind of great."

"So Sammael's going to do something really great for us, is he?" said Danny. "Right. Don't be an idiot. He's going to open up Chromos so it covers the world, and it's going to be chaos. Horrible chaos. We've got to stop him."

"Chicken," said Cath. "You haven't even seen it. You couldn't even go there 'cause you were too scared of it."

"No," said Danny. "I couldn't go there because I'm normal. And you're a freak."

Cath shoved him hard, and he fell over, sitting down heavily on the exposed tree roots. She turned and walked away. If she left him behind, sitting in the woods alone, then Sammael would do what he'd promised and Cath would be able to live in a world full of color and strange life, and she'd find that house between the mountains and the sea, and stay there, and not have to live and die on the dead, gray estate.

"Why are you leaving him?" said Barshin, hopping after her, and for the first time since she'd been a tiny kid, Cath felt a scalding heat run up her nose into her eyes until something threatened to dampen the corners of them.

"He's a loser," she said. "He's a goody-goody, snotty-brained, pathetic little loser. I ain't doing nothing with him no more. You showed me Chromos, didn't you? What did you do that for?"

"To help you escape," said Barshin.

"Yeah. And so now it turns out that it was great, the best place I've ever seen, and he wants to screw it all up just 'cause he doesn't like it, and I'll still be down here running away from my blimmin' dad until I'm old and dead."

"He doesn't want to ruin Chromos," said Barshin. "He just wants to make sure it stays where it is, that's all."

"Yeah, whatever," said Cath, shrugging. She blinked once

and saw, straight ahead, a bank of clouds swallowing the trees, freezing the forest in a sucking mist. And then she blinked again and it was gone, the world normal again, white and green and brown, a few fragments of blue breaking up the sky overhead.

If only she could keep going, leave them both far behind. But there was the question: where would she go?

She looked down at her feet and turned, and kept turning until she was facing Danny O'Neill again. Then she walked back to him.

✦ ✦ ✦

Danny told her what the stag had said, about the story of Phaeton and Sammael's boots. Cath listened in silence, picking at threads on her frayed cuff.

"So what are you going to do?" she asked, wiping away more dirt from her face with the sleeve of her sweater.

"I have to make sure Tom's safe first," Danny said. "You're right—I should try and make a bargain for his sand. So I have to get Kalia. But apparently I can't get into Chromos because I'm too scared."

"You reckon?" said Cath.

"I don't care." Danny shrugged. "It's normal. That's what being brave is, isn't it? Feeling scared and doing things anyway."

"Except getting into Chromos," Cath pointed out.

Danny looked at her, frowning as though he couldn't quite work out how all the bits of her face fitted together. "Are you really not scared to go in there? Not at all?"

"No," said Cath. "Why would I be?"

"Oh, I dunno. Because you've no idea what's in there, or what it might do to you? Something like that?"

Cath shook her head. "It's fine. I know it is. It feels . . . *brilliant*. Like I can do anything. Like the whole world is *mine*."

Danny's fists clenched against his legs, and for a second his face was still and sharp. "Let's try again," he said. "Tell me about it as we're going in. Maybe if I listen to you, I'll feel the same. I *need* to get there. That must count for something."

So Barshin gave his strange growling shriek and the air began to shimmer, although it wasn't as strong as last time—closer to a harsh heat haze than a tremendous shaking of the air's very particles—and Zadoc's hooves began to appear. They had changed color, to a gluey purple, and his legs were now the browny-green of a stagnant pond. His eye was still bright with the thousand colors of Chromos and he still tossed his head, snorting. But Cath thought for a second that she caught a brief glimpse of the world through the other side of him, as if for a moment he had lost all his colors and become one with the forest.

She ran to his side.

"Come on!" she shouted to Danny. "Get on! We'll go to my house!"

 177

"What's it like?" Danny gasped, pushing himself up off the ground and approaching Zadoc. But his face was white and he was biting his lip.

"Away from everywhere. Between the mountains and the sea . . ." But she stopped. She didn't want to tell Danny where it was, even if it would help her in the end. Nobody should know except her and Barshin.

It didn't matter anyway. Danny's arms were up and he was yelling something about dogs, and staggering backward, falling over a tree root, tumbling down onto his butt, kicking his legs out, fending off something she couldn't see.

She let go of Zadoc, and he vanished out of the air with a hissing snap. Barshin, who had come forward in readiness to throw himself into her arms, dashed back to the safety of a bush and crouched under its fringes, peering out at the place where Cath now stood alone.

"Stop it, idiot," Cath said to Danny. "Everything's gone."

Danny's arms and legs stopped waving, and he brought them down to the ground and then sat up, looking around with suspicion. Eventually, when he had seen that only Cath, the hare, and the forest remained around him, he stood and brushed off his clothes.

"I couldn't hear you," he said. "Kalia just went for me. She hates me too."

"Seems fair," said Cath. "If you killed her and all."

"I'll never get her," said Danny. "She's the actual thing

stopping me from getting into Chromos. Going in and thinking her up, giving her to Sammael—it's never going to work."

He stood, shoulders sagging, staring at the ground. The tips of his ears had gone red; Cath couldn't see his face. She ground her teeth, wanting to kick him, then jumped as Barshin came leaping out from under the bush, scuttling to a stop at her feet.

"He's going to the farm! He's going there soon!"

"What? Who?"

"*Him.* He's going to see Tom! The hares that were watching the farm—they say he was there yesterday, and they've seen him again nearby. We have to go and stop Tom from talking to him! We *have* to go and try again! Now!"

Cath told Danny, whose shoulders sank so low that she was sure his knuckles touched the ground for a second. He looked at her, his eyes rimmed with red, although he wasn't quite crying. Yet.

"It's too late," he said. "All of it. It's too late."

"No it ain't!" Cath saw her house in her mind's eye, just beyond the fringes of this little woodland. It was out there, waiting for her. She knew it. All they had to do was save Tom.

"What do you care, anyway?" said Danny. "You'll be fine, whatever happens. You can just go home and wait for Sammael to rip Chromos open. You'll have a great time when everyone else has gone insane."

"I ain't got time to wait!" Cath snapped. "I. Can't. Go. Back. Get it? I gotta get to Chromos before my dad catches up with me again. And Tom's your cousin, ain't he? You can't just hang around with a face like a bulldog's butt going on about how you can't do nothing. You've gotta do *anything* you can! Come on!"

Danny lifted his eyes and stared at her, and she saw a hardness come over his face, sweeping away the pale uncertainty. Whatever doubts he had battled with, they had been stomped on, for a while.

"Okay," he said. "We'll do it. We *will* make him listen to us. Sammael is *not* getting my cousin. I can't let it happen. Wait here."

He stalked off into the woods. Cath threw a piece of grass at him. The wind caught it and batted it back to her. She turned to Barshin, expecting at least a disapproving look, but the hare merely kicked a fly off his ear and waited.

After a while, there was a loud rustle from the direction Danny had gone, and the sound of light *thud*s against packed earth, and then the bushes swung themselves aside and an animal with a reddish-brown hide stepped out. It had thin legs that came delicately down to shiny hooves, deep black eyes, and a wide forehead crowned with a pair of business-like antlers.

Cath knew it was a deer. But she'd never been close to such a large wild animal in her life. This wasn't Zadoc, friendly and welcoming, inviting her to climb aboard. The deer was silent and aloof, and although its eyes were calm, they had a look in them that suggested a certain unwillingness to be doing exactly what it was doing.

Danny was sitting astride its back, his feet dangling below its fawn belly. His hands were on either side of its neck and he looked a bit precarious, but he had a small smile on his face as though he was quite satisfied with the place he'd managed to get to.

"Meet—" he said. The word was a mess of sounds and Cath didn't hear any of it.

"What?"

"Isbjin al-Orr," said Danny. "He's not massive, but he says he can run quite fast."

Cath stared. "You what?"

"Oh, I'll explain later. Get on, let's get this over with."

The deer came forward another pace. Cath watched as its hoof hit the ground, and suddenly she could feel how it would be underneath her, those hooves beating against the earth, flying across the fields and roads and hillsides. Her heart began to thump inside her ribs, quicker and quicker, until her hands were shaking and she was scrambling toward the animal, desperate to be on its back and soaring away so fast that nothing and no one would ever catch up with her.

The stag threw up its head and snorted.

"You'll have to go on the doe," said Danny, pointing behind him. "We'll go faster if they have one of us each."

Cath didn't want to go on the smaller, female deer. She

wanted to sit on that stag and see the antlers ahead of her, raking through the air. For a moment she considered kicking up a fuss, but then she saw the wary suspicion in the doe's eyes, and it cut down into her chest as though she'd inhaled the smoke of burning-hot curry powder.

"She's called Teilin," said Danny. "Isbjin al-Orr says she's the fastest of all the does, but she's a bit nervous."

The doe shook all over as Cath approached her, but she stood still. How had Danny done it? The deer seemed to be listening to him, obeying all his requests and commands. He was weird, there was no doubt about that. But this kind of weird—it wasn't a bad thing.

Cath scrambled onto the doe's back from the stump of an old fallen tree, and then she could feel all the bunched nerves under the animal's skin, and hear its racing heartbeat through the nerves of her own legs.

She reached down a hand to give Barshin something to scramble up onto, but the hare was staying well back from the deer's shifting legs and he didn't advance.

"I will run beside you, thank you very much," was all he said in a tight voice.

"Okay?" said Danny, and without waiting for an answer, the stag he was riding shot forward to the edge of the wood.

Cath almost fell off with the doe's first leap, but she clutched at its short coat and managed, somehow, to keep one leg on either side of its light, bounding body, so that when they galloped toward the gate she was ready for the fact that they weren't going to stop—nothing, indeed, could stop them—and she clung with her knees to the doe's sides and braced her body against the punching kick of hind-quarters and the jolt of forelegs crashing onto the road over the other side. She was still on its back.

This was nothing like riding Zadoc. But the wind was in her ears and her eyes, forcing stinging tears down her cheeks, and the beat of the hooves hitting the solid earth pulled more forcefully at her heart than the loudest drums she'd ever heard.

If she hadn't been on the earth—if she hadn't known at every moment that she was in the real, old world, and that here you could run and run and run but you always got caught in the end—if she hadn't still thought of that in every second that she breathed, it would have been perfect.

## CHAPTER 17

# HIDING

The deer were fast but it was well into dusk by the time they stepped out of a wood and looked down on Sopper's Edge farm, squatting just under the crest of the hill.

Seeing the farmhouse, the deer stopped dead. Danny slid off Isbjin al-Orr's back, and Cath copied the way he leaned forward and threw his leg over the deer's rump. Her knees buckled as she tried to stand and she fell to the ground, sending Teilin skittering away.

"Seriously, you idiot, I've been on your back for hours. I ain't gonna murder you now, am I?" muttered Cath, but the doe's eyes stayed watchful.

Danny stood for a moment with his hand against Isbjin al-Orr's shoulder. Was he talking through his hands? Was he some kind of animal whisperer? Cath watched as Danny's hand fell away and he stepped back from the stag, and then she heard a shout from the farmhouse.

Aunt Kathleen had come out of the back door and was running up the hillside toward them waving her arms. The deer shot into the dark woods but Barshin stayed crouched at Cath's feet, waiting.

"Danny! Danny!"

Then the tatty old woman shouted something that neither Cath nor Danny understood.

"What?" yelled Danny down the field. Aunt Kathleen shouted again, but all Cath caught was the name "Tom!" until she was standing in front of them, resting her hands on the grubby thighs of her overalls and panting.

"Have you . . . seen . . . Tom? Is he . . . with you?"

She breathed in deeply, and Cath saw that she had run all the way up in her socks.

"No," said Danny. "Where is he?"

Aunt Kathleen closed her eyes and her cheeks went all blotchy as though she was crying but there weren't any tears. Just deep breaths, in and out.

"He's gone," she said.

"Where?" said Danny.

Aunt Kathleen straightened up and looked him in the eye.

"I don't know," she said. "You tell me."

Danny stared at her, horror in his face. "He can't have gone already. He can't be . . ."

Aunt Kathleen raised an eyebrow. For a long moment neither of them spoke. And then the woman said, holding back any blame from her voice, "You know Tom. He goes anywhere he wants to. But the cowsheds are filthy. Have you ever seen him forget to clean them out? And it's long past time for evening milking."

Danny shook his head and kept his mouth shut.

"Where's he gone, Danny?" said Aunt Kathleen, her voice low and sharp. "This is serious. You kids are your own people, and I've always respected that. But this is serious."

Danny looked like he might be about to say something, but then Cath saw his lips tighten in a stubborn line of silence.

Aunt Kathleen grabbed him by the collar. "I'm calling the police," she said. "You're going to tell them everything you know."

She dragged him down the hill. He slipped and slid around on the muddy path, trying to keep his footing, but stayed with his aunt, feet trotting beside her.

Why didn't he try to get away? Cath watched for a few seconds in complete disbelief. Did Danny O'Neill really think he still had to obey adults, just because they were adults? He really did need help.

"Chaos," said Barshin, staring after Danny.

"What?"

"Chaos. Make some."

"No problem," said Cath. "I can do chaos."

She ran down the path after Aunt Kathleen and Danny, but stayed back a few steps. They didn't look around; they seemed locked in some kind of old struggle that had nothing to do with her.

When they'd passed the lowest field gate and were almost at the house, Cath stopped by the gate and lifted off the baling twine that was looped around the gatepost. She swung the gate wide and ran into the field, but Barshin was there ahead of her, leaping and sprinting toward the herd of shaggy black cows.

The cows didn't need much encouragement: they knew that the barn where they went to be milked was full of tasty food. They wandered slowly toward the open gateway and tramped through it, mooing for Tom. They pattered along the wet path, tails swinging, hooves squelching into the fresh cowpats left by the leaders.

Aunt Kathleen heard them and turned around. From her face Cath saw that she'd half expected Tom to be there, and that seeing he wasn't made everything worse.

"You stupid girl!"

But Aunt Kathleen didn't let go of Danny. The cows weren't doing anything bad, just mooching down to the barn.

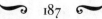

They needed to get scared. Cath picked up a sharp stone from the gateway and hurled it into the herd. It hit one of the back cows on the rump, and the cow leapt forward, giving an agonized squeal. Cath yelled and ran down after it, grabbing another stone to throw, hitting the same cow, and then the cow was trying to run forward, and the other cows were slipping in the mud, scrambling away from one another, trying to get up speed. For a moment the herd was a writhing mass of legs and clambering bodies, and then the front cows set off at a snorting gallop.

Cath didn't stop to watch. She was halfway up the hill before Danny had even gone ten yards from the house and she saw him sliding and slipping over in the slick of mud by the chicken sheds, but she didn't stop or go back to him. She ran with Barshin through the fading dusk, making for the cover of the trees on the hilltop.

Rain began to fall just as they reached the place where Tom had begun his new fence. Fat drops the size of coins came tumbling down from the sweating sky. A growl of thunder riddled through the clouds and gave a swollen burp, and suddenly the last of the iron-gray daylight disappeared.

Great. Rain. That was all they needed. Cath began to shiver as she put the wide trunk of a tree between herself and the farmhouse and stood with Barshin at her feet, waiting for Danny.

The first fork of lightning came stabbing through the air

like a hunting spear, and the storm swung full in front of her across the valley below. It caught at her breath just as the sight of the stag had caught at her heart. She forgot to be cold; she forgot to shiver. She watched the dark sky and willed the lightning to come again.

"You idiot," panted Danny, reaching her. "Those cows— Do you have any idea what happens when cows stampede?"

Cath shrugged. "Got you free, didn't I?"

"It's serious. They'll damage stuff. Aunt Kathleen'll go mad. And it's going to storm."

"It's wicked!" said Cath. "Did you see that lightning?"

"I don't like storms," said Danny. His teeth were chattering, raindrops running down his dirty face.

Cath thought he was just cold. But he shook and shook, and when she tore her eyes away from the clouds to peer at him through the darkness, she saw that his eyes were closed and his hands clasped around his arms in a tight hug. He looked miserable.

"Come on," she said, although she wasn't sure that she really wanted to leave the hilltop. "Let's go down the other side. Find somewhere we can hide."

The night had come so swiftly that she could hardly see where to tread a path between the trees. She tried to keep an eye on Barshin's pale shape ahead, but both she and Danny kept stumbling into holes and falling to their knees, then getting their hands pricked and stung as they pushed themselves up again. After five minutes, Cath didn't even know which direction they were going in—they might have been stumbling back toward the farmhouse again, or they might have been climbing a scrubby slope into the storm clouds themselves. It was impossible to tell.

She heard a new sound, rattling and brittle, like gravel thrown onto a car roof. At first she wondered if it was just the rain getting harder, but there was some kind of flapping noise too, and she listened to hear where it was coming from. She tried to shut out the thousand spattering *smack*s of raindrops on leaves and branches and soil, and then it appeared through the darkness in front of her—a shelter made of a tarpaulin stretched across a frame.

"Danny," whispered Cath. "There's some kind of tent thingy. Come on!"

"No!" said Danny. "What if there's someone else there?"

"Who cares?" said Cath. "I'm going in."

She ducked to the ground and felt around for an opening, crawling on her knees until she found that half of one side was open to the air. There was a panicked rustling and something furry shot past her, then vanished soundlessly into the forest before she could even guess what it might have been.

The rest of the shelter was empty. She crawled inside and sat listening to the rain rattling overhead.

"You coming in?" she said after a moment. "It's dry, sort of."

The shapes of Danny and Barshin came crawling into the little space. Barshin pressed himself close to Cath's legs for warmth, but Danny sat huddled in the other corner. Cath could hear him sniffing. Was he crying? Or just trying to get the water out of his nose?

"You okay?" she said.

"I hate storms."

"Why? They're only storms. They're not gonna hurt you."

"Shows what you know," said Danny.

Cath listened to the raindrops again. But suddenly they weren't the sounds she wanted to hear.

"Go on," she said. "Spill. Tell me everything. We're doing this together, ain't we?"

"Are we?" said Danny.

"Yeah."

"Until you go over to *his* side, you mean?"

Cath knew that he meant Sammael. But it didn't matter who he meant, really. The answer was the same.

"I ain't on no one's side," she said. "Never. Only mine. But we've gotta find Tom, ain't we? So for now, I guess, I'm on yours too. So tell me."

"Tell you what?"

"How you got them rats to chew down my door. How you got them deer to bring us here. It ain't Chromos, is it? Because you said you didn't know what that was."

"It isn't Chromos," said Danny.

"Go on," said Cath, shifting around so she could curl up on the earth. She was suddenly very tired.

"I've told you most of it," said Danny. "But the other bit . . ." He trailed off.

"You still reckon I'll go back to school and tell everyone?" said Cath. "Don't be stupid. They hate me more than they hate you."

"They never used to hate me," said Danny. "All I did was tell Paul some of the stuff that happened. I mean, it was weird stuff, but it did happen. And he just went all mental, saying I was a freak and making fun of me every time he saw me. Every day. Every stupid minute."

"Paul," said Cath succinctly, "is boring. He's a boring person and he's going to be boring all his life, him and all the rest of 'em."

"It doesn't make any difference," said Danny. "He's horrible to me now."

"Well, I won't be," said Cath.

"Swear?"

"I swear. I'll swear on my blood, if you want."

"No," said Danny, but Cath was picking at one of the scabs on her knees.

"Here." She trailed her finger through the blood and held it out to him. "I swear on this, I'll never tell anyone what you tell me. Not even Paul."

She was serious but Danny laughed, just a little bit.

"Okay," he said. "Can you see this?"

He moved, but the darkness was clambering too thickly around Cath's eyes.

"See what?"

"It's a stick. It's got a bit of storm inside it. When I hold it, I can talk to everything that's alive. I can hear them all, too, if I listen in the right way."

Okay. Cath could see why Paul had thought this was weird. It *was* weird.

"What, like, animals?" she asked.

"Everything. Animals. Trees. Plants. Storms, even."

"Storms? Then how come you're scared of them?"

"Because I know what they are. I know what they can do. What they can be made to do. We think they're natural and they don't mean all the bad stuff they do. But they do mean it! They know they're hurting us! And they still do it."

So? Cath wanted to say, but she didn't want to annoy him now that he'd started talking. Because she believed him. Danny O'Neill wasn't exactly normal, but he wasn't making things up to make himself look great. Or at least if he was, it had gone pretty badly wrong.

"Okay," she said. "So you can talk to things. Can I try it?"

"No!" There was a sudden scraping sound as he moved away from her. "No, you can't touch it! It's mine!"

"I won't nick it," she said. "But if you want people to believe you, why don't you prove it?"

"Because you'll die," said Danny flatly. "This old man tried it, right in front of me. He just . . . burned up. I'd have made Tom use it, if I could, to show him I wasn't lying. But I couldn't."

"So why don't you die, then?"

Danny sighed. "It's a mistake. It was all a mistake. I picked it up before Sammael could get it, and then it was mine. And Sammael knows that the only way I can not have it anymore is if I'm dead. He can't kill me—he can't kill anyone who doesn't belong to him—so he's doing all he can to make me go mad, or make me give up my sand to him. That's it, I guess."

"Your sand? That's your soul, ain't it? That's what you said to Tom."

"Yeah, sort of, I think. It's the bit of you that doesn't belong to the earth, anyway. The bit that's just you. It's what Tom's promised to give Sammael in return for that book. If I promise mine to Sammael, then he'll be able to kill me once I've got all I ask for, but I'm never going to do that. Never. So it won't ever end. Unless I kill him or something."

"How?"

Danny shrugged. "I don't know. Yet. I guess I've got to try and find out."

Cath was silent, considering this. She could see it from Danny's point of view. He thought Sammael was terrifying. And yet . . .

"Do you know what would happen if Sammael wasn't there?" Cath asked, feeling the frown deep across her own forehead. "If he didn't do all that stuff with Chromos?"

"No," said Danny. "But I know what will happen, sooner or later, if things stay as they are."

Cath closed her eyes. She thought back to that tall, thin man in Chromos with his hand on Zadoc's neck. She hadn't liked him. In fact, hadn't there been something about him that reminded her of Dad?

But out here, safe from the rain in the little shelter, she could remember how Dad's face went gentle when he looked at Sadie and the other kids, and the desperate feeling she got when she saw that and wanted—so badly it hurt—him to turn the same look on her.

She set her jaw against the night. It wasn't simple. Only idiots thought it was simple. Idiots like those teachers at school who called her "neglected" and said she only needed a "loving family" for everything to be okay.

Cath knew where everything would be okay: in that house between the mountains and the sea, where Dad could be just a memory and not a real person she had to live with. She could imagine his face and never have to stand in front of him.

She curled herself around Barshin's drenched body, tucked her hands up against her chest, and touched the skin that was marked with the pattern of yellow flowers.

## CHAPTER 18

# NIGHTMARES

The path through the dunes was scattered with small lumps of quartz that caught the sunlight and bounced diamond sparks back at her as she wandered down to the sea. She normally left the cottage door open—why not? There was no danger of anyone coming along and breaking in—but this evening she had looked up into the sky and decided to close it behind her. Clouds were gathering, purple-gray, over the sea. A wind picked up and hissed through the miserly fringe of grasses that clung to the edge of the dunes. The waves were rising, too—white horses had begun to gallop along the rolling crests, kicking up sprays of foam.

As she left the dunes behind and stepped out onto the

flat beach, she saw hoofprints in the sand. That wasn't unusual—wild horses sometimes came through here. Occasionally she thought about trying to tame one. But these prints were different. A single line of them, unevenly spaced, as though the animal had been speeding up, then slowing down.

She followed the prints until she came to the edge of the water. They came straight out of the waves.

Cath turned around and ran back along the prints, trying to match her own strides to the strides the creature had taken. It had stretched out its legs in some places, and bounced deep into the sand in others. Here and there a pair of prints were set into the beach where the animal had reared up on its hind legs and come thudding down.

The sunset and the night overtook her, but the moon shone silver along the sand. Shadows clustered inside the hoofprints so they stood out, black and solid. She followed tirelessly, knowing that the animal would be worth the chase.

Bright reddish gold, it was standing on top of the highest dune, looking down its nose at her and snorting.

"You took your time," it said.

"So?" she said. "You weren't going anywhere. Why are you gold?"

"I have stolen the color from the sea," it said proudly.

"Why?" she asked, feeling a chill against her neck. But perhaps that was just the sea air.

Could things be stolen here? Could they be stolen from her?

"I wanted it," the creature said.

"What if I want it?" said Cath.

The creature tossed its head. "You don't want it," it said. "Go into the waves. You'll see that you don't."

Cath turned to look at the swelling sea. The waves were rolling over now, hair curlers as high as her own head. She didn't feel like a swim.

"Will you take me in?" she asked, but the creature snorted again and stepped backward, its gold hooves marking the dune with inky prints.

"No way," it said. "I'm not giving the sea a chance to steal all this gold back. And the moon is rising now. Beware the moon on the sea! Beware the silver waves!"

It reared up and turned on its hindquarters, racing away, gold coat defiant against the flat moonlight.

Cath watched it go, and then watched the waves gathering for a moment. What had the creature meant? How had it stolen a color?

There was only one way to find out. She stepped forward to the edge of the sea and began wading into the water.

The sea began to shriek. Above the dry roar of the waves and the crash of the breakers rose an agonizing, dreadful shout that wailed around the air. Her ears began to sting, and she put up her hands to protect them, but the spray from the waves had become a whirling mass of banshees, salty hair trailing, wide mouths blaring out. They wailed until their faces were puce and their veins were bulging and their tongues were black with spit.

Cath tried to shout over the top of them just to hear a noise that was her own, but the effort of trying to shout brought spots dancing in front of her eyes until she couldn't think how to breathe anymore, and somehow she was drowning in airlessness and everything was going white, and she was thinking, Is this what it meant, is this the place . . .

✦ ✦ ✦

It was Danny who was screaming. Next to her in the tarpaulin shelter, his body was rigid, his legs and arms pushed out as if defending himself from an army of demons, and he was screaming with every breath of air his lungs could hold.

Cath knew in less than a second that she was awake and fine, and that she needed to wake him up because the terror inside him was so enormous that in a second it could twist around his heart and squeeze it to a stop.

She reached out a hand to shake him.

"Danny! Danny! Wake up!"

He woke up and hurled himself away from her, crashing against the tarpaulin. Two of the poles fell and the sheet flooded down onto their heads, so that for a moment the world was a choking mess of plastic.

When Cath finally got her face out into the cold air, she saw that it was almost morning. A thin light had broken through the trees and was curling around the earth.

Behind her, Danny found a way out of the crumpled tarpaulin and got to his feet, rubbing his eyes. He was very pale.

"Sorry," he said. "I get a bit scared when people wake me up. The nightmares . . ."

"Where's Barshin?" said Cath, spinning around to see if the hare was trapped in the fallen shelter. But Danny pointed to the base of a tree, and there was Barshin, crouched.

"We've got to get going," said the hare. "We can't waste time like this. Tom must already be with Sammael—Sammael will make sure he gets to the end of the book even quicker. We need to get after him."

"Use that stick!" Cath turned on Danny. "Let's call Zadoc, then when Kalia comes, talk to her with your stick. Tell her you're going to return her to Sammael. I mean, if you could always do that, why didn't you try talking to her before?"

"She had her jaws around my face," said Danny. "It wasn't the first thing on my mind."

Cath tapped her foot impatiently. "Come on, Barshin. Let's do it."

Danny put his hand in his pocket and shook his head. "It won't work," he said. "Nothing works."

Barshin called, and Zadoc came roaring out of the air. The young morning leapt back in terror as the horse pushed his way into the world, bigger than ever, just a little more transparent. He stood before them, a mottled mess of purples and browns and dark, oily green, as though the colors he wore were designed to refute any suggestion that he could be fading away. But fading he was. Cath saw quite clearly the outline of a tree through his rib cage. He pawed the ground for a second, head thrown up, but his mane was matted and his ears drooped.

It was too much. She wanted to run toward him and leap onto his back, ride him away into the air, leaving Danny behind fumbling with his endless problems. But something made her turn, one last time, to catch a glimpse of the boy and the hare.

Barshin was crouched on the ground watching Danny. Danny had his hands up, the stick clenched in one fist, and his eyes were shut. His face was red, as though he had forgotten to breathe. Both arms were waving desperately, but he was standing his ground, standing firm—

"Quick!" Cath said. "Get on Zadoc! He's gotta go—"

Danny took one pace forward and then gasped. It was the sound of water rattling around a plughole, the swell of waves against a fierce sea. When he opened his mouth, Cath half expected to see a great river pouring out, flooding the earth at their feet. Instead, a mist of dragon's breath hissed from his lungs and he opened his eyes again, and Cath realized that Zadoc had gone.

"Get him back!" she said to Barshin. "We was nearly there. He's getting it!"

But Barshin looked at Danny, and Danny shook his head.

"I couldn't talk to her," he said. "It didn't work."

"What d'you mean? You wasn't screaming. You wasn't scared."

"No. I pushed her back, but I couldn't get past. She was standing her ground, just like me. Stalemate."

"Well, how'd you push her back? Do it more. Stronger."

Danny shrugged. "I don't know. Every time I thought words at her, with the stick, I just saw . . ."

He trailed off, and Cath grabbed a tree branch so that she could fix her hands around something that wasn't his scrawny little neck.

"Saw *what*?"

"I saw the sea," Danny said, tasting the words carefully. "I saw this beach, and the sea, and a line of footprints going into the sea. No, not footprints—"

Cath's heart froze and then seemed to coat itself with something hard, something that shone—

"Hoofprints?" she asked.

Danny looked at her and nodded. His hair stuck out from his head, like the feathers of a windblown bird. "Did you see it too?"

Cath shrugged. "I dreamed it. Last night."

Danny shuddered and wrapped his arms around himself,

holding tightly to his sweater. "It was Sammael, then. He's brought sand here. It's in both of us. He must know what we're trying to do . . . it's no use against him. He can read minds."

"No, he can't!" Barshin took a couple of lopes toward them. "You can hear me now, can't you, Danny? Sammael can't read your minds. And he doesn't plant every dream you have in there either. He puts in the grains of sand to begin with, but it's your mind that grows them into ideas. It's like planting a seed—if you plant a seed in the ground, the flower that grows is always the same kind of flower, for sure. But the way it grows is different, depending on if it has good soil, or strong sunlight, or too much rain. The same is true of Sammael's sand. *You* shape the ideas that come from his sand. And this time, both your ideas are the same shape. You both *know* what you need to do. You *know* where you need to go. You need to look down inside yourselves and read your own knowledge."

Danny looked down at his sweater. Cath looked at hers. Neither spoke for a long time, and the nearby birds began to chatter again, gossiping sharply about the unwelcome intruders in their quiet morning woods.

"Is there—"

"The water—"

Cath broke off as soon as she heard Danny speak. If he was finally getting to the point, she didn't want to hold him up.

He was still staring down at his belly. His dark blue sweater was covered in bits of twig and leaf, which he picked at slowly.

"I think . . . ," he said, "I think it's the sea. That's what we both saw. I nearly died, once. And when I came back, I thought I was swimming up through this water, a really long way. And I felt I could breathe in there. I was strong. I wasn't afraid of anything. I knew I was coming back to life, and that whatever happened, I'd face it, I'd fight it . . . and I did. I think if I went into the water again, I might feel like that again. I might not think about being afraid."

*Because I am afraid.* The admission hung between them, unspoken, and Cath understood that, although Danny had admitted to being a coward before, he was finally saying that his fears ruled him, and he couldn't overcome them by himself. She wondered how on earth it was possible to be like that. And when he looked up at her, he was shaking his head.

"It's normal," he said, shrugging helplessly. "That's what Sammael was telling you, wasn't it? We're all like this, us humans. It's only you who's different."

Cath stared at him, and bit back the "Idiot!" that was on her lips. It didn't matter. What mattered was to find some water. If he thought that drowning himself was going to make him feel brave, then good luck to him.

"Okay," she said. "Let's find some water, then. Best make it deep."

"It's crazy," said Danny. "But this is all crazy. Insane."

"Sometimes—" said Barshin.

"None of that wise-hare stuff!" snapped Danny, turning on him. "I'm not as stupid as you all seem to think, you know."

And, giving Cath a crooked half-smile that suggested he was in no way certain of whether what he was doing was right or not, he walked off toward the middle of the forest to fetch the deer.

## CHAPTER 19

# TO THE SEA

The following night, they slept in a copse of trees. The night after that, they crept behind a deserted house and curled themselves up behind some bales of straw, which at least were warm. By the fourth day, they'd grown so used to being filthy and hungry that they couldn't think of doing anything else apart from scurrying from place to place, keeping their heads down, and spending long minutes crouched behind hedges and walls and fallen trees, waiting for people to disappear from the way ahead. Cath stole food—she was light and small and ran faster than the shop alarms.

Every night Cath dreamed about the sea. And every night they had to make sure they found a place to sleep that wasn't close to people because Danny would have nightmares and Cath would wake up to hear him screaming. But once he'd woken, he'd find something to laugh about, and then everything was okay for a while.

On the evening of the fourth day, Cath came back from a food raid with a newspaper. She handed it to Danny. He read the headline: " 'Fears Grow for Missing Children'? That's it, then. They'll be out looking for us. Everyone will. We'll never get to the sea. Maybe I should just call my parents—they'll be worried."

"Don't be daft," said Cath. " 'Course we'll get there. We're miles away from home now. No one'll look here."

"Yeah, they will. It says the search has gone nationwide. Your dad's even made a TV appeal."

Cath's heart seized up. She clenched her fist so hard that the corner of her chocolate bar dug painfully into the corner of her hand.

"Yeah," she snarled. "He likes talking. Everyone always believes him."

"But he's horrible." Danny turned his wide-eyed face on her. "What he did to you at the farm—that was horrible. People must know he's like that."

Cath stared at him. But, really, why should Danny have any idea about it? He was another kind of person.

She shook her head and kept her mouth shut.

Danny persisted. "Why don't you tell them? Or go to the police, or Social Services, or something?"

Cath unclenched her fist from around the chocolate bar and tore open the wrapper to get the last bit. It was starting to melt.

"Because I'm not a stupid little coward who gets everyone else to do everything for me," she said, and she put the chocolate in her mouth. Then she got up and started walking again, her eyes fixed on the horizon.

"It isn't cowardly to ask for help!" shouted Danny after her, scrambling to his feet. "It's what *normal* people do!"

But Cath kept on walking and didn't turn around.

✦ ✦ ✦

Isbjin al-Orr, who had taken to roaming ahead on his own and reporting back as to the lay of the land, came trotting over the crest of a hill toward them through the fading dusk. Danny's hand shot to the stick in his pocket and Teilin scooted backward a few feet as though she'd been deafened.

Danny and Isbjin al-Orr stood in silent conference for a few moments, and then Danny turned to Cath. His face was wide with a rare smile, his teeth white against the growing darkness.

"He says it's close! Only one or two miles. Let's go!"

Cath thought, How didn't we notice before? There was a

sharpness in the air that, now that she knew what it was, tasted like salt.

Her heart began to race. Down there on the beach, was she going to find her house? No, of course not. There weren't any mountains here. The whole point of her house was that no one could get to it. There wasn't room for Danny O'Neill. But still—she'd see the sea and be a little closer somehow.

✦ ✦ ✦

And Cath couldn't believe the sea. Whatever she'd expected, it had been nothing like this—nothing so strong and dark and vast. She'd never dreamed of the angry wrench of the waves, or the roaring growl of the endless swell, or the way the silver moonlight would dance in a ceaseless frenzy as it shimmered over the water. She'd never dreamed it would look like the edge of the world, and that she'd know for certain as she stood before the sweeping tide that this was entirely real, entirely beyond her imagining.

It was like staring Dad in the face. It was like seeing him appear in the doorway, taking his belt off. It was like seeing him walk toward her, his fist raised, and his eyes full of hate. The sea was too big and too fierce, and she wanted to hide away from it.

"You okay?" asked Danny.

"Yeah, 'course." She scowled.

"Okay, we're here. What do we do?"

What did they do? She hadn't thought for a moment that she'd be so scared. She hadn't thought that she wouldn't want to go in. She swallowed. Sometimes it wasn't enough just to do things no one else would do, she told herself. Sometimes you had to do things you didn't want to do, either.

Who had told her that? For a second she had a vision of someone with long black hair, like her own, someone who smelled of warmth. But it was gone before she could reach out to it.

She controlled her voice. "We go in and then Barshin calls Zadoc."

"What, now?"

They both looked at the blackening waves. Drifting behind a thin cloud, the moon softened and began to stroke the water with a paler, steely light. Of course it was now.

"Yeah."

"Okay then. Let's go."

Suddenly, she wasn't sure that she could. Those waves were so dark—and it was Danny who knew what the dog looked like. He was the one who should go into Chromos and find it.

"I dunno," she said, holding her arms tightly to her chest. "I dunno if I should."

Danny laughed. "Neither do I," he said. "I mean, it's a massively stupid idea, isn't it?"

Cath glared at him. He stopped laughing.

"You still scared?" Her voice came out in a thin whisper.

Danny shrugged. "I guess so. I . . . don't really know. You?"

Cath shook her head. " 'Course not," she said, lifting her chin high. "S'only the sea, ain't it?"

Danny looked at her. He opened his mouth as if he were about to say something, and then he stared back toward the sea. The moonlight had stolen all color from his face: his cheeks were snow white.

"Yeah," he said, nodding. "Let's do it. Come on."

He held out a hand to her. How could she say no? The sea was boiling, as black as tar. A streak of moonlight broke through the waves, as vivid as the stripe on a badger's head.

Palms thick with clammy sweat, she looked down at her feet. And then there was Barshin, his thin face steady.

"It'll be fine," the hare said. "We'll all go in together, and then I'll call Zadoc. I really don't think he'll be able to carry both of you. But if he can't, Cath can swim back to shore once we've gone to Chromos. We won't go far out. She'll be fine to get back on her own."

Cath looked out at the sea. She couldn't even swim very well. She'd only had a few lessons at school.

Isbjin al-Orr stepped along the shingle beside her. He had his head up, his antlers cast back, and he was sniffing the air. He turned to look at her.

What was he trying to say? He must know that she couldn't understand.

"What's he saying?" she asked Danny.

Danny shrugged. "Nothing. But he'll help us."

And then she understood. He was offering to take them in. Isbjin al-Orr wasn't brave. He was without fear. And he knew it.

She closed her eyes and breathed in once, then opened them. "Give me a leg up," she said to Danny.

Danny held his cupped hands out, and she stepped into them and sat on the stag's back. His antlers were soft in the sharp air.

She put down her hand for Barshin, who came to sit in front of her, and then again for Danny, who jumped up behind her. And Isbjin al-Orr began to run toward the sea.

✦ ✦ ✦

The stag's hooves hit the water and threw up a cloud of spray. In a second Cath's clothes were soaked and her hair was streaked over her cheeks, sticking to her skin. The water was quickly up to the height of Isbjin al-Orr's chest, and then too deep for him to run through, and he began to swim, striking out at the sea with smooth fury.

A huge wave came without warning, swelling and rearing up in front of them. It held back for a moment, then curled over their heads and hurled itself down, streaming over their faces.

Cath choked, struggling for air. She heard one dreadful, dry snort as Isbjin al-Orr blew hard through his salty nostrils. Barshin struggled up her shoulders and curled himself around her neck, his long legs hard against her throat, front paws clinging to her face. Danny threw his arms around her waist, nearly dragging her off backward. She grabbed for the stag's neck—whatever happened, she mustn't let go, mustn't lose him—but his coat was slippery and her hands found nothing to hold.

A pain stabbed her cheek and another wave tried to pull her into its inky belly. She reached out, trying to fend off the pain and the water, and then she could no longer feel the soaked hair of Isbjin al-Orr's short coat or the warmth of his body. She kept her head up, desperate to breathe, to stay above the surface, but Barshin was heavy around her head and Danny's arms were tight about her, anchoring her down, and neither would let her go so she could breathe, both pushed her farther down into the water . . .

Another black wave broke over her head. She saw that Isbjin al-Orr hadn't disappeared, but that his head was right next to her and his crown of antlers was high above the water. His antlers shone silver as the moonlight caught them.

Isbjin al-Orr was swimming purposefully out to sea. He shouldn't go too far—what if Zadoc couldn't carry her as well as Danny and she had to swim back alone?

No. Cath kept her chin above the surface of the sea and

set her jaw hard. If anyone else was going to Chromos, she was going with them. Even if she had to hang off Zadoc's tail.

"He's coming!" shrieked Barshin, squirming around Cath's face and pushing a foot into her ear to steady himself.

Zadoc breached from the waves like a seal, hair slicked down to his skin. He was entirely black in the moonlight apart from his glittering eyes, shining with all the colors of Chromos.

"Quick! Get Danny to him!" Barshin's legs scrambled against Cath's cheek, raking her skin with hard claws. If they had drawn blood, she couldn't tell beneath all the flying spray.

"Danny!" Cath yelled. "Go on! Get on!"

But Danny was already swimming toward Zadoc, his face turned from the battering waves. He reached out a hand to the horse and touched it.

Nothing happened. No flames, no Kalia. Nothing but a boy's hand pressing against a horse, its muscles strong and warm.

His fingers found safety in the horse's mane, and he swung his leg easily over Zadoc's back. Poised above the foaming sea, he tilted his head and looked up into the black sky. His body seemed to grow, and his wet shoulders shone in the moonlight, as if he had shrugged on a suit of silver armor.

"Take me to him!" Barshin screamed. The hare was

shaking violently, with fear or cold, Cath couldn't tell which. He seemed to have gone a little crazy. She swam the few strokes to Zadoc, and Barshin leapt to the safety of his back.

Zadoc plunged, and Cath saw that he was about to dive down into the sea. She grabbed at his mane but missed as he swiftly began to disappear. His tail was still behind him though; she swiped out and found it, a few strands of coarse hair. She snapped her fists shut and clung on for dear life.

Almost at once she felt the water grow thin, and then a pair of teeth snapped shut on the back of her sweater and she was swinging up onto Zadoc's back, landing behind Danny. Barshin leapt gratefully into her arms, and together they disappeared into the inky depths.

CHAPTER 20

# REVENGE

"Are you sure it'll work?" Tom whispered, crouched under the dark trees. "I don't think I'm very good at the stoat noises yet."

"It'll have to, won't it?" Sammael raised his hand. He was kneeling behind the tree root in exactly the place Johnny White had lain. Sammael wasn't shaking with fear, though. He was listening to the night sounds of the small woodland: rustles, low squeaks, the clacking of owls' beaks around beetles' skins, the distant barks of farmyard dogs chained to kennels.

The light buzzing of a motor was winding its way toward

the far side of the hill. That was where the baiters had parked before.

"Is that them?" Tom strained his ears toward the sound.

Sammael nodded. "Ready?"

Tom was ready. Confidence surged through him. Before, with trembling Johnny White beside him and burning outrage tearing at his guts, he'd been afraid, desperate. Now he was going to get them by calling up an army of stoats.

For days he'd lain low in ditches waiting for their calls, and he'd tried to imitate their chirping and barking sounds, straining to distinguish friendly calls from warning ones. He wished he could be more like Sammael, who sat with Iaco on his arm, stroking her back with a finger and making a low noise in his throat to her while she stared into his thin face. Whether this was really talking, Tom wasn't sure. But the stoat had often disappeared for a time into grasses and banks of scrub, chattering away, and then returned to Sammael's arm. Sometimes other stoat faces had peeped out of the grasses and viewed Tom with their hard black eyes, then withdrawn once they had satisfied their curiosity.

It made Tom smile, to be stared at by stoats. He'd spent hours himself watching for them on the farm. What a business. But if it worked—well, he'd always said nature was amazing.

"Get down!" Sammael gave a silent gesture downward and retreated behind the tree.

Tom watched. The trees were mottled olive green in a sea of shadows; the earth was as dark as tar.

And then he heard their footsteps.

They were quicker than before, but it was the same men. The coward with the terrier, the short man with the double chin, and the taller one with eyes as cold as moonlight. They knew the way, and the terrier was pulling them forward, eager to get at her business. Tom's fingers tightened on the earth as the coward bent down to unclip the terrier.

"She'll do the job," the coward said. "Off you go, Julie."

They hung a bright light on the bough of a birch tree and turned the beam toward the badger sett.

The entrance, carelessly earthed up days before, had been reopened by the badger, so Julie the terrier only paused briefly to scratch at the dirt, sniff it, and give a little whine before snapping her jaws and scrambling down into the hole.

To distract himself from the horrible thought of what was going on underground, Tom tried to commit the men's faces to memory as they leaned back against the trees and waited for the terrier to flush the badger out. The coward had a twisted smile of eagerness on his lips; the short, paunchy one was fatly satisfied; and the taller man with his big belly and blank eyes had a face so emotionless it made Tom shiver.

A flurry of yelping barks shot up from the hole, and a yowling so loud it seemed to shake the earth. The terrier's tail and wriggling haunches appeared, then the rest of its yapping body, shaking with aggression.

This time, it hadn't managed to bite a badger underground. The old boar erupted into the night, its jaws half-open in a vicious snarl. Lamplight caught its white fangs and raking claws as it charged toward the barking terrier and threw itself into the attack.

The men unclipped the other dogs and let them go.

For a second, Tom froze. His neck broke out into an icy sweat.

Stay still, he told himself. Just a few more seconds. Make sure everyone is distracted, then—

Then what? Call some stoats?

It would never work. What use were stoats against dogs like these? It was a stupid plan, bound to fail. The badger would die—

No. He would never let that happen. This time, if the stoats failed, he would throw himself forward. The men would get far worse punishments if they let their dogs attack a human.

As though men's lives were worth more than animals', thought Tom. As though these cruel men were worth more than that desperate badger.

He held his breath.

The dogs plunged toward the badger.

The big old boar wrinkled up his graying face, opened his mouth wide in a full, angry roar and showed them the size of his teeth. And it was the badger who flung himself first into the fight, growling like a bear.

But wherever the badger fought, claws and teeth and snapping jaws, there was another dog he couldn't reach biting at his belly or his back.

"Go on!" whispered Sammael from somewhere behind Tom. "Call them! He'll fight, but he can't win."

Tom tried to bring up the barking noise of the stoats in his dry throat. He could barely hear the sound over the snarling and growling of the fighting animals, but he felt his throat move. Was that it? Was that even the right sound?

And then, catching the lamplight, to the left of him he saw the small glint of a pair of black eyes on the other side of the tree trunk. Farther to the left, another pair. Farther on, another and another and another, until everywhere he looked, the night was glowing with bright black eyes.

He made the hissing bark in his throat again. It was right—it had to be right. He hoped desperately that he wasn't telling them to go away.

But the eyes came running toward him.

✦ ✦ ✦

Behind Tom, Sammael reached into his pocket and pulled out a few grains of gray sand. Putting them to his lips, he blew them forward onto the night breeze, which carried them toward the badger fight.

The lamplight died. Above the growling and barking, the hissing of stoats rose in a crescendo to the sound of a fighter plane stuttering with gunfire. The stoats' eyes, dimmer now, caught only traces of light reflected from the moon and stars.

A swarm of inky shapes, knitted together in a rattling blanket of fury, rushed over the lunging dogs, clinging to their legs, their necks, their ears, hanging off their heavy jaws and biting into their skins. The dogs leapt in the darkness, trying to bark, trying to howl, thwarted at every twist by a dozen sets of claws and tiny teeth.

The badger backed away, stiff-legged, confused. It sat back on its haunches and reared up a little, pawing at the empty air.

Tom watched the creatures in the darkness of the night, fighting to protect one another. He wanted to see them as they really were: nature fighting for the right to live in peace against the evils of men.

And then the badger began to grow.

It happened so quickly that before Tom could even understand what was going on, the badger was as tall as a man, high above the stoats and the increasingly frightened dogs. Its paws were the size of dinner plates, each claw as big as a curling coat hook. It swiped at the air, crouched, and sprang toward the three men.

The men screamed and ran. The two smaller goons shot away fast, but Cold Eyes was caught by the badger's swinging claws and dashed into a tree. He crumpled to the ground, fists up to defend himself, but even through the darkness Tom could see how tiny he was, cowering in the shadow of the massive badger. The badger stood back on its haunches again, its huge gray body as big as a car.

"It's going to—"

Kill the man? Of course it was. He'd been trying to kill it, hadn't he? But something hard inside Tom broke and his anger flooded away. It wasn't right to kill anything without a good reason—not badgers, not men.

The air lightened and a pale glow spread downward from the treetops. The dogs had stopped snapping and were curling up into tiny balls, whining to themselves. The badger stood, a growl in its throat, and Cold Eyes held his hands up to cover his face.

From above the treetops a spark of wind and starlight dropped into the rough arena, followed by the sound of beating wings and a high, clear call.

Two tawny birds flew down, their wings spreading wide. They swooped through the trees, feathers glinting with the gold of the burnished sun, and curled their claws around the shoulders of Cold Eyes's coat, lifting him off the ground. He was in the air and out of the clearing before Tom could blink, or name the birds, or even think to follow them into the sky.

The dogs uncurled and shot away into the darkness. The hard-eyed stoats vanished back into the wood. The huge badger—but it was huge no more, just a normal size, snuffling at the ground and trundling back toward its sett.

Iaco was the only stoat to stay behind. She came trotting toward them. To his right, Tom saw Sammael's hand stretch forward and the little stoat leap nimbly onto it.

He sat up, feeling for the rough lumps of tree root. They were solid and anchored to the earth. Some things were still real, then.

"What . . . was that?" he said.

"Looks like we got some help," said Sammael, sitting up himself, then rising to his feet.

"No, I mean, what was that? The badger—getting so massive—and the light, and those birds . . . Where did they take that man? Is he dead?"

"Oh no, I don't think so. Not that it matters either way. They were golden eagles—I had no idea they ever came this far south. I should think they'll just drop him somewhere, but I doubt he'll ever speak sense again, wherever he lands up. At least we got the baiters, didn't we?" He held out a hand to help Tom up. "That's what matters, isn't it?"

"But . . . I . . ." Tom tried to play over in his mind what he'd just seen. Had he really seen it? Or just imagined it?

"Shall we walk across the hill and over to town? I know it's a bit of a way, but we might see some good night wildlife. And then you can report the men to the police as soon as the station opens."

Tom stared up at Sammael, and the shape of the man and the offered hand. How could he be so casual? He must have seen nothing out of the ordinary. Apart from the eagles and the stoats, of course.

Rising to his feet, Tom didn't quite know what to say. Perhaps he shouldn't mention the monster badger again. He must have made that up, out of shadows and fear.

"Do eagles fly at night, then?" he tried, still not seeing anything clearly in his mind's eye.

"Those did. Did you hear what they were saying?"

"No," said Tom. "I haven't learned their calls yet—they're the only ones I haven't done. I didn't know where to go to find them."

"Ah, I know the very place! We must go there. And then you'll know all the calls, will you?"

"All the birds," said Tom. "I've still got a couple of pages of the animals to go. But the eagles were the last birds. What were they saying?"

"They were singing!" Sammael's face shone with happiness in the starlight. "It was an ancient eagle song about flying—about their wings being made of cloud silk and the sun setting fire to their tails. Did you know they can fly at one hundred and twenty miles an hour? And they can dive even faster—closer to one hundred and fifty miles an hour. Imagine being able to fly like that."

Tom laughed. "You'll be telling me I could persuade them to take me for a ride next."

But Sammael didn't laugh back. "Isn't that the kind of thing you'd like?"

"Of course it is," said Tom. "Who wouldn't like that? But come on, be serious."

"No, you're right," said Sammael, beginning to walk along to the top of the hill. "It's daft to think that anyone who could learn to talk to stoats could take that even further and learn to talk to eagles, isn't it?"

"But . . . flying?" Tom strode to keep up with him. "I'm nearly six feet tall. Really?"

"You remember what I said?" Sammael stepped through a couple of closely growing trees, and for a second his silhouette looked exactly like the shapes to either side of him.

"About what?"

"About imagining."

Tom pushed his own way between the trees. He wasn't sure about imagining. Monster badgers? Golden eagles?

But in the dark woodland, in the black spaces and the branches and the leaf shadows, he saw Cold Eyes's feet lifting off the ground, and the powerful wings of the eagles, and the starlight, and he heard the sound of feathers beating the air.

He opened his mouth to say, "Don't be daft."

But what came out was, "Do you think it's really possible?"

CHAPTER 21

# BEYOND THE SEA

Darkness opened its jaws and tore away the sky in one savage bite. Clouds flashed with lightning, rain snaked through the treetops overhead.

Trees? Yes, they were in a forest, the way upward barred by a mesh of twisting branches, and Danny didn't have to look to know that each and every tree was a sycamore. The lightning would get them all, one by one, and then it would get him.

He pulled at Zadoc's mane. "Please!" he begged. "Please stop! I hate storms—I've done enough of this. Don't take me into a storm. Take me back!"

Zadoc plodded on. A bolt of lightning sparked and thudded into the tree just ahead, yapping out a harsh sneer of triumph. The tree cried, long and high, and hissed into flames. Danny tugged at Zadoc's mane again, harder this time.

"Stop! It's all going to burn! You've got to stop!"

And Zadoc stopped.

For a second, the storm also stood still, holding its breath at Zadoc's motionless body. And then it began to roar. The trees were culled as fast as twigs on a bonfire, each great trunk flaring into orange fire, curling over into a twisted prawn, and exploding into a pile of gray-white ash.

It was snowing. No—those were the ashes, drifting through the air, clasping Danny's eyes and lips, choking up his mouth. He tried to breathe in, but his throat was papered with bitter smoke.

"Danny! Breathe!"

Cath's voice behind him was soft. He listened to the sound of her words in his head. And his breath came, sweet and clear, and the ash fell down to the ground so that he could see the world around him again.

They were wandering through a lamp-lit village at dusk, the houses' windows drawn over with softly glowing curtains. Danny knew this place. It was the village he'd come to in the search for the Book of Storms. Before, the houses had lined his way, still and silent, but now they sneered at Danny as he went past, and opened their doors, letting out a furious stench of moldy potatoes, sports socks, and eggs. He held his hand over his nose and mouth.

Dark blue birds with pointed tails began to shoot past his ears, clawing at his face.

"Coward! Stupid fool! Too slow to fly properly! Too slow to do *anything* properly!"

Swallows? But when he'd met them, they'd helped him. Why had they turned against him now?

A clump of fur shot down from a tree and launched itself at Danny's face, clawing at his mouth. Not the cat too? Not his friend Mitz?

"Blind buffoon!" Mitz screeched. "I've seen better guts on a violin! Only way to deal with nasty, selfish boys like you is to bite out your lying tongues!"

"No!" Danny let go of Zadoc and put up both hands to push Mitz away. The cat arched her back and reached for his neck with her hind claws.

"Danny! They're not real!"

He knew Cath was lying. His ears were covered in birds, and his face was covered in cat. Four sets of claws latched on to his head and neck; countless tiny wings beat at his ears. He scrabbled at them, trying to pull just one of Mitz's limbs away from his skin, trying to wheel his arms out around his head to knock the swallows away, but no sooner did he clear one patch of skin than it was being clawed at or flapped at again, until he could neither hear nor see nor feel anything except the gouges of cats' claws and the dry scratching of swallows' wings, and his eardrums were buzzing so loudly he knew they were about to burst.

✦ ✦ ✦

"What am I supposed to do?" Cath hissed at Zadoc. "He's gone mental. I dunno what he's looking at. I can't see it."

"Of course not!" said Zadoc. "Of course it's not the same! In order to see the same things in here, you'd have to have the same mind! And the same heart! Or at the very least, be thinking about the same thing. That might help you for a while, I suppose. You must both be thinking a little bit about the same thing, or else I wouldn't be moving at all, you know. I can feel you're both pulling me in the same direction. Or rather, you're pulling, and he's going along with you."

"We need to find a dog," said Cath. "That's the thing he needs to help this guy Tom."

"Well, you know what to do," said Zadoc. "We've told you what goes on in here. Come now, help him before he chokes."

But how could she make Danny see through her eyes?

Cath found her voice. "Danny, don't think about them," she tried.

That wasn't any good. Remembering what he shouldn't think about wouldn't help Danny now. She needed to tell him what he *should* do.

"Look past them," she said. "Let them do whatever they're doing. They ain't real, you know it. Just look over them. What's there?"

Danny gasped and choked. "Cat," he said. "Cat on my eyes. Can't see."

"She ain't. We're in Chromos. You're just making her up."

"No!" insisted Danny. "On my face! I can *feel* her! Get off!"

Cath thought hard. Could she try and see the cat? Could she pull it off him, if she knew what it looked like?

She tried. "What color is it?"

"Tabby." Danny sounded as though he were trying to strangle himself. "Gray . . . and brown and . . . white . . . on paws."

"Gray and brown?" said Cath. And then she had it. He just needed to make the cat into something else that couldn't possibly be real. Then he'd see it wasn't here.

She smiled at the back of his head. "Nah. Cats ain't normal colors in here. She'd be blue and green in here, with orange paws. Maybe red."

"No," said Danny.

"Yeah, she is. Just look at her!"

"No," Danny said again, but a little more weakly. Something in him was shifting.

"Purple ears. And yellow tail. And bits of her you'll see through. Her guts! Cats have windows in their guts here. All of 'em. Honest!"

"If I could see through her . . . I'd see her blood," said Danny. "And intestines. All that."

"You'd see forward," said Cath. "You'd see where we're going."

"But I can't." Danny sniffed. "There's a cat on my face."

"There ain't!" Cath held herself back from thumping him between the shoulder blades. "God's sake! There's whatever you want! Just dream up something you want. Just . . . just *want it*. You'll get it."

"That's impossible," said Danny.

"This ain't the other world, stupid. This is Chromos. Just do it yourself!"

Her fist, without any kind of permission, snaked out and punched Danny square in the back of the head.

Good, thought Cath. At least even he might reckon that a fair way to dislodge a cat.

✦ ✦ ✦

Danny's head snapped forward, and he had to cling to Zadoc to stop himself from falling off. The back of his head smarted, but at least Mitz had dropped from his face. She couldn't have gone far though. Would she be able to jump straight back up?

He wrestled with the smoke in his brain. One thing that he wanted. A single thing. Apart from an end to all this, he couldn't think of wanting anything else.

Ahead of them, a woman leaned against an oak tree, shabby and greasy-haired. She turned warm red eyes onto Danny's face.

"What did I give you?" she said.

Danny didn't know who she was. But suddenly a book came to his mind. A book of his own, made from the pictures he'd drawn. When he went home again, he'd start drawing Chromos. He couldn't hope to understand it now. But once he sat down with a pencil in his hand and made Chromos his own—he'd know where he was then.

He closed his eyes. How would he do it? Which bit would he draw first? Here, it would be the leaves along the tops of the hedges on either side of the lane. Then Mitz: the real, kind Mitz, her tabby stripes bent into the shapes of tiny tigers running across her coat to show her bravery. Shimny the horse, sleek-backed and proud, her bored old eye rolling at him. And the swallows would be away at the highest point of the sky, wheeling in joy.

It isn't much, he thought. Maybe it isn't enough. Cath would be dreaming of a whole new world in here. That's what I want though.

He forced himself to open his eyes.

And Chromos was shining.

✦ ✦ ✦

They were still in the forest; as dark and glossy as Isbjin al-Orr's tiny woodland, but a million times larger. Now the trees were warm and breathing, and they called out to him as he passed by. The forest was full of animals, and Danny thought he saw Mitz again. But instead of launching herself at him, she stalked along one of the low branches and stood watching him pass. Her eyes were yellow and defiant, and her fluffy tabby coat was in perfect order.

"Mitz!" Danny called out to her.

"Cat-torturing weasel!" spat Mitz, arching her back. "You deserve to be boxed into a corner and pelted with rotten haddock! If I were your mother, I'd roll you in fox poo and hand you over to a slobbery Rottweiler!"

This time, Danny didn't let himself be upset. He grinned at her. Some of the things that had happened to her really were his fault. One day she'd forgive him, probably if he just bought a special piece of fish for her.

"See you at home!" he called.

"Not if I see you first," spat Mitz. For a long second she stared at him and narrowed her eyes, and then she said, "I am partial to meatballs in gravy."

Danny's heart soared, and he thought, Cath *was* right. There is everything here but there is also something special—something entirely belonging to me.

And then, from between two trees in a darker corner of the forest came a spindly gray dog, a lurcher narrower than a sapling, its woolly head pointed and earnest. It looked up at Danny with round black eyes that held a single, unanswerable question.

"Is it you?" said Danny. "It is, isn't it?"

He held out a hand.

"Careful!" warned Zadoc. "You can't touch anything in Chromos. It'll become a part of you."

"She's already a part of me," said Danny. "I killed her. She's already in my blood, I can feel it. Come on, Kalia."

The lurcher didn't answer. He tried again.

"Kalia, please. Will you come with me? I'm going to take you back to Sammael."

Her thin head high, she watched him steadily, and he saw dark shapes detach themselves from the tree trunk and come drifting around her. Formless and papery—what were they? He tried to catch one, but they dissolved as his hand reached out to them. Drawing his hand back, peering, he saw that the shapes were scraps of burned paper with trails of writing faint across their brown pages.

"Is it the Book of Storms?" he whispered, the words half catching in his throat.

Kalia's lips drew back—was it a snarl or a grin? She gathered her legs underneath her, and for a second Danny thought she was about to spring at him. He braced himself.

But instead of jumping, she sat down. Zadoc carried on walking.

"Stop!" Danny said to Zadoc. "I need to take her back! She's the only thing Sammael will leave Tom for. Oh, please stop!"

Zadoc ground to a halt, grumbling. "What are you going to do? She doesn't want to come to you."

"But . . ." Danny tried to think of a way to persuade Kalia to come to him. There wasn't one. He would have to go to her.

He swung his leg over Zadoc's neck.

"What are you doing?" yelped Zadoc. "Don't get off! You can't get off!"

Danny looked down at the forest floor. It was a boiling mass of dark brine, bubbling and steaming.

He glanced back at Cath clutching Barshin in her arms.

"You can't do it," she said.

"I need Kalia," Danny said. "I need to save Tom."

Cath shrugged. "What if I try to see her, too? Maybe if we both see her, she'll be a strong enough thought to take down there. Tell me what she's like."

Danny looked at the dog. "She's gray," he said. "Really skinny. Kind of hairy, only the hair's like an old scrubbing pad. And her eyes are really big."

"But what's she *like*? Maybe . . . what sort of stuff does she like?"

He tried to see through Kalia's eyes. "I . . . I'm not sure. She must have liked Sammael. I don't know why. She stayed with him. They had some kind of bond, some bargain. She wanted to be his dog until she died. He wasn't that nice to her, but she stayed with him. And sometimes he was nicer to her than to anything else. But only sometimes."

"But she was always loyal?"

"Yeah, always. He didn't deserve it, but she was."

Cath snorted. "Deserve it? That's what kids say."

"No," said Danny, noticing how Cath's fingers had tightened around Barshin's fur. "If someone's that loyal to you, you should be good to them."

"But some people don't know how to be good. Or some dogs, neither. And sometimes you're just loyal to them no matter what. It ain't wrong."

Danny stared at her. "It is wrong," he said. "It shouldn't be like that."

"Or maybe you're wrong. Maybe Sammael isn't all horrible."

Danny shook his head. She had twisted his thoughts around so that he couldn't even think them properly anymore. He knew how important it was to try and say that you shouldn't believe people are allowed to hurt you, you shouldn't believe that Chromos is the only place of peace in this world—but the words balled up like clumps of hair in his throat and he couldn't cough them out.

He swallowed the hair balls and forced himself to say, "It doesn't matter. Do you know enough now? Can you imagine Kalia?"

"Maybe," said Cath. "I reckon I can try anyway."

"Okay. Let's call her together then."

They tried it. Kalia continued to stare at Danny, but threw a couple of glances toward Cath and Barshin, mistrustful.

"She's not coming," he said. "I don't think you've got her right."

"It's you who ain't got her right, idiot. You're still thinking about how wrong everything is. She'll never come to you."

"I can't help it," said Danny. "Sammael and her—it is wrong."

"Sometimes right and wrong ain't important," said Cath. "Sometimes it only matters what you do."

Danny looked at Kalia. "If you were my dog," he thought, "I'd never kick you. I'd never be mean to you or drag you around. I'd be nice to you, and I'd love you."

"It wouldn't make any difference," said Kalia. "Love is a steadfast arrow. Once the bow is fired and the barb has gone in, it can't be pulled out again. At least, not back the way it went in."

And she came toward him and put her paws up onto Zadoc's shoulder.

"Pull me up," she said.

She was no heavier than paper, and for a moment Danny thought he was gathering up a parcel of snakeskin. He didn't understand how they'd done it but he had her, cradled in his arms. She wasn't a real dog, solid and warm. But she looked like the animal he'd killed on that windy hillside.

He wrapped his arms around her as tightly as he dared. She rested her scraggy head against the side of his neck.

"Take us down, Zadoc," he said. "We're ready."

And then the air got thicker and became slimy and wet

until water was running down their faces and arms, and they had to close their mouths because they were breathing in air so wet that it made them cough up splatters of salt.

Just as his lungs were starting to feel painfully tight, Danny's head broke through the surface of the sea and he gasped, gulping in the night air again. Cath appeared beside him with Barshin crouched around her head, and they looked around for Isbjin al-Orr.

"Swim!" Cath yelled. "Swim for shore!"

"What?" Danny readjusted his grip on Kalia. She felt so fragile he was sure she was about to dissolve.

"Swim!" Cath screamed again. "Don't go into the moonlight!"

What was she going on about? Danny couldn't understand the fuss. They'd survived Chromos; they were back on earth again. Not solid earth, not quite yet. But nearly. What was the panic?

"The moonlight!" Cath waved her arms wildly. "It was in my dream!"

Danny managed to turn his head for long enough to see a vast, white wave sweeping toward them, soundless and soft. It was almost transparent, except that on the other side of it, instead of more sea, he could see shapes. There were tall things that looked like buildings, and other shorter shapes lower down.

As the salt water drove harder into his eyes, the tall shapes formed into separate things. What were they? Some kind of apartment buildings, like the Sawtry? He tried to look, but the wave was shining too brightly, rolling too close, and then he was in a dip with the whole white wall in front of him, and it was curling over, just as an elephant would curl its trunk around a log, and it was lifting him, Kalia, Cath, and Barshin together, raising them up into the sky as though they were weightless enough to fly.

Then they were streaming downward and the white wave was pushing them underneath the surface of the sea, and this time there was no Zadoc to carry them away, and they were going down and down and down, far too deep to ever swim back up again.

And the white water closed over their heads.

## CHAPTER 22

# THE ETHER

They were kneeling behind rocks, their legs and arms drained of strength. The world was white and stark, and the air was so thin that they had to draw hard at it, like thirsty people trying to suck water from mud.

Ahead, a path snaked from left to right in front of a steep rock face with a narrow white door set into it. When Cath tried to see where the path went off to once it had passed the door, her breath stopped working and her eyes clouded over with stars.

She heard a low rasping from her chest, as rough as a rusty blade biting into metal. Barshin slipped from her shoulders and dropped to the ground, panting weakly. Beside her, Danny's head was turned away downward, his mouth open in search of oxygen. None of them would last long here; only Kalia, under Danny's arm, seemed unaffected. The dog gazed calmly out to the path; her gray ears pricked.

And Sammael came along.

He had a big lump swung around his shoulders, which he threw to the ground with a silent shrug, raising a puff of dust from the white earth. He wasn't white—in fact, the back of his shirt seemed to be catching some kind of reflection of peacock blue from behind him, but there was a whiteness about his edges that seemed to fix him to this colorless world.

They'd found him in the moonlight on the sea.

But this wasn't the sea, or the earth, or Chromos. This was another place entirely. How many different worlds were there?

Cath had to pull her thoughts back toward her breathing, which didn't seem to want to work on its own. Were they still in the water, drowning? Had they *died*?

Danny's eyes were as bright as flint. "We're in the ether!" he whispered.

Kalia twitched and strained for a second out toward Sammael, but Danny's arm held her close.

"What?"

"The ether," Danny repeated. "It's his place—the top of

the sky. A river told me once—but it said I could never get here. Sammael's *made* of ether. Don't you see? Everything feels like him!"

*The top of the sky?* Wasn't that Chromos? Cath looked down to see what surface she was crouching on, but it was only white dust, with no fragments of color in it that she could see. It seemed undisturbed by Barshin's long, panting shape.

"Look!" Danny nudged her sharply.

She followed the direction of his pointing finger.

Sammael was stooping outside the white door, putting his arms around the lump he'd thrown down. The door was open and he was going inside and taking whatever it was with him. Kalia tried to free herself again, paws scrabbling in the thin air.

"What is it?" said Cath. "What's that thing?"

Danny shook his head, putting a hand over Kalia's paws to keep them still. "Can't see," he said.

The air around the lump had a darkness to it. Cath couldn't look for any longer than to run her eyes over it, and then her brain couldn't explain what she was seeing.

Sammael disappeared through the door. Cath's breath became heavier and heavier, her skin clamping in a band around her rib cage. She turned to Danny to see if he was having the same problem.

Danny's eyes were bulging, but he was still fighting to

keep breathing. Of course he was—had Cath expected that he'd lack the courage even to do that?

Yeah, she thought. Yeah, I did. And in a minute, he probably will. He'll get really scared and lie down in a ball, and give up and die.

"Go on!" she whispered. "Go out! Show him the dog!"

Danny drew in a hoarse breath and tightened his arms around the struggling dog. He half got up onto one leg and then hung his head, shaking with the effort.

"I . . . can't . . ."

A black shadow drew itself across Cath's mind. Of course he could. He was just afraid to, that was all. He couldn't make himself stand up and face Sammael, so he was going to hold on to Kalia and agonize about what to do, and end up choking to death instead.

At least if he died, she could have his bike. She'd command the deer to take her back to the wood and get the bike, and have it at home with her, so no one could steal it. She deserved it more than he did anyway. What had Danny O'Neill ever done to deserve a bike, except be a pathetic wimp with stupid rich parents? And if he died, they could forget all this rubbish about stopping Sammael. Sammael would let more of Chromos onto the earth, and Cath would be able to bathe in it and watch its colors spreading over the world.

She could reach over and press down on his chest, right now, and he'd just stop breathing. It would be easy.

But when she turned to him, his eyes were on her in the same way. Not struggling, not giving up, not thinking of asking for help. They were burning with hatred.

She reached out toward him, her hand flexing in a claw, ready to latch on to his neck.

And then in a blinding flash of light, a great, pitted ball of silver came stinging across the white sky. Instead of a shadow, a stream of fire was racing over the white ground beneath it. The flames roared up the path, squealing over the stones and dust.

Sammael stepped out of the doorway, looking up at the silver ball. His face was sharp and calm.

"What's this?" he said. "Dropping by? I'll put the kettle on, will I?"

The trail of fire swept toward his head, blowing at his black curls with a thousand orange mouths, trying to chew him and scrape at him and scour away his face, but he was laughing.

"I've missed you!" he said, his arms spread wide. "I've missed you up here!"

And then he took off his boots and stood barefoot in the sheet of flame, laughing as it tried to burn him.

"I don't need you yet, my beautiful!" he shouted. "Bide your time! Soon I'll have him! I'll spread out his moon-kissed sand and we'll burn great craters in the floor of Chromos. Then we'll see what waterfalls we can make!"

A second later, the ground under Cath's feet dissolved and she fell through an endless, thickening air that darkened to pitch-black. The roaring of the fire became the roaring of the sea and the grinding of waves, and the blackness was because her face was pressed against the soaked hide of Isbjin al-Orr, her arms tight around his neck, and he was swimming and swimming, his legs pawing against the wild sea, his patient head pointed in the direction of somewhere only he knew.

There were paws around Cath's neck and an arm around her waist. Of course. Barshin clinging on and Danny O'Neill dragging her down. But suddenly she was glad to feel Danny's heavy grip about her. At least he was still there. At least she hadn't reached across in the ether and closed her fingers around his neck . . . and if they ever reached dry land again, she'd be able to ask him about that silver thing and the fire, and what kind of a creature Sammael was that he could stand in those flames and not get burned.

✦ ✦ ✦

The beach came upon them hard and relentless, and even Isbjin al-Orr struggled to stay upright as his hooves scrabbled on the shingle. Cath let go of him and then she had to twist free from Danny's grip so that the weight of his body didn't pull her and Barshin back underneath the waves.

Once she'd found her feet again, Cath reached up and

lifted Barshin gently down from her shoulders. Lowering him onto the beach, she ran back into the edge of the sea for Danny. His arm was still clasped around the gray dog, which shone faintly in the moonlight. Cath dragged them both up the pebbles to beyond the limit of the tide, and waited for Danny to stop coughing.

Back here, she was shocked that she'd imagined wanting to kill him for a bike. If she'd done it, there'd be only her and Barshin and the stag on the beach now, and somewhere in the darkness among the crashing waves, an empty space where Danny might have been.

Danny sat up, spitting out seaweed and running his hand over Kalia's bony head.

"He took his boots off," he said. "We could have used Kalia to distract him, and run out and got them. Damn! Why didn't I do that?"

"Yeah," said Cath. "Why didn't you? You could have got Tom back by now."

"I couldn't breathe," said Danny quickly, hugging the spindly dog to his chest. "And I'd have gotten caught in that fire."

"It didn't burn him," said Cath.

"Well, he isn't human, is he?" Danny snapped.

"I don't reckon it was real fire. You were too busy pissing your pants, that's all."

"No I wasn't," said Danny.

"You so were."

He didn't argue back. Cath didn't blame him.

"It was the moon, wasn't it?" said Danny. "The silver-fire thing, I mean."

"I guess . . . yeah, it was the same color as moonlight. What did Sammael mean about 'moon-kissed sand'? Was that Tom?"

Danny thought for a while, the moonlight glistening off his wet face. Cath suddenly didn't like the way the silver light touched everything, as though no secrets could be hidden from it. But it was only light. It couldn't hear them.

"I think it might be," Danny said slowly. "There were these dogs that chased us last summer—the Dogs of War. They belong to the moon. I escaped, but they bit Tom. Maybe that . . . changed him. Made his sand special. So that means . . . Sammael's not just playing with Tom to get at me. He really needs him . . ."

"If he gets Tom's sand, he can open Chromos," said Cath. "But if not, then he's stuffed."

Danny looked out to sea, out to where the moonlight still flickered across the waves in an endlessly shifting dance.

"We have to take his boots," he said. "Then he won't be able to go into Chromos at all. And then he won't need Tom's sand anymore—he won't be able to use it how he wants to if he can't get to Chromos. It can't be that hard, now that we know when he takes his boots off."

This time Cath didn't argue. Sammael hadn't looked like he was wishing anything good on anyone, back in that dusty white world.

"Okay," she said. "How can we get through the fire, then? Any ideas?"

Danny shook his head. "I could . . . ask something, I guess."

"Maybe Isbjin al-Orr knows?"

They all turned to peer through the darkness at the stag, who was standing a few feet away with his head down, breathing heavily. Danny put his hand in his pocket to take hold of the stick, and Isbjin al-Orr pricked up his ears. There was a short silence.

"He says he doesn't," said Danny. "He says we should ask the sea."

"Well, go on then," said Cath.

Danny was very still. Cath wanted to launch herself at him and tear the stupid stick from his hand. Why couldn't he just get up and get this over with? If it all had to end—Chromos on earth, the colors, Sammael—why couldn't it just happen quickly and be done?

But suddenly she was aware that they were all watching her—Danny, Isbjin al-Orr, Barshin—and although she couldn't see their faces clearly in the moonlight, she could feel how strongly they were willing her to stay on their side.

Danny got up and held Kalia out to Cath.

"Here, take her."

Cath accepted the thin gray dog, curling her arms around its bony body, and Danny moved away to the tufted grasses at the edge of the beach. He turned the stick over in his hands, looking up at the moon.

For a long while there was only the sound of the breaking waves and the night breeze through the grasses and the distant whine of cars from up on the road.

Eventually Danny said, "I'm sorry I can't show you how it works. You'd probably be better at it than me. But I don't want to see anyone die ever again. I'll ask the sea."

And, hugging the paper-light shape of Sammael's dog, Cath watched as Danny wandered back toward the edge of the sea alone.

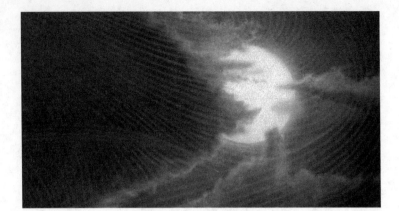

CHAPTER 23

# TALISMANS

**D**anny reached the edge of the sea and gripped the stick. "You're probably the worst thing of all to talk to, aren't you?" he said in as small a voice as he could think. "You must know pretty much everything. More than I want to know, anyway."

The sea laughed and gave a loud, watery burp.

"Sorry!" it said. "Porcupine fish scraping at my guts. They really can't keep their spines to themselves, you know. It's always scratchety, scratchety, here, there, and everywhere. Well, now. I am honored. I'd heard you'd fairly well gone to ground, young sir. Strange occasions, strange times."

Danny let this pass. Most creatures said weird things, in his experience.

"We got into the ether through you," he said. "We fell into a moonlit wave and ended up there. We saw the moon trying to burn Sammael with silver fire, and we just wanted to know what it was, so we can get through it and, you know . . ."

"Oh! I see!" shouted the sea, so loudly that Danny's eardrums rattled together inside his head. "You think I would know what goes on up there, do you? And why would you think that?"

"I . . . er . . ." Danny floundered. "I only thought . . ."

The sea shrieked with laughter and then quieted.

"Of course I know," it said. "I am the sea. I'm not so distinct from the sky as you might think. The moon paints my waves with her silver and, therefore, what is in the sky is also on the sea, if you see what I mean."

"No," said Danny politely. "I mean, the moon is actually *in* the sky. It's just a reflection in the sea, isn't it? But never mind, if you don't know anything about the fire . . ."

"Hold on!" boomed the sea. "Hold on!"

Danny, who had been about to turn away and return to the others, stayed for a nervous moment.

The sea curled a few waves and stretched out a little, catlike. "You know, I take it, that Sammael and the moon are old friends?"

Danny nodded. He'd heard this before.

"And like all old friends, they have their arguments. But arguments are sometimes just a way of letting someone know the strength of feeling that they inspire in you. Sammael and the moon—well, their friendship will last as long as they do. But they don't always agree, and the moon is a terrible sulk, you know. Sometimes she keeps herself to herself and won't talk to Sammael at all. And then she comes to the point where she can't bear it any longer and she tries to hurt him—to scorch the ether, to burn her mark across his land. Moon fire is the strongest, hottest, and coldest kind of fire that there is, but she can't hurt him as long as he is connected to the ether, which is the source of all that *he* is. So he takes off his boots, stands on his own ground, and steps into her fire to show her that he can bear anything she throws at him."

"So . . . we couldn't survive it, could we?" asked Danny. Perhaps the power of the stick might protect him?

"No, no, you'd be cooked, of course."

"Oh," said Danny, his heart sinking. "I guess there's nothing we can do up there, then."

"You certainly couldn't go through it," said the sea. "But you could get it to go around you, if you needed to. You only need a talisman—the moon's very respectful of that sort of mumbo jumbo. She loves all those wafty women who drape crystals everywhere and burn candles in her honor. Just take something like that and she'll avoid torching you."

Danny frowned. "What? Just a bit of crystal? Really?"

"Oh, no, no—you need something she's had her hands on first, something she recognizes. Don't you know anything that's been touched by the moon?"

Yes, he did. They came after him in his nightmares and woke him screaming into the dark.

"The Dogs of War," he said, barely whispering.

"Well, that would be a good start, certainly. Could you get hold of one of them?"

Danny's throat was bulging with salt granules scratching and scraping together.

"No!" he said. "Never again! They chased me last summer, but I got away. Tom got bitten."

Please tell me I'm wrong, he begged silently. Tell me that the moon's got nothing to do with Tom. Please say it.

"Perfect!" said the sea happily. "If he's got the saliva of the Dogs of War mixed with his blood, then the moon's a part of him now, isn't she? He's your man. Just take something from him—a finger, maybe, or a toe. Or an ear, something small like that."

So that was it. Tom was the center of it all. Danny would have to find him again and get something off him, regardless of Tom's scorn. Tom would never admit that he was wrong because he didn't think he was. He thought only that Danny was weak and small, and not worth being friends with.

Danny felt coldness sink down his chest and tried to struggle against it. "But I've lost him. He's gone."

The sea was silent for a second, settling itself flat and seething, and Danny knew that he had run out of excuses. If the wise and endless sea told him to get something belonging to Tom, then the only choice he had left was to set out and get it. Not a toe, though. He'd think of something less gruesome than that when the time came.

"Well, sir," said the sea. "Your business is your own and you will deal with it as you see fit. I think you know that happiness is seldom found in the surrendering of a difficult quest, and I think you may be learning under which circumstances it is imperative to keep fighting. But if you hope to be successful, I should caution you to beware of one thing."

"What's that?" asked Danny, thinking it would be just another possible hazard in the ether.

"One can always see the fire ahead. But often it's easy to be blind to what's behind you. Sometimes you don't see it until the flames are licking at your ears. So beware, sir. When you are dazzled by what's before you, don't forget to look around."

✦ ✦ ✦

Cath had fallen asleep on the tufted grass by the time Danny got back, her arms around Kalia, Barshin tucked against her legs. Danny was jealous of the way she could sleep anywhere, not noticing that the ground was hard or the night cold. Maybe she didn't have so much to worry about, he thought.

It must be kind of nice to know that you could go wandering off whenever you liked and no one at home would care.

What if Tom was miles away already? If someone saw Danny and Cath and called the police, and they were sent home, no one would believe how important it was for him to find those boots. No one knew what Sammael was planning to do, or how terrible it would be for Tom and for everyone else.

Again it was all up to Danny. He was so tired of hiding in hedges and not eating enough, and of the dirty world of mud and fields and rain. He was tired, even, of the sea—it felt like the end of a day on the beach when all the fun was over and the sun had gone, and the gathering clouds made you suddenly realize you'd stayed too long.

One more thing, he thought. I will find Tom. And then I'll get back into the ether and take the boots, and it'll all be over. As long as I get the boots, everyone will be safe.

He lay down beside Cath for a moment and looked up at the stars. There were more than he'd have guessed, out here in the countryside. Thousands of them. Were they in front of the ether or behind it? Danny didn't know. Was the ether even a real place? Was Sammael even a real creature? Or was he, Danny O'Neill, actually crazy and inventing everything?

Cath was with him, so he didn't feel alone, at least. But he didn't understand how she could think so differently from him, and always seem so certain of herself.

Five minutes' rest, he thought. And then we'd better go

and find Tom. He looked across at Cath, asleep in the faint moonlight. Was *she* even real?

There wasn't a way to answer that. One day all this would stop and it wouldn't matter anymore.

As long as there was still a world left to live in.

✦ ✦ ✦

Seagulls were wheeling and cawing in the sky when Danny woke up. An early mist lay heavily on the stone-gray sea. He shivered and scrambled to his feet in alarm. A whole night, gone! Perhaps it had already happened . . . Perhaps Tom was already dead, Chromos already open . . .

No, it couldn't have happened yet. The sky was still a dirty white and the air was thin. No mad screams carried over the breeze toward them, and the only colors to be seen were the tiny pinpricks of flowers in the tufted fringes of the beach.

He shook Cath to wake her up, but she was hardly asleep. Her face looked even grubbier in the clear air, and her hair was a wild bush.

"Food," she said, sitting up and hooking her wrist under Kalia's armpits. "We've got to get something to eat."

"We've got to find Tom," Danny said.

"Eat first!"

Danny shook his head. "There's no time. We've got to find Tom."

Cath clenched her jaw, gripping the gray dog tightly. "I ain't going hungry," she said.

Danny felt her watching him as he took the stick from his pocket and fixed his eyes on the coarse grass around his legs. He spoke inside his head so that nobody but he and the grass would hear it.

"Grass," he said. "Please listen to me."

The grass bristled, chattered, and then the single voice of the chosen speaker emerged.

"Danny O'Neill," it said. "What is it you want from us?"

Danny didn't bother to ask how this grass knew who he was. The grasses had undoubtedly been watching his every step for days.

"I need to know where my cousin is. If I tell you what he looks like, can you track him down for me?"

The grass paused and muttered to its neighbors. There was a dubious tone to the muttering.

"We know he is involved with Sammael," the grass came back with eventually. "We don't want Sammael to blame us for assisting you."

Danny looked over at the edge of the sea. It was calmer this morning, white foam lapping softly at the stony beach.

"Do you know about Chromos?" he asked.

An excited shudder ran through the tough grasses, as though they'd been struck by a tiny typhoon.

"The land of colors! The land of endlessness! Of course

we know of Chromos. They say Chromos is a wide green plain, full of grass. Have you been there?"

Danny felt his face redden at the lie he was about to tell. "Yes," he said. "I've been there. All the grass dies and dries up, and lies around all twisted and brown, all over the floor. Chromos is full of the screams of dying grass. It's awful."

The grasses let out a thousand small gasps of agony.

"It can't be true!"

"It's true. I've been there. I've seen it. And Sammael wants to tear open Chromos and let it pour all over the earth. He's found out how to do it—he's going to use my cousin. So if you can find out where Tom is, I can stop it from happening." Danny crossed his fingers inside his pocket, hating the lie. If the grass found out and got angry with him . . .

There was more discussion among the grass. Some of the voices were scared, insistent on helping. Some were scornful, full of disbelief. But eventually the lead grass spoke again.

"We will send the messages. We will find out where he is."

Danny, already trying to think up more stories he could tell to persuade them, swallowed in surprise. "Er . . . thanks. Great."

But the grass hadn't finished. "It does not matter if you are lying to us, Danny O'Neill. We are the grasses, and we cover everything in this world. The scars. The lies. The fires and the battles and the marks of destruction. We are the stability and the guardian of the earth, and whatever some of us might say, that is our first and foremost duty. Therefore, if there is a threat to the earth, we will help you counter it."

Danny let go of the stick, afraid that the grass might hear some of his thoughts. He looked out to sea again, tasting the clean salt air, shivering as the breeze blew flecks of sea foam against his sweater and pushed damp spots into his skin. What if Tom was miles away? What if it was too far for Isbjin al-Orr and Teilin to carry them? Would he have to face going back into the sea again and trying to travel swiftly through Chromos?

He picked up the stick and waited. The message took several minutes, but it came quickly enough to be reassuring.

"Not far! Not far! Not even a day's journey."

Danny's breath shot so fast from his lungs that it made his jaw hurt, and he realized that his teeth had been clenched tightly shut and all the blood had drained from his face.

✦ ✦ ✦

"I cannot take you. We have strayed too far from our herd already. Many days' journey and another many to return. I will have to fight every young stag in the neighborhood to regain my position. And I am graying and old, and I do not have the strength I once did. I cannot do it."

Isbjin al-Orr looked down his fine nose at Danny. The wind tugged at the whiskers around his soft lips, and his eyes were half-closed against flying drops of sea spray.

"Please?" Danny tried again. But the stag dipped his muzzle in regret.

"I cannot. I have responsibilities. To Teilin. To my herd."

The doe, standing as always with her head tucked against his flank, raised her face. She said something so quietly that neither Danny nor Isbjin al-Orr understood it.

The stag turned his head to her. "What? Speak up, sister. Your words are of no use while they stay in your mind."

Teilin, her small hooves unsteady on the shingle, stepped forward a pace or two. She looked up to the grass-covered land, following the line of rough fields toward the north. It was the way they had not yet traveled.

"We should take them," she said.

Isbjin al-Orr flicked his antlers against the gusty wind. "No," he said. "It is sufficient. We have done our duty and can return. You need not endure any more."

But the doe kept her gaze on the north, and her eyes were steady. "Why return?" she said. "We know what is back there. Onward—it could be anything. Adventure at the least."

"But . . . you didn't want to leave," said Isbjin al-Orr. "I only demanded it of you because I knew you were the strongest of the does. You only left because I demanded it."

"Ah yes," said Teilin. "But then I did leave. And the world is so large."

Isbjin al-Orr looked at her for a moment longer, then he

too turned in the direction she was facing and sniffed at the wind.

"It seems we go," he remarked. "I fear there is no turning back from here for any of us. Come, let's run."

Danny and Cath, eyes stinging from tiredness, found large stones to stand on and scrambled up onto the backs of the deer. Danny took Kalia from Cath, holding her close against his side. The dog seemed less substantial every time he lifted her, as though her wiry coat and fine body were slowly disintegrating back into the air.

The deer put their muzzles to the north, lifted their hooves, and plunged off the shingle beach, striking hard against the tufted grasses. Barshin kept a pace clear of them, skimming close to the ground and dodging the clods of stony mud that flew from the deer's hoofmarks. So they ran, five earthly creatures clinging tightly together, never once looking back at the growling sea.

CHAPTER 24

# BY THE LAKE

Mist curled up from the silver lake, reaching out to the mud-fringed shore. Sammael and Tom stood together, looking across the water. Both were very still, listening for something.

"Look!"

Cath kept her voice low as they crouched behind a heap of stones halfway down the valley side. They weren't close enough to be heard—the figures of Sammael and Tom were still tiny and distant, but she didn't want to scare Danny. He was already as pale as the morning clouds, his trembling arms clutched around Kalia's scrawny body.

A giant, golden-brown eagle soared overhead, swooping

down toward the lake. Sunlight flared up across the little valley, catching at the burnished golden feathers and the yellow-blond of Tom's hair.

The bird came to a gentle landing on a mound of rocks and tucked in its wings.

"It's massive!" Cath was struck, for a second, by the weight-less grace of the eagle. The ground dwellers around her seemed coarse and heavy in comparison. Even Barshin, just a little.

Kalia whined, and as Cath tore her eyes from the bird, she saw the lurcher's gray head snap backward and its lips draw back from its teeth. With one savage dart, the dog lunged up at Danny's face.

Danny threw up his hands to protect himself and let go of Kalia. She scrabbled free soundlessly, and shot out onto the purple heather of the hillside, sprinting madly down toward the figures by the lake.

"You *idiot*!" Cath ground her fist into the dirt.

"I couldn't help it . . . ," said Danny, his face almost broken by tears. "I just thought . . . it was what she'd do, wasn't it? She was his dog. I knew she'd go, I just thought it—"

"No matter," said Barshin. "She won't last long out of your arms, remember. As long as she survives long enough for him to see her, I think it'll be enough."

✦ ✦ ✦

Sammael shaded his eyes from the sun and looked up the far hillside, toward the sky.

A figure broke out from behind a clump of bushes and came sprinting toward him.

His heart spun itself into a whirling carousel.

It wasn't possible.

He knew it wasn't possible.

It was against every single law of nature.

And yet she ran and ran toward him, and he saw by the long, lollopy swing of her scrawny legs and the low lurch of her head that it was her. No other dog in the universe could look so similar.

His vision went black, then red, and he fought it as hard as he could, because there was still something in his head that told him this was a trick. But the spinning of his heart crushed the suspicion.

Kalia was running toward him, her face full of happiness. Her eyes were shining and her mouth was hanging open as she panted.

He almost reached out to her, except that had never been his way, so he kept his arms at his sides and waited for her to press herself against his boots, for the warmth of her body to curl itself around him. The redness of his vision faded and for a second he saw her in her exact colors—gray coat, black eyes, purple paws—only the paws were nearly gray again, so something must have healed her.

He struggled. Kalia's paws had been purple for years. How could they be gray again? But she had nearly reached him and the longing to take hold of her was so powerful that he couldn't organize his sharp thoughts.

A brilliant surge of hope exploded into his mind, blinding him to anything but the wonderful sight of his dog, racing toward him once more.

"Kalia?" he managed to say, but as soon as the word left his mouth the shape of Kalia, so merry and solid, began to dissolve.

His hand leapt out, trying to grab hold of her fur. A cloud of colors puffed at every point he touched. He pulled his hand back sharply, knowing the nature of these visions. She was disappearing into Chromos—a dream, nothing more.

But something had brought her out of Chromos. Did that mean there was enough of her left in there to be brought out somehow? Could he go in there and do it himself?

He forgot everything. He was no fool. But he was a creature, and every creature has a limit.

Sammael took three steps up into the air and vanished into Chromos.

✦ ✦ ✦

"Quick!" said Barshin. "You won't have long."

Danny, Cath, and Barshin left the two deer lurking behind the bushes and ran down the hillside toward Tom, slipping and catching their legs in the tough stems of heather. The golden eagle started in alarm, but a sound from Tom quieted it, and it sat on its rock, staring with hostile eyes at the new arrivals.

"Tom!" said Danny, scrambling to a halt. "You've got to believe us! He's going to kill you and use your sand to melt the floor of Chromos."

"What?" Tom threw up his hands and tried to laugh. "Not this again! How'd you get here? Did you follow me all this way?"

"There's no time to explain," said Danny. "You've got to come with us and leave the book behind. Please!"

"No way!" said Tom. "I've only got one more page to go. And he's starting to show me even better things—we came here through all these crazy secret tunnels left from the war. Miles of them! Nobody even knows they exist! No way am I stopping now. You're just jealous."

"*Jealous?*" Danny gaped. "Of what? You think I couldn't have made a bargain with him a thousand times over if I'd wanted to?"

"Probably not," said Tom. "There's nothing you want, is there? You haven't got the imagination to want anything worth having."

"Oh, for God's sake!" shouted Danny. "It's nothing to do with jealousy! He's going to kill you, and use your sand—"

"Yeah, yeah, you already said that," said Tom evenly.

"Because my sand's so special, isn't it? So different from *everyone* else's?"

"But it is! Because of the moon—you know, when those black dogs bit you, they changed you. Your sand *is* different. But I can't explain it all now—we've got to get out of here!"

"It's nonsense," said Tom, staring at Barshin. "You're making it up."

A breeze picked up. Was it the stirrings of Chromos, about to belch out a furious Sammael?

The air began to shake.

"Quickly!" begged Danny. "Come on!"

Tom shook his head slowly. The golden eagle spread its wings.

"We've got to go," said Cath. "We don't know what he'll do. Use that stick. Call up something. Just get us out of here."

Danny looked around the valley, his heart beginning to pound.

"Please, Tom," he said again. "Please . . . we'll take you into Chromos. When we've gotten away from Sammael, I'll take you in. You'll see it all, in there."

Tom snorted. "Maybe I wasn't giving you enough credit," he said. "You do seem to have developed a bit of imagination. But I think it's probably just lunacy."

"Tell him to call the wind," said Barshin to Cath. "Tell him to call it up and have it take us away."

"Can't we get Zadoc?" tried Cath.

But Barshin snapped, "Zadoc isn't an omnibus. You won't all fit on his back. Do as I say."

"The wind!" Cath said. "Barshin says—"

Danny remembered, for one terrible second, what had happened to his parents, and then he forced himself to shut everything else out of his mind, and gripped the stick in his pocket.

"Wind!" he shouted, loud inside his head. "We've got to get away! Please take us!"

The golden eagle held out its wings and launched itself off the rock, soaring into the wide sky, feathers beating strongly against the air.

If only it was going to be that easy for us, thought Danny.

"Are you sure?" hissed the wind, whispering and scuttling into his ears. "Are you sure you want this?"

"Yes," said Danny, holding every single muscle tight. "It's the only way, isn't it? Please don't kill us."

"Can't be sure of that," rattled the wind.

"Hey!"

Danny swung around at Tom's shout to see Cath dodging away, holding something.

"Give that back, you little cow!"

It was the book. Danny's heart soared. Good old Cath. While he'd been busy worrying, she'd crept up and stolen the book out of Tom's pocket while he was watching the flight of the golden eagle.

"Brilliant!" he shouted across to Cath. "Don't let him get it!"

"No fear!" She grinned at him, and shoved the little book into the waistband of her jeans. And then the wind picked her up off her feet.

Cath wheeled out her arms and legs, fighting against the punching gust, spinning and struggling up into the air. Danny had only a moment to think that he really didn't want to go the same way himself, before the wind caught him, too, and he was sucked into the air, reaching out to hold on to anything he could touch, feeling the world under his toes and fingertips vanish away. He tried to get his hand into his pocket, to take hold of the stick and beg the wind to stop, but his arms wanted only to stretch themselves out and flap, as though somehow his sticklike bones might steer him with the same grace as the golden eagle's feathers.

Below, he saw Barshin leap into Tom's strong arms, and then Tom was yanked off his feet, too far away to shout to over the whining moan of the wind.

I should have talked to the wind first, Danny thought. I should have made sure I was holding on to the stick. I should have known what I wanted and asked for it.

But whatever he had done, it was too late to worry about it now. For the first time in months, he felt both terrified and full of fight. He struggled to keep his head higher than his body. Blood rushed to his toes, then surged back to his ears, filling his vision with tiny spots. Far below him, he faintly made out the lake that they had left, and then the wind rolled him over to hang on his belly for a second, just long enough to see a lone figure reappear on the lake's shore.

Even from this distance, he could see how still Sammael stood, and how that stillness made the air around him grow darker, full of tightly restrained hate.

Sammael raised his face to the sky. Danny caught the narrowness of that black-eyed face for a single moment before the wind flipped him over again, then spun him and spun him until he began to feel so sick that he was sure he was going to vomit.

And then he heard a cracking, spitting sound above the grating sighs of the wind, and he felt a breath of warmth against his shoulder. He couldn't turn to see it but he smelled pine resin and ashes and toast all mingled together, all climbing into the sky behind him, and he knew it was fire.

Fire. But a fire of Sammael's making, surely? Then he was safe from it. Cath was safe. Barshin and Tom were safe. They were all their own people; not even Tom belonged to Sammael yet. No fire made by Sammael could hurt them. Besides, they were so high in the air that they must be beyond the reach of any flames.

Then the wind turned him over again and pulled his head back and his shoulders back, as though forcing him to look at something outrageous he had just done. It held him still and rigid, and he could not turn his face away.

Below, the sheet of flame bristled. On the ground, he saw Isbjin al-Orr and Teilin fleeing for their lives, heading away from the burning scrub and up to the high hills. For a second his heart choked him, for that was surely the last time he'd ever see them—how would he know where to find them again, so far from home? But at least Cath was safe, well away in the sky to his right, hanging upside down and flapping about like a puppet. And Tom, a little farther away, clutching Barshin up to his face, keeping the hare tucked away from the currents of wind.

Then Tom's arms opened and Barshin was dragged free, the hare's light little body spinning away in a mess of limbs and ears and bony feet.

Tom's arms spread wide and his legs kicked out so quickly that he looked like he was dancing. But he wasn't dancing. He was trying to kick away the flames, whose soft orange tongues lapped toward his feet. He was trying to lift himself into the air, to swim higher, to push away, but orange fingers were catching at his ankles now, poking up toward his knees.

The fire can't get him, thought Danny. It can't get him. That isn't how it works. I know it can't get him. Sammael can't kill him, not yet—that's what everything's told me. They can't all have been lying. It must be true. He must be safe—

And then Tom's legs stopped dancing and he threw back his head in a choke of fear, and he was trying to say something to Danny, trying to shout out against the fire and the wind and the vast space of air between them, but whatever the words were, they were too faint for Danny to hear.

Tom stopped moving. The wind released its hold on him and he dropped through the clear air and fell into the sheet of flames.

He must be safe, thought Danny. Sammael can't kill him. He must be safe . . .

From the flames rose a streak of dark fire, purplish-black, with streams of green edging its pointed leaves, and Danny heard the last call of Tom's deep voice, roaring out a terrible scream of pain and fear and sadness.

Away to the east, a figure stood on the crest of the hill. For a second, Danny thought it was Isbjin al-Orr, and then he saw that it was a human shape: the old woman with straggly gray hair and red eyes he'd seen in Chromos. "What did I give you?" she'd asked him. He hadn't understood. But here, now, he recognized her for who she was. She'd given him life, a year ago, although he hadn't been aware of it at the time. That had been a one-off though. She wasn't a mysterious creature with strange and fantastical powers.

She was Death.

And she was here for Tom.

CHAPTER 25

# DEATH

Danny's heart stopped beating. Oblivious to the rages of the wind, he hung in space and stared into the flames below. He thought over and over on that sight of Tom vanishing into the flames. Couldn't he have reached down and pulled him out? Couldn't he have got his hand to the stick and begged the wind to carry Tom upward?

The terrible knowledge came to him that if he hadn't used Kalia, then Sammael wouldn't have been so angry. He might not have tried to kill Tom.

But he shouldn't have been able to kill any living creature that didn't belong to him: Death would refuse to take them.

And yet she was here.

"I don't understand . . . ," said Danny, letting the words dribble out of his mouth. "I don't understand."

And he couldn't even put his hands up to his face to hide the shame of his tears. He was crying—a soundless gape of horror because Tom was dead, marvelous, brilliant Tom—and he would have to tell Aunt Kathleen that Tom was never coming home, and she would die of sadness, and his parents would never speak to him again. The world was over.

Then the wind was still and the old woman was walking toward Danny, up a broad beam of air that had laid itself flat underneath her feet. Her gray hair lifted gently about her tired face and her red eyes shone as softly as the embers of a dying fire.

"Hello," she said. "You saw me. I generally avoid talking to you lot, but since you saw me, I thought it would be less frightening if I said hello."

Danny gulped. "You've come for Tom," he managed. "Please don't take him."

"I'm not going to. I can't. He belongs to Sammael, and Sammael will take him now. I came here because I thought Sammael was making a mistake, but alas, he isn't."

She smiled regretfully and held out a hand to Danny.

"B-b-but he is. He must be. Tom didn't learn all that stuff, he said he hadn't finished—"

"Take my hand," Death said. "Don't worry, I've no business with you. I saved you, remember?"

Danny took her hand. It was warm and dry and it felt like his grandma's hand, old and wrinkled and rough from work.

"I don't remember," he said. "But I know you did. If you saved me, can't you save Tom?"

Death squeezed his hand with both of hers. "I can't," she said. "He chose Sammael—it was his own wish. It's possible that you'll never understand that—to you, Sammael must seem like an evil, cheating destroyer of light. But I can't take Tom from the death he chose."

"No!" Danny pulled his hand away. "You've got to! He can't die! Sammael's cheated him—it isn't how it works. You've got to stop him!"

Death put her hands up to the breast of her worn old cloak and fiddled with the pin.

"I don't like how he goes about things," she muttered. "But I did come here, and now I see that there's nothing I can do. I'm sorry."

"Why not?" Danny wanted to grab her, shake her until her red eyes rolled.

"I just can't. Some things are beyond the understanding of humans. I am Death—I have one job, and I can't interfere with the schemes of other creatures. If you want an answer, you'll have to ask Sammael."

She half turned to leave.

"I'm not going to ask him anything!" Danny yelled. "I'm going to kill him!"

Death turned back. "I doubt it," she said. "But listen. I

dislike Sammael's kind of unfairness. I presume you have some plan in mind. For you, I'll pretend I haven't understood about Tom. I'll go and argue with Sammael over him for a short while. If that helps you with anything, then all to the good. If not—I am sorry for it. Sammael has indeed been unfair, but it is not my job to redress the balance. Farewell, Danny. I hope we do not meet again for a long time."

She turned and walked swiftly back along the air to the hilltop. As soon as her feet touched the wiry heather, the wind sprang back into life.

✦ ✦ ✦

The wind shook Danny until his neck made a thousand tiny tearing sounds, and he tried to keep his head still for fear it would fall off. Then something came cannoning into his ribs, reached out, and hooked itself onto him, and he struggled in panic for a moment until he realized that it was Cath's twiggy arms gripping tightly to his sweater. She was trying to speak, but the screaming wind dragged the sounds from her mouth as fast as she could shout them. Her hand crept down his sweater, reaching for his pocket, and he kicked her viciously away.

"No! No! Don't!"

She shouted something more and tried to reach again, but Danny brought his foot up higher and shoved her in the stomach and she was snatched free of him by the wind. Thank

God she hadn't got to the stick. But if Cath could wheel all that way through the air toward him, surely he could get his own hand into his pocket?

With an effort so great it nearly split his shoulders in half, he pulled one of his arms down to his side. More by accident than anything else, his fingers got caught in the material of his trousers, and then they were brushing the top of the stick and the howling of the wind turned to a stream of swearing.

"Please," Danny begged, "please put us down. We'll die . . . we can't—"

"Hmph!" snorted the wind. "More than you could chew, eh? Told you, didn't I? Told you."

"Please!"

The wind grumbled and coughed like a bronchial horse and then chucked Danny high into the air, cackling as he turned a pale shade of olive.

"Heh-heh! I heard about you and the storms. Thought you could tame me, did you? Thought that taro—that little stick—would have me at your beck and call?"

"No," said Danny, tears still streaming from his eyes. "No, I never thought that. Please put us down! Please!"

"Hmph!" said the wind again.

It dashed him against a pile of rocks and vanished.

Danny held on to the earth, his cheek pressed into the gravel around the rocks. There was nothing around but emptiness, and he was the smallest creature that had ever existed.

He closed his eyes. This wasn't his earth. It was a new earth, a world without Tom. Danny didn't know what he was supposed to do in it. He didn't trust the way it felt so solid and reassuring.

A *thump* and a few painful curses made him aware that Cath had landed too. At least they were still together. Except—if it hadn't been for her, he'd never have started on all this; he'd never have tried to trick Sammael, and Tom would still be alive. If it hadn't been for Cath, he'd be safely at home and so would Tom.

He kept his face turned away from her and watched the far horizon. Sea, again, though whether it was the North Sea or an east sea or a west sea, he had no idea.

"Where's Tom?" said Cath, making scrabbling sounds as if she was sitting up.

Danny couldn't answer her. How could she be so stupid? Her and that wretched hare. He hated them both.

"Danny? You okay?" Cath reached over to shake him.

He jerked himself away from her. His ribs and stomach hurt. He wished he had broken into a million pieces.

"Oi, weirdo, where's Tom?" she repeated.

Danny didn't want to answer. He didn't want to give her anything, not even a word. Why hadn't she been the one to fall into the fire instead of Tom? Nobody would care about her being dead.

"Oi, you freak. Answer me!" Cath chucked a pebble at him. It bounced off his shoulder blade.

He grabbed the biggest stone that came to his hand and swung, launching it toward her face. She got a hand up to it, but not before it had hit her on the cheek, splitting open the skin under her eye.

She swore, wiping the blood with a filthy cuff. "Jeez! What's up with you?"

Danny was surprised she didn't make more of a fuss. The cut was bleeding freely. He shouldn't have done it. Seeing Cath bleeding didn't make him feel any better.

Still, he couldn't say sorry or tell her what had happened to Tom. There was only one thing he could do now.

"I'm going to kill him," he said, pushing himself to his feet.

"Tom?" said Cath, looking around in confusion.

"Sammael," said Danny, spitting out every syllable. "Where's Barshin?"

The hare appeared from behind Cath, treading a little gently as though his paws hurt.

"Can I get to the ether through Chromos?" Danny demanded. "Is it linked to it? It is, isn't it? It must be if Sammael goes that way."

Barshin was silent, his eyes wide with alarm.

"Tell me!" Danny snapped, grabbing at the stick in his pocket.

But the hare only gulped and shivered.

"Oh, what the hell," said Danny. "Get Zadoc." And to Cath, "Give me that book."

She gave Tom's little book to him without argument. Danny didn't look at it. He turned on Barshin, his eyes hard.

"This is something of Tom's, right?"

Barshin crouched low on the stony outcrop, dipped his nose to the rocks, and stared up at the book, his ears twitching.

"I know Sammael made it," snapped Danny. "But it belongs to Tom, doesn't it? It will protect us against the fire."

"I don't know," said Barshin. "I don't know."

"Where's the moon?" said Danny, peering up into the sky. But it was still daylight, despite everything that had happened. The moon wouldn't be around for a while yet.

Blood sang in his ears. No matter, he thought. This was no time for holding back.

"We could wait?" tried Barshin, but Danny wasn't listening anymore.

"I'm going up there," he said to Cath. "I'm going to get into the ether and I'm going to steal his boots. And if that doesn't kill him, I'll find out what will. Maybe if he's dead, they'll all be brought back to us—all the creatures he's taken. All those people—"

But he couldn't say any more. Instead, he made a grab for Barshin, but the hare jumped backward.

"Get Zadoc!" Danny shouted. "Get Zadoc now!"

Barshin cowered against the stones, and Danny yanked the stick out of his pocket.

"Wind!" he said, deliberately out loud so that Barshin could hear him. "It's this hare that thinks he can control you. He's got a taro of his own. Don't believe me? Pick him up and chuck him in the air and throw him against a rock, and it'll burst out of his stomach when he dies. Go on, try it! He's been telling me all about it for days!"

"No!" yelled Cath, leaning over to take hold of Barshin.

The wind stirred again. It wouldn't take much to shift the tiny hare.

"Get Zadoc!" Danny bellowed, his white face turning purplish-red. "Get Zadoc or I'll kill you!"

This was nothing like the terror he'd felt for his parents. This was a blinding, white rage. He would do anything. He would get Zadoc by himself if he had to. Chromos was there for all of them, wasn't it?

The wind snatched angrily at Barshin, trying to tear the small creature from Cath's grip. She slipped against the stones and nearly fell backward.

Barshin struggled. "Stop it!" he squeaked. "Let me go!"

"I can't," said Cath. "The wind'll get you."

"No, no, I'll do it! I'll call him."

The hare leapt down from her arms and glared at Danny. Danny kept his mouth shut, crossed his fingers behind his back, and told the wind that he'd made a mistake, he was sorry.

Zadoc came. He was so transparent that the whole landscape was visible through his body, and he had taken on only the colors of the earth this time, the purple of the heather, the iron-gray of the rocks, and the bitter dark green of the undergrowth. Danny scrambled up onto his back first, and then Cath, neither of them talking, neither of them looking around.

Cath held out a leg to Barshin, but the hare shook his head. "I can't go there again," he said. "I'll see you back here on earth."

"No—" Cath tried to say, but Zadoc was trying to take off, his legs slipping on the stones beneath him. He came crashing down onto his nose.

"I'm sorry . . ." He gasped, and he tried to right himself. His creaky limbs flailed on the loose gravel, and he fell again.

"You're . . . much . . . heavier . . ." He panted. "Much heavier than last time."

His fading coat was damp with sweat as his legs tried to straighten and again buckled. Danny wanted to kick him.

Cath grabbed at his arm. "It's the book!" she said, pulling his sleeve urgently. "It must be. He can't carry the book! You've gotta leave it behind!"

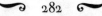

"Don't be stupid!" hissed Danny. "We need it to get past the fire. It's the only thing we've got left of Tom's."

"Well, tear it up! Take a little bit of it! He can't carry it—look at him."

Zadoc was down on his knees, nose squashed against the ground. He was gasping.

"Got . . . to . . . get . . . back . . . up . . ."

"Quick!" said Cath. "He can't stay here! You're trapping him on earth! He'll die too—is that what you want? Idiot!"

She hooked her arm around Danny's neck and squeezed the breath out of him, using her other hand to grab the book.

As soon as it was out of Danny's hands and in Cath's, Zadoc scrambled to his feet. But Cath, not trusting the little book, ripped out the last page and let the rest of it fall onto the stones at Zadoc's feet. A page was the same to them as the whole book, wasn't it?

Zadoc launched himself frantically into the air and the world fell away.

CHAPTER 26

# THE FIRE

D anny's demons swarmed around him. Gone were the
forests of Mitz and Kalia. Rivers of anger swirled,
bloody and dark. Chromos was a hazy mist of farmhouses
and cows and fences and ham pies and warm sofas, all burning with flames of green and black. Danny himself was
everywhere—wading through lakes of black runoff from the
muck heap, falling forward into manure-soaked straw, lying
motionless and screaming as great herds of dangle-tongued
cows loped steadily toward him. Their cloven hooves clacked
over the rutted concrete yard as they would soon clack over
his head, crushing the grass as they would soon crush his
skull.

How had he done it before? How had he gotten through this? He couldn't remember, couldn't even begin to think. And then the whole landscape in front of them opened up and they were streaming back down into the valley with the lake where they had seen Tom and the golden eagle, and everything for a second seemed familiar, until he realized that they were heading down toward the lakeshore.

Only it wasn't a lake now.

It was cows.

The light shining on the surface was nothing but a trick. What looked like ripples were the fast-moving backs of black-and-white cows packed together in a tight bunch, stampeding toward him.

He tugged at Zadoc's mane. "Stop! Don't go in there!"

But Zadoc plunged onward, desperate to leave the anchoring earth far behind him, and water began to pour out of Danny's mouth in a great jet, aiming itself at the cows, trying to scatter them with the force of its pressure.

The water made the cows charge faster, their eyes swelling up in anger. And Danny couldn't breathe through it—he started to choke until a familiar touch on his shoulder pierced him with the heat of lightning.

"You're rubbish at this, ain't you?" said Cath's voice, scornful and calm. "Just shut your mouth. I'll get us there."

Her hand came up to his chin and pushed it sharply upward, cutting off the jet of water. The cows in front of him slowed, although Zadoc still ran on toward them.

"What's the worst they can do?" said Cath.

And then the cows were fading into silver, and Zadoc's hooves were clambering up the wide currents of the air.

"I can't go in there!" panted Zadoc. "I can take you to the ether, but you'll have to go in alone. I belong in here, in Chromos, not up there."

The whiteness spread in a great cloud above them, and breathing became harder, and Zadoc's legs swung heavily, as if he were swimming through custard.

Zadoc stumbled, pitching them forward over his shoulder, and before Danny could reach out to grab a tuft of mane, the horse had dodged away from him.

"Zadoc!" called Cath, her voice thin with something close to a sob, but Zadoc was quickly out of sight.

✦ ✦ ✦

It was the same place as before—the piles of white rocks, the path, the cave, and the door. Cath was sitting next to him, rubbing her elbow and looking after the last sight of Zadoc's heels.

"How did you know the way?" Danny asked.

Cath looked at him for a second and he couldn't read what was in her face. Was she still angry with him about how he'd threatened Barshin?

"I'll call the moon, if I can," he said quickly.

The stick didn't like being in the ether. It felt cold and

clammy. He knew instinctively that his voice would be quieter through it. Didn't it want to be used in here? Was he doing something that would change the nature of the stick, or even of himself?

There wasn't time to think about that now.

"Moon!" he called silently, thinking out toward the silver ball of the moon, wherever she might be. "Moon, are you there?"

The moon was there. He couldn't see her, but he felt her silvery voice gently stroking his hair.

"I'm here, soldier," she said. "What are you doing here, I wonder. You don't belong here."

"I'm going to . . ." He wondered if it was worth lying. He had no idea if the moon and Sammael really disliked each other as much as their fiery arguments said they did. She sent her dogs out for him, didn't she? So they must be friends sometimes. In which case it definitely wasn't worth telling the whole truth.

"Going to what?" the moon asked.

"I'm going . . . to get into his cave. He's stolen something from me."

"Really?" The moon lingered over the word. "What is it? What could you possibly hope to get back from him?"

"It's a secret thing. I can't tell you," said Danny. "But it's important."

"So why should you need my help?"

For a second he wondered how much she knew.

"Just . . . to distract him. So he doesn't come in and find me there."

The moon whistled with soft laughter.

"Lying's not one of your strong points, Danny O'Neill," she said. "But I love annoying Sammael. Love it. Love him. Hate him. Nothing better than annoying him as much as possible. Watching his cross little face as he gets full of anger and tries to stamp his pointy little feet at me. Love the creature. What would life be without a bite to it? What do you want me to do?"

"Just . . . um . . . that thing you did before. With the fire and stuff."

"And you? What will you do?"

"We'll just . . . go in, get it back, and run."

"But you'll be burned. Nobody can survive my fire."

"We'll be fine," said Danny. "We've got something, something from Tom. I don't know if you remember him, but you got the Dogs of War together—"

"My actions are not for you to question," said the moon, in the same tone that his mum sometimes used when she was trying to warn him off a subject.

"It's okay," said Danny. "I wasn't going to say anything about that, but we've got something of his. You know him now, don't you? The sea said you wouldn't harm him . . ."

He tried not to let himself think that there wasn't anything left of Tom to harm now.

"I know the traces of my own touch," said the moon. "If it's true that you've got something I once touched, then my fire will skirt round you. But don't go thinking you can run straight through it. The heart of a fire is a very different place from the tips of the flames."

"I won't go into it," said Danny. "I really don't want to. I'll just go around the edge, that's all."

"Very well," said the moon. "But mind you do. If anything happens, you can't say I didn't warn you."

"Nothing will happen," said Danny, wishing he believed it. "It'll be fine. I know what I've got to do."

✦ ✦ ✦

In seconds, Sammael was there with a lump slung around his bony shoulders. His face showed nothing of the grim satisfaction that it wore in Danny's dreams. For a moment something tweaked inside Danny's stomach, and he thought, Did I do that? Is he *sad*? But then he looked at the darkness of the lump, and he knew it was Tom.

His stomach nearly threw itself out of his mouth, but there was a huge choking mass in his throat that kept it down and he closed his eyes for a fraction of a second, steadying himself against the white rocks.

Blindness made the world spin. Danny forced himself to open his eyes again.

Sammael stopped and threw the dark lump onto the ground, reaching out to push open the white door.

And the moon fire began. It wasn't at all like the fire that had swallowed up Tom; that crackling, hissing yellow blaze had burned the air and flooded across the whole world below. The fire of the moon was hard and full of nervous energy. It flared up like the sudden headlights of a truck on a darkened road, swooping over the whiteness of the ether with a brilliance so sheer that both Danny and Cath had to put their hands to their eyes.

Sammael spun around, yanking off his boots and throwing them back toward the door. He cast a swift look around the ether.

"Oh, you've come, have you?" he snarled. "What timing! If you'd given me ten more minutes, I'd have been ready for something far grander. But if you want me now, let's dance! I'm in the mood for a quickstep!"

He raised his arms and stepped forward into the moon's brilliant fire.

✦ ✦ ✦

Danny sprinted out, but the heat swept him viciously back. What was wrong? Of course! He didn't have the page—Cath had it, still crouching behind the silent rocks.

He ran back to her.

"The page!" he hissed. "Give it to me!"

She offered it up without a word, grubby and crumpled, and he didn't dare look at her as he snatched it away and ran once more toward the rock face, skirting the tongues of the silver fire.

The boots were lying on the white ground. He hesitated for only a second before reaching out to grab them. The scuffed dark leather was soft and warm under his hands—too soft, too warm, as though the boots were made of fragile baby animals and the desperation of Danny's grasp was squeezing the life out of them. He was sure he felt them wriggle in protest. But they were a pair of boots, nothing more. It wasn't possible. And he sprinted back to Cath, hurdling the rebounding flames, breathing hard against the heavy atmosphere.

"Take us back!" he said.

"How?" said Cath, her eyes reflecting the fire behind him.

"I dunno. You know. You always know!"

She shook her head. "No Barshin. No Zadoc."

"But they're just helping you, aren't they? It's you who knows!"

Cath shrugged and shook her head again. And then she opened her mouth as if to speak and a plume of thick black smoke came streaming out.

They both stared at it in terror. Cath's face turned red and she clawed at her throat, trying to open her mouth wider and wider, trying to rasp air into her chest. And Danny saw that something vital had broken inside her.

She couldn't breathe.

He stared wildly about the white world, looking for any kind of exit, any other creature that might help them.

But they were alone there, and the moon's fire was already dimming. Soon Sammael would step from it and reach for his boots, and find them gone.

## CHAPTER 27

# THE GREAT PLAIN

Danny tried to think—how could anyone get out of a place like this? There was the door but he didn't know what was through it, and he couldn't risk finding out. He'd heard no legends about this place, only that it was Sammael's home, away in the uppermost air.

The boots trembled in his hands. Were they trying to kill Cath? They were Sammael's boots, after all. Who knew what kind of power they might have picked up from him?

Danny found his finger was running itself over the dull leather. It was as soft as a kitten's fur. What if he put them on? Would he become like Sammael, nasty and hateful and full of spite? Or would they eat him alive, feet first?

He closed his eyes. Cath's choking rasp was slowing as the last air shivered out of her lungs and her blood began to fizz from lack of oxygen. She was going to die. Cath, too, on top of everything else.

The boots were the only thing he had left. They let Sammael walk through Chromos. Was there any chance they might do the same for him?

Danny kicked off his shoes and dragged the boots onto his feet. They were too big for him and they came up to his knees, but they clung to his feet in a gentle way, as though promising they'd try not to let go.

He grabbed Cath under her shoulders and tried to lift her up, but the effort was too much for his spinning head, and he couldn't do more than twist the thin material of her sweater into his fist and grip it tightly, hoping that it wouldn't rip.

How did the boots work? He had no idea what to wish for, or hope for, or whether there was a thing he should do with his feet to break through the edge of the ether and spin out into Chromos. Cath was the one who knew how to break through these walls between worlds. He was only Danny, a boy of the earth, and nothing more. Maybe if he thought hard enough about earth, he'd get them there, somehow . . .

Nothing happened. He had to ask Cath—she had to tell him—but she couldn't speak.

He took one hand off her shuddering body and reached into his pocket for the stick.

"Save us," he begged. "Whatever you know, tell me now."

Her voice was fainter than the hissing of the flames and he had to strain his thoughts toward her to pick it up.

"Don't wish back. Idiot. Just—only—forward. Outward. Onward."

He had no time to argue that she was wrong. He made himself look up at the sky of the ether and the white stars that sweated in the white heavens, and he fixed on one of them and made himself wish . . .

If only I could get there, somehow, all the way up there— I'd fly up in a plane or a rocket, and I'd fly it myself, and I'd burst through the atmosphere and find that it was nothing like this place, nothing like any of these places, and it would be full of—

And quickly, because his imagination was failing him in the face of his terrible fear, he stepped forward as if to step up toward the white stars. The ground at his feet dissolved and he was climbing a steep, steep hill, dragging the heavy burden of Cath along the roughening air, pulling at her sweater, pulling at her arms, and the air was taking on a sweeter note, full of the perfume of some old flower his grandmother had put on her porch in springtime.

For a moment he was sure he felt a sword clanking against his leg and heard the thundering of hoofbeats and the snort of a charger. But then Cath was struggling to stand up, holding on to him, and he saw that she was breathing again and her skin was just dirty instead of blotchy and red.

Where were they climbing now? Into another world entirely? A fourth place, beyond the uppermost air?

"Where are we?" he whispered, looking around at a great expanse of pale green and sparkling blue.

"Don't you know?" She frowned in surprise, keeping hold of his wrist.

"It's not Chromos," he said. "It can't be."

Chromos had never been like this. Chromos had never been so calm.

"Wanna bet?" said Cath, and she pointed back over his shoulder to something in the far distance.

It was Zadoc galloping toward them—Danny could see by the way the horse moved that it was Zadoc, but this was a different Zadoc entirely, a young, proud giant of a horse, his gray-brown mane flying in the wind. His head was stretched out, nostrils flared, and the hair of his legs was gleaming in the sunlight as he raced over the plain, drawing nearer with every flash of his hard brown hooves.

Zadoc, raised to glory, by what? By Danny's thoughts? Or by Cath's?

Or by his rider, tall and straight, sitting upright on the horse's flying back and driving him on toward both of them?

Danny didn't know whose eyes he was looking through. But he knew what he was looking at.

"Run!" he screamed at Cath. "Keep hold of me and run!"

And Sammael kicked Zadoc viciously on.

✦ ✦ ✦

"Through here!" said Cath, yanking at Danny's wrist, tugging him sideways.

"Through where?" Danny couldn't see where she was going.

"The door! Quick!"

"What door?"

"This door!"

Cath pulled with all her strength.

"There isn't a door!"

"Well, imagine one!"

He did his best. There it was—a door, dark blue with a gold number, like his own front door at home. Cath pulled it open, and they stepped through into the hall of his house.

Except Cath wasn't there.

"Cath!" Danny yelled, trying to run to the stairs and shout up them. His wrist was anchored to the door frame. He tried to wrench it free.

Something screamed in the air, as piercing as the buzz of a mosquito in a silent room. He wrenched at his arm again, and the scream tore into his ear.

"Cath! Where are you?" He struggled to reach the living room—she must have run in there, or straight into the kitchen. But he couldn't free his arm from the door frame. If

only he could reach the banister, pull against it, and get some leverage—

"Danny!"

Something trickled out of his ears, hot enough to be blood.

The door frame was pulling back. He fought it, braced his legs against it, but it tugged and pulled until he fell forward and banged his face against the front step.

And then, raising his face in the dust, he was back in the green plain again with the blue sky wide above him, and his arm was being tightly held, not by the door frame of his house, but by Cath.

"Well, you did tell me to keep hold of you," she said, her face dark and scornful. "We imagined different doors. 'Course we did. You went back again."

"I don't know what's in your stupid head, do I?" Danny spat out dirt. "I can't read your mind."

The hoofbeats were loud enough to feel now. The ground trembled.

"We need something we both know!" said Cath, readjusting her grip on his arm. "Come on, think!"

"School?" Danny tried, but she pulled him to his feet, stamping her foot.

"No! Stop going back! Forward—what's up there? Tell me a story!"

Danny closed his eyes. His head hurt. Sammael was

nearly on them. Sammael who knew everything. Was there nothing bigger than Sammael?

Of course there was. What about those stories he'd heard? The beginnings of the world and how it had come to be as it was.

"Remember . . . Isbjin al-Orr?" he managed to say. "Remember his story? Apollo, and Phaeton who stole the chariot, and the stags that pulled it—"

"Imagine it," said Cath, gripping his wrist so tightly he was sure she'd stopped all the blood moving in his arm. "Imagine every bit of it."

Danny brought the story back to his mind. He pushed away the fear he'd felt as he heard it. He pushed away the horror at the idea of stealing a chariot, of holding on to eight huge stags, trying to control them with a thin leather rein. He thought of eight Isbjin al-Orrs, each one bigger and more beautiful than the last.

"It's gold!" shouted Cath, beginning to run. "With two massive black wheels!"

"Taller than me. Taller than both of us put together," Danny tried, stumbling over a tuft of grass.

"Not that tall. Just tall enough for us. And covered in pictures," said Cath, skipping more nimbly beside him.

"Pictures of the sun!" Danny added.

"And the moon!"

"And planets, and the stars!"

"The stags are in pairs, four pairs, and the front ones are red—"

"The second are black—"

"Then white—"

"Then brown!"

Danny stumbled on another tussock and nearly pitched into a bare strip of dirt. Long and linear, it stretched out before him in a dusty ribbon, marking the way.

"It's a rut!" he gasped. "A wheel!"

"It's coming!" yelled Cath. "Run!"

Without letting go of him, she began to sprint alongside the wheel rut, and the distant sound of Zadoc's drumming hooves swelled up in a rumbling roar of pounding feet against bare earth, all jumbled together over the song of wheels running sweetly along a humming road.

The chariot was next to them before Danny had time to trip up again.

"Grab it!" yelled Cath.

Danny smelled the heat of eight galloping stags. The dust filled his eyes in a second as they rushed past him. They were going straight on, heading for nightfall—he'd never be quick enough to get on, never even manage to touch the gleaming gold of the chariot's sides—

And then Cath shoved him almost underneath the giant black wheels so he had to put his hand out to save himself, and somehow he was holding on to the side rail of the chariot and hauling himself up onto the running board. First one foot, then the other was standing on the bumping, rackety floor, and Cath was scrambling up beside him, shoving the reins into his hand.

"You do it!" he shouted over the thunder of the stags' hoofbeats and the rattle of the wheels. "You take them!"

He tried to give the reins to her, but her other hand was around the front rail of the chariot and she wouldn't let go.

"*You* do it!" she yelled back at him. "Get some guts, for once!"

Danny balled the reins in his fist, trying to pull back against the massive stags. They were careering madly forward as fast as they liked, spurring one another on to greater speed. He wasn't controlling them at all.

He had imagined them here, hadn't he? Couldn't he just slow them down by imagining it?

With cold horror he remembered Isbjin al-Orr's words.

*The stags, free from any restraining hand, at once doubled their speed. With no charioteer to guide them, they galloped closer and closer to earth, the flames roaring out in their wake, and the mountaintops began to scorch and shrivel as they passed overhead.*

And he wasn't even Phaeton. He wasn't the son of the Sun God. He was Danny O'Neill, and his dad sold farm machinery, and neither of them had any kind of special powers.

"Steer them!" yelled Cath. "He's coming!"

Sammael and Zadoc were only yards away, Sammael's bare feet hanging at Zadoc's sides. Danny felt the boots twitch around his ankles.

Picking up the reins, he slapped them across the backs of the last pair of stags.

"Go up!" he begged them. "Up! Or down! Or any way! Just faster! Faster!"

The stags leapt up into the sky and Danny felt a huge heat blaze out behind him. It must be the sun! He didn't turn his head to look. He was driving the sun across the sky—he, Danny, driving the chariot of the sun!

He risked a glance at Cath. She was half smiling, half scowling, but a light reflecting in her eyes told him the truth, that she was as happy as he was, as terrified as he was; that for the first time, they were in this together, blazing the same path through Chromos.

"Did you see it?" he yelled to her. She looked at him, brown eyes shining.

"The sun? It's behind us!"

"I know! On the back of the chariot!"

"Don't look! You'll go blind!"

"So will you!"

She shook her head and smiled, and with surprise he realized he couldn't remember having seen her really smile at another person before. But then, it probably wasn't a person she was smiling at now.

"Is he still there?" he yelled.

Cath looked down, leaning out of the chariot as far as she dared, to see what was happening on the plain below. She clung to the rail like a monkey.

Sammael was there, galloping beneath them, his right arm raised as if he were about to release a spear.

"You've picked the wrong story!" he called, and the smile on his face was tight. "I know how this one ends, too. Remember?"

And when Cath pulled herself back up, the smile had gone.

"He's gonna shoot us down," she said, in a thin, matter-of-fact voice.

"No! We'll go faster!" Danny slapped the reins against the stags again, but Cath shook her head.

"It's what happens, ain't it? In the story. The sun gets hotter and then Phaeton gets shot down by a thunderbolt. Sammael calls the storm."

"But we're not Phaeton. We're us. Danny and Cath. Don't think about it—it won't happen! It's *our* minds that make this place!"

"We stole his story though. We know it's what happens." Cath closed her eyes for a second, but they both saw it before them—the rolling clouds, the dark thunder.

"We should have made our own story," yelled Danny. "We can still—"

"It's too late!" Cath smacked her fist on the chariot rail and gestured down at Danny's feet. "So what are you going to do with them?"

"What?"

"Them boots. What are you going to do with 'em?"

Danny felt a desperate urge to keep the boots. As long as he had them, they could still run. If they were caught, it would be terrible. But as long as they weren't caught . . .

"Burn them!" yelled Cath. "Throw them into the sun!"

He turned on her. "No! No way!"

"Fine! Give them back to Sammael then! If you're too yellow to do what you want, let him do what he wants!"

"No!" Danny gripped the rail, trying to steady himself. What was she saying? She couldn't mean it.

"Go on, then! Burn 'em! Get on with it!"

He struggled against his own clenched feet. "Would you?" he yelled at Cath. "Would you burn them?"

She shook her head. "I told you," she said. "We're different. This is your call. You've got ten seconds I reckon."

Danny tried to see where Sammael was, but when he leaned out of the chariot to look behind, the scorching rays of the sun singed all the hair off the front of his head.

In despair, he pulled his feet out of the scuffed boots, looking at them for the last time. Like Sammael's old coat, they were as unremarkable as the leftovers from a yard sale. Just a pair of old boots. If he'd gotten them sooner—if he'd had time to find out what new strength they gave to his feet—what could he have done with them?

Nothing, thought Danny hopelessly. I'd have done nothing, like I always do. But that's going to change now. I'm never going to do nothing again.

And he threw the boots behind him. He didn't have to throw them carefully, or risk blinding himself by turning to check that they really had been swallowed up by the gigantic fireball of the sun. He knew that nothing else could have happened to them. Sammael had destroyed so many parts of Danny's world—his peace, his safety, the happiness of his family—and Danny had got his revenge. An eye for an eye, he thought. A tooth for a tooth. That's what he'd done.

And then the dark clouds flashed and a great crack of thunder rang out. One of the stags seemed to stumble over the currents of the air and its antler-crowned head crumpled forward, dragging the harness down among the other stags until they were a great kicking mass of legs and antlers and thrashing bodies. They tumbled toward the great plain, the chariot lurching in their wake.

Danny and Cath clung to each other and to the sides of the chariot, pulling themselves against the gold rails, watching the wheels spin like wild tops. There was nothing else to do but cling on, and wait, and hope.

The chariot hit another gust of wind and spun madly until Danny and Cath couldn't hold on anymore. The front rail tore itself out of their hands and they fell through the air, hanging on to the leather reins and each other, trying desperately to slow themselves, to climb back up, to fly away . . .

But they knew they were falling, and the floor of Chromos melted into olive-black brine.

## CHAPTER 28

# A MISTAKE

Sammael pulled Zadoc to a halt. His palm was stinging, but it wasn't the thunderbolt that had burned a heavy mark in his skin. He hadn't touched it; it had been summoned up by two other imaginations, not his own.

Perhaps it was his own fury that had burned him, and the stinging sensation was a sharp rush of hatred.

For he hated Danny O'Neill; there were no two ways about it.

It was impossible to believe he'd stolen the boots. And before that, Sammael's coat. They were two of the most precious items that Sammael possessed, and Danny O'Neill had destroyed both of them. But he would never get his hands on anything else.

Because this was the end for Danny O'Neill. This was the last place he would ever see. As soon as he hit the floor of Chromos, he would be eaten by his worst nightmares. Whatever happened to the shell of his body down on earth, his mind would devour itself and leave nothing but a few trails of dribble soaking across the Chromos plain.

Sammael edged Zadoc closer to the place where the chariot would fall. He wanted to watch Danny O'Neill die. It was a shame about the girl—she had imagination and she was brave, and the world needed more people like her.

But a lot of things were a shame. One more wouldn't make much difference.

Zadoc's legs began to shake. Sammael kicked the horse roughly with his heels to keep it still. Stupid animal. Always afraid, looking for a way to flee. Chromos should have had a clever, courageous guide. But then, Chromos was a place to rightly fear. Even Zadoc, once, had been brave and full of heart.

What did it matter now? The stupid animal had been scared for hundreds of years. Just a beach donkey, fit for nothing but the glue factory.

The chariot was almost at the floor now. Another second or two . . .

Sammael kicked Zadoc on, not looking down at the

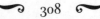

horse's feet. He knew this place, every inch of it—it was all too familiar.

The tangle of stags and wheels and harness crashed down before him. Leather straps whipped through the air, curling in high arcs around his shoulders. Hooves flashed past his impassive face.

He waited for everything to dissolve, to leave only two children lying on the plain, sinking into its darkening slime.

The hooves kicked and the legs struggled, and the tangle carried on falling. It should have stopped by now. It should have come to a crashing halt on the floor of Chromos—

A strip of harness snaked out and caught Zadoc's leg. The horse tried to shake it off.

Another leather strap coiled around Sammael's ankle, and before he had time to resist, they were pulled down into the tumbling carnage.

With a terrible, piercing agony, Sammael suddenly knew that the swift look he had cast around the ether before he'd stepped into the moon fire had not been long enough. For it had been his final look.

The plain of Chromos had gone dark gray, and he was being pulled through it, without his boots, onto the earth below.

A wide expanse of blue-gray flashed up, chopping at a narrow strip of pale brown—and beyond it, a field, some woods and mountains . . .

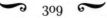

It was that girl. She'd seen something up here, she'd remembered it, and she'd well and truly done for him.

Not entirely perhaps. But well enough for now.

His jaw set in grim satisfaction as he was dragged from Chromos onto the hard, cold ground of the earth.

CHAPTER 29

# THE BEACH

The last rays of sun were sinking into a great sheet of sea as Danny pushed his face up from the sand. Cath was a short distance off, already sitting up and looking around her. She was grinning from ear to ear.

"Made it!" she said, dusting off her hands.

Danny thought she was talking about the fact that they'd survived, and then he looked farther on behind her and saw a path over the back of the dunes leading to a tiny cottage with steep mountains rising up behind. Was this where she'd been trying to get to all along?

Well, she was welcome to it. He was going to find Tom and go home—

And then he remembered Tom, and his heart sank into the sand. Sammael had cheated.

"I told you, *I* never cheat," said Sammael. But his eyes were on Cath.

She got to her feet and shrugged. "You made them paths."

"Paths?" Danny looked from one to the other. "What paths?"

"Just paths," said Sammael. "Gray ones. Rather like the one we just fell through."

Danny frowned. "There are still holes in Chromos?"

"Oh, only those small ones from the bargains I used to make," said Sammael.

"We fell through a hole *you* made?"

"Correction. Your friend dragged me through it," said Sammael, but there was a note of admiration in his voice. "She took us all through it, in fact. Including Zadoc, which saved you mere mortals from having your brains leak out through your ears. Rather clever, don't you think? A somewhat unfortunate strength of mind."

"But then, you—you defeated yourself?"

Sammael stopped looking at Cath and turned his shrewd gaze back to Danny. "One man's flaw," he said, "is another man's beauty spot. Which of us is which in this case, I wonder."

Danny looked up at him. The tall, thin figure didn't look quite so threatening down here, standing barefoot in the sand. He held out a bony hand, as if offering to help Danny to his feet. Danny got up by himself.

"We did it then," he said. "We stopped you."

"You," said Sammael thinly, "are the worst example of your species I've ever had the misfortune to meet. Look at yourself."

Danny looked at himself. In his mind's eye he flew around his body and took a good summary of what he saw. Okay, he hadn't exactly embraced his fears, but he'd gotten the better of Sammael, hadn't he? He looked Sammael squarely in the face.

"So what?" he said, feeling his cheeks burn red. "I still beat you."

Sammael laughed. "Lost anything along the way?" he asked. "Like, I don't know, a cousin?"

Danny's jaw and fists clenched tight to themselves.

"You cheated," he said.

"Not at all."

Sammael reached over his shoulder, into the collar of his shirt, and yanked out a stringy ball of brown fur and dangling limbs.

Barshin.

He dropped the hare at Danny's feet. It crouched, looking out toward the sea, avoiding Danny's eyes.

Cath, treading silently, came to stand beside him. Danny didn't dare look at her.

"Hey, Barshin," she said. But she didn't follow it up with, "How did you get here?"

Danny pulled the crumpled page of Tom's book from his pocket. The last page. He smoothed it out and read it. What had Tom said? *I've only got one more page to go.*

On one side, the page was headed "Hares." And on the other—

Blank.

"You killed him," Danny said to Barshin. The words seemed impossible.

Barshin turned his black eyes up to Danny for one inscrutable second, and then looked back at the sea.

Danny tried again. "You talked to him when we got picked up by the wind. Hares were the last thing he had to learn."

The hare didn't answer.

"So all along you weren't trying to save Tom?" asked Cath in a slow voice. "You just wanted—"

"To get Danny into Chromos for me," said Sammael. "Correct. He was acting on my orders. I knew if I could only get that sniveling boy onto Zadoc's back and into Chromos alone, he'd be sure to oblige me by imagining up a whole army of terrifying things to kill himself. You know, I'm quite keen on Danny dying a miserable death. I'm sure you're aware by now that he has stolen three things from me, none of which I can get back."

"Three?"

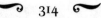

"A dog. A coat. And a taro, in the form of a small stick. Oh, and apparently a fourth thing now. My boots. A bit greedy, when you think about it. More than one small human really needs."

"But if he was working for you . . . all that stuff about telas . . . Is it all crap, then?"

Barshin held his head high. "You can talk to me," he said. "That's not a lie."

"But I can't talk to other hares?"

"Not unless they've gained the ability to speak to you from me," cut in Sammael. "It's always illuminating when the ones we trust most turn out to be traitors, isn't it?"

Cath didn't look at him. She was still staring at Barshin as though she were having difficulty distinguishing his brown coat from the coffee-colored sand.

"I don't get it," she said. "Why'd you need to get me involved?"

"Danny wouldn't listen to me on my own," said Barshin. "And we knew that he'd never be able to get into Chromos if he didn't really want to either. So we decided to use you to draw him in. We tried showing you how good Chromos could be so that you might persuade him. And you did help him find enough strength to get into Chromos in the end."

"No I didn't," said Cath. "He just figured out his way was through the sea, that's all."

"Oh, don't be naive," snapped Sammael. "Of course he

didn't figure it out. I sent you those dreams, both of you. He only got to Chromos through the sea because he believed he *could*. Without you beside him giving him confidence, he'd have stayed being the same sniveling little ninny he's been all his life and he wouldn't have got there through any route. *Anyone* can get to Chromos! But they have to want to, and they have to be *brave* enough."

Cath looked at Danny. He kicked the sand defiantly but didn't meet her eye.

Barshin carried on apologetically. "So, you see, it would have worked. But you did something more than we planned—you gave him true courage, the kind that only flashes into the heart on those rare occasions when it casts off all doubt and feels invincible. He *wanted* to go into the sea, even though he knew he should be scared. And I didn't get the chance to warn Sammael that you'd fallen into the ether by mistake and found out about the boots. Neither of us ever thought Danny would last two seconds if he got into the ether."

"But Sammael was trying to pull Chromos onto the whole earth, wasn't he? Why didn't he just wait till then to get Danny? Danny would have gone mad along with everybody else, wouldn't he?"

Barshin looked at Sammael. Sammael tilted his head.

"Ah, yes," he said. "Revenge. Even the best of us lose our heads over it sometimes. Why didn't I lump Danny in with all the rest? Because I hate him more than all the rest. He is an unimaginative, stodgy, stiff-necked coward. Even when he tries to be brave, he's still as curled up and scared inside as a fledgling bird. He deserves to be eaten up slowly by his fears, bite by bite, and I wanted to see him suffer."

Cath's fingers tightened as though she were still holding on to the chariot, trying not to fall. She was silent for a long moment, and then she said, abruptly, to Barshin, "So you used me, then? You're just like Sammael. You're the same kind of thing."

Barshin gazed up at her, his black eyes still. "I am not like him at all," he said. "I liked and respected you from the start. I tried not to involve you too deeply—I tried to keep you out of Danny's attempts to get to Chromos by telling you that you wouldn't fit on Zadoc's back if he was there. But you were determined to come."

"So there wasn't ever a problem with the number of people on Zadoc's back. It was only that stupid book that slowed him down," Cath said, although she knew that Barshin wouldn't deny it. He was just telling her another way in which he'd lied.

"Indeed." Barshin nodded. "The whole world would fit onto Zadoc's back, if only they wanted to. But I had business to do. And doing that business does not make me the same as Sammael. Not in any way. I am a real, earthly creature who made a bargain with him. That is what I am."

"What kind of bargain?"

But Barshin flicked his ears and tilted his head. "That is the deepest secret of my heart," he said. "The knowledge of it belongs to me and to nobody else. And if I tell you, it will seem as if I'm trying to excuse myself. And I am not."

"You evil little scumbag!" Danny kicked at Barshin, sending him skittering back onto the sand. "Without you we'd have had more time! Tom wouldn't have died!"

"Forget it," said Sammael. "You'll forget it soon enough anyway."

"No, I won't," said Danny, and tears began to drip down his cheeks. "I'll never forget him, never."

"Yes, you will," said Sammael. "He's mine, remember? All his memories are mine. Didn't you learn that last time? I can take them away or leave them here. What do you think's best?"

Danny gaped up at Sammael. "What do you mean? Take them? Take what?"

"All the memories of Tom belong to me," repeated Sammael. "I can take them out of the earth so no one will remember that he was ever here. His mother will think she only has a daughter. You'll never know you had more than one cousin. Look on the bright side: no one will grieve or be sad that he's gone. And no one will blame you for coming back without him. Because they're going to blame you, you know that."

Danny did know. He was terribly afraid of it. Tom

gone—that was a hole torn in his stomach, and each time he had to tell someone else, it was going to be like tearing another hole, and another, until there was nothing left of his stomach but holes. Nothing good would ever be held in there again, only a constant stream of lumpy sadness.

He swallowed and looked at the ground, and Sammael spoke again.

"Go on then, I'll give you the choice. What do you want? I think I know the answer to this one."

Danny wrestled with himself. But already he could feel the vision of bright Tom growing duller and darker in his mind. Already he was thinking, Whatever Tom did, it wasn't my fault, was it? It wouldn't be fair for me to be blamed for things he chose to do. He chose to sell his sand. I even tried to help him, but he still chose to go with Sammael . . .

"No," he said. "You can't take him. It's not right."

Sammael grinned, catching the last rays of the dying sun in the whites of his eyes and teeth.

"I thought your voice would say that," he said quietly. "But it's betrayed by your face, I'm afraid. I know what your cowardly heart really wants. Well, off you go. Don't look back, mind you. Your friend's told you that enough times, hasn't she? If only there were more people like her."

And you? What will you do? Danny wanted to ask, but he didn't dare. There was a closeness about the way the shadows were drawing around Sammael's face, and a silence in the air that could only have been the quiet at the beginning of a long wait.

"Oh, I'm not going anywhere," said Sammael. "How can I? I'm stuck on earth. You've burned my boots, and Zadoc has all but vanished. I don't think he'll be leaping to answer my call anytime soon."

"Good," said Danny. "You can't go back to Chromos then. We're all safe."

"Safe?" said Sammael, raising a thin eyebrow. "Do you really think you're safe? You've got a world without anymore Chromos now. You took away the darkness because you were afraid of it. You never had the courage to try and see what it really was. But there are some things a lot more dangerous than darkness in your earthly world. And those, my friend, are the *shadows*. What color are they? You'll find out. Now if you'll excuse me, I've a meeting arranged with a stoat. I don't think she'll take it kindly if I'm late."

He gave an elegant bow, turned on his heel, and walked off down the sand.

Danny watched him go. Why did he feel like a great weight had launched itself off his shoulders? Had he been scared of that tall, thin man disappearing into the distance? Of course he hadn't. That couldn't have been the terrible Sammael. It must just have been a stranger passing by, looking for his lost dog.

Anyway, it was getting dark. He ought to be going home. His parents would be frantic by now—he'd been away for days.

He turned to Cath.

"We should go," he said. "It's time to go home."

She shook her head. "I'm stopping here," she said.

"But you've got to come back! They're looking for us."

"So? I ain't going back to my dad. No one's gonna tell on me, unless you do. No one's gonna find me here."

He looked around at the bare beach, the low dunes, and the little cottage with the wild mountains beyond.

"Where are you going to live then?"

Cath shrugged. "Here."

She held out a hand to Barshin, beckoning him to follow her.

"You can't take him!" said Danny. "He's a traitor."

But quite why this was, he wasn't sure. It was just a feeling he had, that the hare wasn't to be trusted.

"He ain't bad," said Cath. "He ain't good. But he ain't bad. And maybe he needs a home too. Call Zadoc for Danny, Barshin. Let him get out of here."

"I'll try," said Barshin. "I don't know if there's enough of him left. Falling through two of those holes should have killed him completely."

He let out the growling shriek, and the air trembled, but with barely the strength of a summer breeze. The shape that shook itself out of the air was a ghost horse, as translucent as a sheet of glass. The only substance to it came from a shimmer around its outline that echoed the dry beach sand with a hint of sea-moistened darkness, and the thousand colors of Chromos in its eye.

"Be quick," was all Barshin said.

Cath shrugged. "So long, Danny. You did what you wanted, I reckon. I'd say see you, but I don't reckon I will. I'm not ever going back, at least not to where you belong."

"You can't—" Danny tried, but she gave a small shake of her head and turned toward the path between the dunes. He watched her walk away from him and could think of no more words to call her back.

And then the sky stirred and he knew Zadoc was going. He felt a strong surge of hope that in a few seconds he'd be flying, soaring up into the wings of his own mind, galloping over the boundless world with freedom at his heels. He'd go anywhere he liked—anywhere he wanted—and nothing was ever going to hold him still again.

He scrambled up onto Zadoc's back, felt the invisible mane and smooth coat under his hands, and clapped his heels to Zadoc's fading sides.

"Go on!" he shouted to the snorting, dying horse. "Go on! Fly!"

And Zadoc leapt up into the green-blue of the sparkling plain, and it was wild, and empty, and wider than the entire universe.

## CHAPTER 30

# FORGETTING

They didn't fuss too much. They were just glad to have him home. His mum made dinner, and even though it was half past ten by the time it was ready, they sat down to eat around the kitchen table, all together.

"We'll go to Aunt Kathleen's next week," said his dad. "It's time we all had a vacation together. I know Sophie'll be back from university soon. You two still get on fine, don't you? She'll be so glad you're safe and sound again."

Danny nodded happily. Even though she was seven years older than him, he'd always gotten on well with Sophie. They were both only children, and only cousins too. It would be great to go on vacation at the farm again—Sophie was the closest Danny had ever gotten to a sibling of his own, and he was the little brother she'd never had.

He picked up the fork and began to eat. Maybe Sophie would take him horse riding. She was always patient with him, even though he'd been really nervous at first. She was much nicer than Cath had ever been on that crazy journey they'd had escaping from her dad.

It was going to be a good summer. Everything was fine again.

✦ ✦ ✦

The night settled around the window frames and the kitchen lights were bright, and Danny ate until he felt so sleepy that he almost fell face-first onto his plate.

"Get to bed," said his mum. "We'll sort everything out tomorrow."

As Danny climbed the stairs to bed, the summer stretched out before him, endless and sunny. He was going to sleep. And for the first time in months, he wasn't going to dream. Not about Cath or Zadoc or deer or hares or the rolling sea or the silver moon. And certainly not about Sammael.

He belonged to himself. And the world was his.

✦ ✦ ✦

Outside in the darkness, the moon slid from behind a cloud and the air began softly to shiver.

8/2/14